"I'm no saint, Ellen," Nick said roughly

"There are times I couldn't care less, patients I want to slam the door on. I'm not some noble doctor from a TV show. Of all people, you should know that!"

She didn't know if she could equal his honesty, but the ache in her chest made her try. "I don't want Dr. Kildare. I want you. I'm a little scared how much."

There was a brief silence. He frowned as he searched her face, his gaze lingering on her mouth with such possessive intent that her own doubts were swept away by intoxicating need.

When he spoke, his voice was thick, uneven. "Tell me I'm not imagining things. You did just issue an invitation?"

Here it was, the moment of truth. Ellen didn't even hesitate. She stepped off the precipice. "Yes," she said. "Yes, it was an invitation."

And then his mouth met hers, and she didn't even feel herself falling.

ABOUT THE AUTHOR

We are pleased to welcome Janice Kay Johnson to the Superromance line. Janice is the talented author of sixteen contemporary romances and young adult novels. She has set her first Superromance novel in beautiful Snohomish County, in Washington State, where she lives with her two daughters, two dogs and five cats.

Books by Janice Kay Johnson
HARLEQUIN TEMPTATION
149—NIGHT AND DAY

HARLEQUIN REGENCY ROMANCE
13—THE IMPERILED HEIRESS

Don't miss any of our special offers. Write to us at the following address for information on our newest releases.

Harlequin Reader Service
P.O. Box 1397, Buffalo, NY 14240
Canadian address: P.O. Box 603,
Fort Erie, Ont. L2A 5X3

Seize the Day

JANICE KAY JOHNSON

Harlequin Books

TORONTO • NEW YORK • LONDON
AMSTERDAM • PARIS • SYDNEY • HAMBURG
STOCKHOLM • ATHENS • TOKYO • MILAN

Published January 1992

ISBN 0-373-70483-6

SEIZE THE DAY

To Mom and Dad, with love
and thanks for your
unfailing encouragement
and support

CHAPTER ONE

THE PLACE DIDN'T SMELL like a hospital, but it looked like one. Hard, shiny floors, long corridors painted a soft peach color meant to soothe the distraught, glimpses of hospital beds through open doorways. The click of her heels was too loud as Ellen Patterson hurried, trying not to see, trying not to hear. She flinched at the sound of a scream, walked faster. A teenage boy slouching in a doorway watched her appreciatively, giving a soft wolf whistle as she passed. His cocky grin was a sharp counterpoint to the muffled groan that came from behind another door.

Ellen stopped at the nurse's station, trying to appear composed to the smiling woman who glanced up from a chart.

"Yes, may I help you?"

"I'm Linda Jarrett's sister, here for the family orientation. I'm afraid I'm a little late."

"Did you get lost? Everyone does, don't worry. Take a left at the end of the hall and it's the last door on the right. Just slip in and find a seat. Dr. Braden won't mind."

Ellen forced a smile. "Thank you."

Beyond the nurse's station was an open lounge where casually dressed adults and a few teenagers watched a football game on television. Some talked quietly or read newspapers, and one man sat up suddenly. "Come on,

ref! That wasn't interference!'' Were they visitors, or
patients? she wondered. They looked so normal. But
then, Ellen knew better than anyone how illusory that
appearance could be.

As she hurried down the corridor, more glimpses into
rooms revealed rumpled beds and gray faces. She was
both repelled and fascinated, praying that one of those
fleeting views wouldn't be of her half sister. Only two
days into treatment, Linda might well be having convulsions; at the very least, she was vilely ill. She wouldn't
want Ellen to see her.

At the last door on the right Ellen hesitated. Through
it she could hear a voice, muffled and incomprehensible,
presumably belonging to the great Dr. Braden whom her
sister admired so. Would he be white-haired and silver-
tongued? Suave and impressive? Ellen impatiently
pushed silken strands of red hair back from her face.
What did it matter? Dr. Braden was unlikely to accomplish a miracle for Linda. There'd been too many other
tries, too many other promises. This was an interlude, a
reprieve. No more.

As she opened the door and slipped quietly into a seat
in the back of the room, Ellen's preconceptions suffered
a jolt. The voice was neither smooth nor suave; it was
rough, impatient, charismatic. And it suited the man
pacing before the group, who she would never in a million years have guessed to be Dr. Nicholas Braden, the
man her sister had assured her was not only the founder
of this hospital, but a highly respected authority on alcoholism.

He was big and strong, with large hands that chopped
at the air as he spoke. His corduroy slacks were rumpled, the tie tugged loose and the sleeves of his creased,
blue oxford cloth shirt rolled up to reveal powerful fore-

arms. Straight dark hair, a little long, raked carelessly back from a face that looked like it belonged to a longshoreman, not a doctor. Broad cheekbones and blunt features, harsh lines cut in his cheeks, all added up to an impression of toughness.

For just an instant his eyes, dark blue and compelling, met Ellen's, and she felt as though she'd been given an electric shock. Whatever she'd expected—bland sympathy, useless coping strategies—would never be offered by this man.

It was a moment before she was able to tune in to what he was saying.

"By the time the alcoholic has been at it a while, he's losing his grip. Hiding it pretty well most of the time, but now he's doing some sneaking around. Maybe keeping an extra bottle tucked away, just for emergencies. Private ones, of course. Maybe generously offering to stop at the store on his way home from work. That way you'll never know how much booze he's actually buying. Encouraging his friends to drink more, maybe even you. Maybe even his kids, if they're old enough. Hey, when other people are drinking, too, he doesn't stand out, does he? He's normal. Nobody else knows that he doesn't wake up in the morning feeling like hell 'cause he's had too much. No, he feels like hell because he needs more. He *needs* that booze to hide his shakiness. Woe unto you if you get in his way when he's headed for that first drink of the day, whether it's at eight in the morning or at five when he gets home from work.

"Our alcoholic used to be able really to put 'em away and stay the life of the party. Now his tolerance is decreasing. He spends a lot of time with his head in the toilet. He passes out sometimes. Has blackouts. Pretty scary stuff." The man paused, swept that electrifying gaze over the audience. "Sound familiar?"

A murmur of agreement rippled through the crowd of parents and spouses. Oh, yes, they knew, thought Ellen bitterly. They all knew what it meant to love somebody who cared more for a bottle than for the people in his life. In *her* life. Ellen heard again her six-year old niece's voice, small and tremulous through the telephone.

"Aunt Ellen? I'm ... I'm scared. Mommy ... Mommy was throwing up in the bathroom and now she's fallen down on the floor and her eyes are closed and she's just lying there like ... like our dog when he died, and she won't answer when I talk to her and ... Aunt Ellen, we're hungry, Patrick and me, Mommy didn't even make us lunch and now it's dinnertime and I made us sandwiches but I put too much mayonnaise on and we don't like the kind of cheese that's already sliced but I can't cut the other kind." She ran out of words. "Aunt Ellen ..."

Hiding her fear, Ellen had said calmly, reassuringly, "I'm on my way, sweetie. You hold on and I'll be there in five minutes."

Anger shuddered through her again as she remembered the tears, the small clinging arms, as Laura and Patrick's mother was carried away on a stretcher. Not for the first time. Oh, no. Linda had been drinking since she was fifteen years old.

The big man with the gritty voice had gone on, was talking about the end, about heart failure and cirrhosis of the liver, cancer and malnutrition. About the *disease* of alcoholism.

"Any questions so far?"

Ellen sat with her back very straight, her fingers gripping each other in her lap. Why had she come? She could do nothing for Linda. She ought to be at home with

Laura and Patrick, learning how to substitute for their mother. This was the first time the children had ended up with her; the other times, Ellen's mother had taken them, since their father, who lived in California, was apparently uninterested.

"They gonna get counseling here?" somebody near the front asked gruffly.

The speaker nodded. "Yes, they are. But let me repeat myself. Our patients have a physiological disorder, not an emotional or psychological one. Yeah, lots of them have lost their jobs, their families, their friends. But problems like that are symptoms, not causes. The behavior of the alcoholic—depression, anger, confusion, denial—is the result of his disease. So we're not treating those symptoms. We're treating the underlying, physiological problem. We offer counseling only because it's a tool in helping the alcoholic learn to cope with the disease he has to live with for the rest of his life. But he—or she—is no more to blame for having the disease than someone else is for being a diabetic. You don't make yourself an alcoholic. You're born one. If the treatment is to be effective, we have to move beyond blame."

Bitterness curled in Ellen's stomach and she surprised herself by saying loudly, "That's convenient. Lives destroyed, but they don't have any responsibility. All is forgiven and forgotten. Wouldn't we all like that?"

With their intensity, the doctor's dark blue eyes pinned Ellen to her seat. "Any serious disease disrupts lives. What if your husband is dying of cancer? Do you hold him to account?"

She hated confrontation, anger, but she couldn't back away from his challenge. "The person dying of cancer can't change anything. Alcoholics can. They make choices every day."

"They're in the grip of an addiction that makes their choices for them."

Her gaze stayed locked with his. "But some alcoholics choose to quit and succeed. You depend on that for your living, don't you?"

He shoved his hands in his pockets and strolled toward her, coming within a couple of rows of chairs, so that he looked down at her, dominated her with his sheer physical presence. Curiously, his voice had become gentler, though still rough-edged.

"Very few alcoholics come here by choice. I've never yet met an alcoholic who woke up one morning and said, 'Hey, this'd be a good day to quit.' Hell, no. The people who come here are compelled to. Maybe the boss tells 'em it's this or else. The average alcoholic would choose the 'or else' except for one thing. Then there'd be no money to buy the booze. Sometimes the wife says she's going to leave him—and she means it. Sometimes the alcoholic is committed by court order. Or she's so sick there's no other choice."

The room was deathly silent, the battle between her and him. "If they don't want to quit, what hope is there?"

"All alcoholics want to be cured. They know they're sick. They just don't have the guts to take that god-awful first step. It's damned painful. But force 'em to take the first step, and they're ready to take the next one alone."

Oh, how simple it sounded. How easy. Ellen tore her gaze from his, swept it over the faces that stared at her. They all wanted to believe it was true, that their loved one could walk out of here in thirty days cured, all of the missing years, all of the anger, gone as though nothing had ever happened. Well, maybe she ought to allow them their illusions.

He still stood watching her, his face craggy and rough, his eyes compassionate. "We have an eighty percent rate of success. And we start with people who'd rather not be here. They need your support. The support of all of you." He began pacing again, his gaze moving from her to touch each person in turn as though he saw into their innermost pain and understood it as they had never been understood before. And perhaps he did. He'd seen it so many times.

Suddenly Ellen wanted to cry. The tears stung her throat. Clenching her teeth, she grabbed her purse and left, not looking back to see if he'd paused, not even caring if they all knew why she had fled.

The hall was blessedly silent and she hurried back the way she had come so that she didn't have to hear his voice, even muffled. How dare he? she thought, shocked at the corrosive strength of her anger. Were Laura and Patrick, bereft of parents, supposed to wait uncritically for their mother who had, of course, left through no fault of her own? Was no one to blame for their desolation, for the tears that wet their pillows, the nightmares that awakened them sobbing in the darkest hours?

Was no one to blame for the fear that had crippled her own life? Like a mantra she told herself that parents *were* responsible; they *had* to be, or what security did any child have?

At the nurse's station Ellen hesitated, with a tremendous effort composing herself again. The same woman looked up, smiling.

"Done already?"

"I'm afraid I had to leave early," Ellen said. "I wonder... could you tell me how my sister is? Linda Jarrett?"

"You really ought to talk to Dr. Braden. I'm sure when he's finished he'd be happy to..."

Ellen broke in, conscious of how desperate she sounded. "But I can't wait. I...I'll call later. Perhaps then..."

"No, that's all right," the nurse said gently. "Your sister is fine. Really. We'd rather that you not visit her for several more days, until she's more herself, but I'm sure she'd appreciate a card, perhaps some flowers. Something to cheer her up."

"Yes, fine." Ellen backed away from the waist-high counter. "If there's any change... Well, you have my number."

"Yes, of course."

"Thank you."

The same teenager whistled at her again as she passed. She only dimly noticed. The sky outside was dazzlingly blue, almost hurting her eyes. Once inside her car she crossed her arms on the steering wheel and leaned her forehead on them, drawing slow, deep breaths until the turmoil inside her quieted. At last she lifted her head and looked again at the hospital, low and rambling with cedar shakes and siding. Typically Northwest, it was nestled between residential neighborhoods in Everett, about thirty miles north of Seattle. Even though she lived in Everett, Ellen had had trouble finding it. Among the trees the hospital was scarcely noticeable from the road.

Now bright fingers of sunlight found their way between the fir boughs, making the beads of water from yesterday's rain glitter on the fronds of ferns clustered beneath the trees. Brave early crocuses bloomed in the dark earth along the front walk. It seemed unbelievable that spring was nearly here, Ellen thought, turning the key in the ignition. She wished it were an omen.

A friend had volunteered to baby-sit the children, since she had a couple of her own and was, as she'd put it cheerfully, stuck home anyway. Ellen was grateful for the time it took to drive to Joanne's, across the valley in Lake Stevens. Laura and Patrick didn't know she'd been to the clinic, and she was determined not to let her mood give her away.

Sheer chaos greeted her when she knocked and, since there was no answer, let herself in the front door. Joanne's living room was wall-to-wall toys. Joanne's four-year-old son Eddy and Patrick were ramming blocks with miniature war tanks and fang-nosed troop carriers. Crashes and roars and whoops accompanied the action.

From the direction of the bathroom came bloodcurdling screams and the slightly more muffled sound of Laura talking.

"Uh...hi, guys," Ellen said.

Eddy didn't even lift his head. Patrick's glance was brief and disinterested. The tank, driven by a small plastic man with bulging muscles and hooks for hands, feinted in her direction before turning back to the battle.

Ellen made a face and followed the screams.

In the bathroom her statuesque blond friend was changing her baby's diaper. Ignoring the baby, Laura stood in the doorway chatting.

"My friend Jill has this great new doll. I want one, too, because she has this dress that can be short or long and these pearly pink shoes and perfume and everything. I'm gonna..."

Raising her voice above the howls, Ellen interjected, "Hi, Laura. Hi, Joanne."

Her elfin niece, blond hair scraped back in a ponytail, turned a look of distinct hostility on her. "I don't want to go home yet. You said we could stay for lunch."

"My errand didn't take me as long as I expected it to." She gave Laura a tentative hug, but the little girl stayed stiff. Pretending not to notice, Ellen peered around the door frame. "I take it Colin doesn't like having his diaper changed."

"The understatement of the world," Joanne said grimly, pitching her voice above the baby's howls. "I tell him all the time that if he wants to use the toilet, that's okay with me."

"He's only eight months old!"

"But with a will of his own." Joanne righted the red-faced child, deftly hooked his overalls, then thrust him unceremoniously at Ellen. "Here, take him, will you? I have to do something with this diaper."

Ellen backed away from the bathroom, clutching the surprisingly heavy and very angry baby boy. She awkwardly patted his back. "Uh . . . it's okay, Colin. Really. I'm not so bad."

"I don't think he likes you," Laura said.

"I'm not his mother."

"You're not mine, either."

Ellen hitched Colin onto her hip and tried to answer calmly. "That's true. You have a perfectly good mother of your own."

Laura stared at her with that disconcerting hostility in her eyes. "You went to see her, didn't you?"

"Sweetie . . ."

"Don't call me that. Only my mom can call me that."

With relief Ellen deposited the baby among the blocks in the living room, then turned to look at her niece. "Laura, I didn't see your mother, but I did talk to the nurse. She said your mom's fine. We'll be able to visit her soon."

Except for a lower lip that trembled slightly, the little girl's face was mulish. "I don't want to see her."

Was it possible to make Laura understand, Ellen wondered, when she didn't understand herself? Unwillingly she thought of what Dr. Braden had said.

"Laura, your mom is sick. I know she misses you. I won't make you see her, but I think she'll feel sad if you don't go."

The six-year-old plopped down on the couch and crossed her arms. "Can we have lunch here?"

Brick wall. Ellen glanced up to see Joanne watching silently from the arch that led to the hall. Her friend pantomimed a yes. Helplessly Ellen glanced at Patrick, who gave no sign of listening but had no doubt heard every word, and then at Laura, who waited with stubborn blue eyes. For an instant Ellen remembered another pair of blue eyes, dark and compassionate, before she gave up.

"Sure. Why not?"

DESPISING HERSELF, still Ellen took the children from Joanne's to the nearest mall and indulged in an orgy of toy buying. Would a new stuffed animal or action figure make up for their mother's failure? But she felt better for having tried. She was so awkward with them; maybe this way she had showed that she cared.

They had barely walked in the front door of Ellen's condominium when the telephone began to ring.

"Can we watch TV while we play with our new stuff?" Laura asked.

"Yeah," her little brother parroted. "Can we?"

Hurrying toward the kitchen, Ellen said resignedly, "Yes, all right. I don't care." The TV leaped instantly to life along with Patrick's whine. "I can't get this open. Stupid thing!"

Behind her, Laura said, "Oh, I'll open it."

On the fifth ring Ellen snatched up the receiver. "Hello?"

She recognized that gritty voice at once. "Ms. Patterson? This is Dr. Braden from the clinic."

Her heart began to thud unpleasantly. "Is . . . is something wrong? Is Linda . . ."

"No, no, your sister is fine." He sounded brusque. "I'd like to have more chance to talk to you than we had this morning. The nurse told me who you were."

Ellen closed her eyes for a moment. "I made a scene, didn't I?" she said quietly. "I'm sorry. I had no business . . ."

He interrupted, "You didn't make a scene. You expressed your feelings. That's what we were there for."

"The others were there to hear your views, not mine."

"They were there to discover that they're not alone. Every one of them feels as mad as you do."

He was disconcerting; that rough, impatient voice combined with his insight.

"Am I that obvious?"

"The family members of an alcoholic are nearly always angry. And why not? They've been let down repeatedly. Humiliated. Hurt. You're not alone either, you know."

Ellen was momentarily startled. Living with an alcoholic had an isolating effect; it wasn't something you readily confided. She had seen the others in the meeting as innocents who had yet to be disillusioned, not fellow sufferers. Perhaps there, at least, she had been wrong.

"I never thought . . ." she began stiffly.

Again he interrupted without compunction. "I'd like to talk to you. Can we set up a meeting?"

The canned voices from the television set in the next room had become hysterical, adding to her tension. "I'm afraid getting away from work is difficult. And I can't really see what good that would do Linda."

"I gather that your sister has little contact with her ex-husband and that your mother is in ill-health. That leaves you as the only relative who she feels she can lean on. Your attitude can have a powerful impact on her."

"Really?" She couldn't help the sarcasm. "It's never had much effect on her before."

"Not when she was in the grip of her addiction."

"Not even when she wasn't. This isn't the first time for Linda, you know."

He dismissed her argument. "Detox is next thing to useless for an alcoholic. They need a hell of a lot more than a few days of drying out."

"She's been through treatment as well."

He grunted. "Never thirty days."

Ellen bit her lip. "Dr. Braden, I don't know if you realize that I have her children, but I really have to be putting dinner on. So if you'll excuse me . . ."

He didn't let her off the hook. "What about tomorrow? Surely you don't work on Sunday?"

"No, I don't," she admitted, scrambling for an excuse, "but getting a baby-sitter can be a problem. I'm sorry. Why don't I give you a call when the children are a little better settled in?"

"Ms. Patterson, is there some reason you're reluctant to talk to me?"

Faced with such bluntness, she didn't answer for a moment. But then she made herself consider it. Why *was* she so reluctant? Did it have something to do with Dr. Nicholas Braden? With those disconcerting blue eyes that saw too much?

She knew the answer, of course. It was hard to say, but she made herself. "Has Linda told you that her father was an alcoholic as well?"

He didn't sound surprised. "Your stepfather."

"Yes. I have very few good memories of those years. The subject is a difficult one for me. Linda owes her children something better. I'm afraid she's long since worn out my sympathy. If it weren't for Patrick and Laura..."

"For their sakes, if not your own, let me have an hour. It won't kill you."

She couldn't withstand his determination. "All right. Tomorrow. At the hospital? Ten o'clock? Fine." Slowly Ellen hung up, feeling battered. How could Linda have done this to all of them? Her father had made Linda's life as miserable as he had made Ellen's, so how could she of all people have begun to drink? It was unthinkable.

Now—somehow—Ellen had to cope with two children. She loved Laura and Patrick in the casual way of an aunt who has to do little but bestow an occasional gift along with a smile and a hug. Now she had to feed them, comfort them during the night, do endless loads of laundry increased by Patrick's regression to wetting his pants.

She was trying to become used to toys littering the floor, toothpaste drying on the bathroom sink, spilled juice and constant chatter. Well, she didn't begrudge them any of it. They were children who didn't deserve to suffer for their mother's weakness.

But apparently Dr. Braden, the all-seeing, thought she also ought to become a prop for her half sister's limp willpower. Thanks, but no thanks, she thought acerbically. This was one hole Linda had to climb out of herself.

CHAPTER TWO

"HEY, FOX!" The teenager was getting bolder, his grin even cockier. Today he sauntered a few steps down the hall after Ellen, giving a low whistle.

For an instant she had a dizzying sense of *déjà vu;* the same suffocating silence closed about her and she caught the same glimpses of rumpled beds and slow-moving, gray-faced patients.

But today the morning sunlight reached into the hall, and the soles of her sneakers were soundless on the hard floor.

The disorientation passed and Ellen resisted the urge to make a rude gesture behind her back at the teenager. Secretly she was a little flattered. She had turned thirty the month before. It was nice to know her body at least didn't look it.

A different nurse was on duty today. She directed Ellen to Dr. Braden's office at the far end of the right wing. Ellen walked quickly, without glancing into the rooms she passed. When she came to the door with the frosted glass insert and his name in discreet letters beneath, she didn't hesitate. He could have the hour he'd asked for, but she wouldn't let herself feel intimidated.

At her knock she heard him growl, "Come in."

He didn't look up immediately, even though he must have been aware that she had entered. His dark head was bent as he dug through a heap of manila folders that threatened to slide off his desk at any moment. "Now where the hell...?" he muttered. "Jane, I can't find..." And then his glance collided with hers.

Nick Braden was very seldom shocked into silence, but the unexpectedness of Ellen Patterson's appearance did it. He had felt something when his eyes met hers yesterday, an uncomfortable lurch that he'd later remembered uneasily. But she had been sleek and remote, her red hair coiled in a smooth chignon, her lemon-colored suit tailored and expensive. Her anger had unsettled him, but he'd faced anger like hers before. That was the woman he had expected to meet this morning—if she showed at all, which he had doubted.

Well, she'd showed all right, but today she wore jeans that emphasized narrow hips and long coltish legs, a coral cotton shirt that exposed a creamy throat and the dusting of freckles on her chest. Her hair, thick and undisciplined, flowed like waves of molten lava over her slender shoulders and back. And her face, without makeup, looked younger, less sophisticated. She had a full, sulky mouth, a small, straight nose, high cheekbones and velvety, chocolate-brown eyes. Her complexion was the matte cream of a true redhead with freckles sprinkled across her nose. Ellen Patterson was stunning: beautiful, sensual, and curiously unapproachable despite the youthful look her casual clothes gave her.

Ignoring a disconcerting surge of pure, unadulterated desire, he asked gruffly, "How old are you?"

She looked startled. "What difference does it make?"

"You can't be older than Linda."

"I am, by three years."

Then she was thirty, he calculated. Which made that air of control less surprising.

He realized he was staring and said abruptly, "Sorry. I'm forgetting the amenities. We haven't exactly met, have we? I'm Nick Braden." Keeping one big hand on the heap of charts, he stood and extended the other. Her hand, small and warm, met his clasp with surprising firmness. His fingers tightened and he felt strangely reluctant to let go. When at last he did, she stepped back, her expression wary. He hated to think what his face showed.

Nick cleared his throat. "Have a seat." After waiting politely until she did, he lowered his large frame into his leather office chair. Unfortunately, the instant he took his hand from the pile of charts and notes, it collapsed in seeming slow motion, sending folders and papers fluttering to the floor.

He jerked forward, too late to save anything, then swore under his breath. Looking up, he saw her press her lips together, failing to quite hide the amusement that danced in her eyes.

"Don't you have a secretary, Dr. Braden?"

He followed her gaze to the untidy heaps of papers, books with ragged markers sticking out the top like spider legs, and manila folders that covered the file cabinet, a small table, his desk, an extra chair and even the floor. Half hidden on his desk sat a couple of coffee cups with dried brown rings inside.

"I know where everything is," he said.

Dimples appeared in her cheeks as she suppressed a smile. "Really."

He couldn't help grinning. "Well, almost everything."

She chuckled and let her smile blossom. Her mouth was so soft, so full, he wanted to reach out and touch her lips with his fingertip. He caught himself wondering how her smile, so warm and generous, would feel against his mouth, whether she kissed as generously.

At last he wrenched his gaze away and cleared his throat. "Fortunately most of the papers are clipped into the files. I'll pick up later."

Her smile faded, leaving him with a disconcerting sense of loss. He'd barely met the woman, for God's sake.

"You wanted to talk about Linda," she said. "How is she doing?"

"Very well," he said. "I'm pleased with her progress."

Obviously she didn't like platitudes, because her tone became crisper. "Exactly what does that mean?"

He had several stock answers, but chose to discard them and answer bluntly, "Just what I said. She feels lousy, but she hasn't had any of the more frightening withdrawal symptoms."

In the first sign of nerves he'd seen, her fingers twined in her lap. "But Linda was unconscious when the ambulance came."

"She regained consciousness at the hospital. She was stable by the time she arrived here, and we've kept her that way. We use medications to make the withdrawal gradual. It's easier for the patient and considerably less dangerous."

Her voice was stifled when she said, "Another treatment center she was in once kept her on phenobarbital for almost the whole ten days she was there. They cut her off just a day or so before she was released."

Nick didn't say what he knew had been the result: Ellen's half sister had gone out and gotten drunk immediately. She'd have had no choice; stranded like that, she had been literally dying for a drink.

Instead, he said, "We use drugs like phenobarbital for only a few days, just to minimize withdrawal. In fact, I think Linda received her last dose this morning."

Ellen didn't comment. She just waited.

After a moment, Nick said quietly, "It's not so much Linda I wanted to talk about, as you."

Her dark eyes had a spark of anger. "I'm not your patient."

"Helping the family members to understand is as essential to the alcoholic as her own treatment."

"I don't even live with Linda. I may judge her, but I keep my opinion to myself."

The chair squeaked as he tilted it back. "You think she doesn't know how you feel?"

Vividly, painfully, Ellen saw in her mind her sister's face as she had seen it too many times, puffy, discolored, the brown eyes that were still beautiful, bewildered and pleading. Linda had always had a gift for eliciting sympathy, using that very look. Ellen had become cynical about it, although invariably after seeing Linda, she would lie awake that night crying for the sister she had loved. But she rejected those painful memories now.

"Of course Linda knows how I feel!" she said tartly. "She grew up in the same home I did. I'll never understand how, of all people, she could have started to drink!"

"Tell me," he said, his voice mild as he clasped his hands behind his head. "Do you drink at all?"

Ellen's answer was stiff. "Socially."

"Why? How could you bring yourself ever to take a drink?"

"I drink rarely. I don't abuse it."

"I don't suppose your sister started out that way, either. Drinking is something almost everybody does. It never occurs to the children of an alcoholic that they don't dare—ever—take a drink. Linda probably despised her father's weakness. *She* wasn't like that. Of course she wasn't." His hands dropped and he leaned forward with sudden intensity. "But guess what? She *is* like her father. Not because she's weak. She may or may not be. I don't know. But what she is, is an alcoholic. She inherited the physiological inability to handle booze. Simple as that. The only thing different between you and her is that you don't have the same genes."

The air fairly crackled with the strength of his personality. Ellen was made uncomfortably aware of him, big and husky, his hands so large they had dwarfed hers. He wasn't the kind of man she usually thought of as sexy; he certainly wasn't handsome. His features were too rough, too lived-in. But the hint of a cleft in his chin softened his face and his grin had been disarming. The force of his conviction, his intensity, looked very like another kind of passion. She had the uneasy feeling that he would be a very hard man to resist.

She hated to argue, wanted to agree with everything he said so that she could escape. But his blue eyes held hers and innate stubbornness made her say, "You sound as though you don't believe in free will. Are our whole lives determined by our genes, then? Is that what you think?"

"No, it isn't. I believe we can change our lives, fight against our physical limitations. But research *is* showing that a great deal of our behavior can be explained by heredity, by hormones, by chemicals in our brain. It's impossible to successfully argue any more that we're born a blank slate, with the capacity to make ourselves. Or even to be made by others. We all have a few ticking time bombs inside. For some people, theirs is the disease of alcoholism.''

A surge of anger stiffened her. "You're very anxious to excuse the alcoholic, aren't you?''

Some emotion that she couldn't read flickered in his eyes, as though she had struck a raw nerve. But his gravelly voice was still very calm when he said, "I'm making that judgment based on knowledge, not emotion.''

Ellen didn't like his implication. "Are you? Or are you reaching the conclusion that suits you best?''

His eyes were suddenly hooded, and it was a moment before he answered. "It's hard to totally discount your own emotional needs. But the research results are very persuasive. I'd like to lend you some literature. All I'm asking is that you read with an open mind.''

Ellen bit her lip and nodded, wondering why she felt so uncomfortable, as though she had hit below the belt. Was it only because she had made the argument personal when it shouldn't have been? She couldn't possibly have hurt him with her accusation, could she? "I'll try,'' she said quietly.

He nodded. "Good.''

There was a moment's silence during which Ellen couldn't meet his eyes. She looked down at her hands. "I'm sorry. I know I have a lot of anger left inside me. I shouldn't have taken it out on you. You're trying to help Linda. Instead of arguing, I should hope that you're right.''

He frowned. "Don't apologize. I was asking for it. Literally. I'm the one who dragged you down here, not the other way around.''

"Still . . .''

"No apologies,'' he said again, his voice rough. "Not to me. I want you to be honest with me.''

Ellen gave a rueful smile. "I've been that."

She was quiveringly conscious of his gaze when it lowered to her mouth and lingered for a charged instant before his eyes met hers again. Tension shimmered in the air as she thought, in shock, I can't be attracted to him.

She hurried into speech. "I really should be going. I promise I'll... think about what you said. Maybe I'm being unfair, I..."

"What's fair is in the eye of the beholder."

Ellen gripped her purse and stood, nervously searching his face, but now his expression was impenetrable. She'd surely imagined that instant of heat. Relaxing by slow degrees, she said, "But even you think I'm being unfair."

He was on his feet now, too. "I didn't say that," he contradicted. "Fairness has very little to do with reality. Haven't you seen that bumper sticker, 'Life's a bitch and then you die?'"

The darker mood of their interview was broken and Ellen had to laugh. "Do you have one on your car?"

He came easily around the desk, stepping over the pile of files on the floor. "Nah. I'm not enough of a fatalist."

"You were going to give me something to read," she reminded as he reached past her for the door.

He shook his head and turned to scan the overstuffed bookshelf. "As my mother used to say, I wouldn't be able to find my head..."

"If you took it off in this office?"

He pretended to be wounded at her remark. "Hey, I'm more organized than I look. Give me a minute and I'll prove it."

When less than thirty seconds later he produced some mimeographed articles and a couple of well-thumbed paperbacks, Ellen smiled, conceding him the victory. Well, as he'd said about this meeting, doing some reading wouldn't kill her. Maybe she would even discover that he was right. Alcoholism wasn't a subject she approached with an open mind. But she could try.

"I'll look at them," she said again, "Thank you, Dr. Braden."

"Nick." He held the door open, adding, "I'll walk you out. I'm going that way."

Somehow in his presence the hall seemed less sterile, her emotions no longer numb. She was very conscious of him beside her. At nearly five feet seven inches she wasn't short, but the top of her head couldn't be much above his powerful shoulders, and next to him she felt fragile. But more than sheer size accounted for his effect on her. Maybe it was that very air of certainty, as though he knew and had accepted himself, that attracted her even while she half resented it. She only wished she shared a fraction of that confidence.

Outside in the spring sunlight, Ellen hesitated, reluctant to say goodbye.

"Will I be allowed to see Linda this week?"

"I don't know why not." He bent to pick a purple crocus from the planter box and surprised Ellen by handing it to her. "To cheer you up."

Their fingers touched as she took it, and she felt his warmth. "Thank you," Ellen said quietly. Obeying a sudden impulse, she reached up to tuck the flower in her hair. His gaze followed her hands, then moved lower to where the thin fabric of her shirt pulled tightly across her breasts. But when her hands dropped, his eyes met hers.

"You look like you ought to be on a beach in Tahiti."

She smiled up at him, ignoring her breathlessness. "Are you craving a vacation in the sun?"

"Sounds good to me. Shall we run away from it all?"

For an instant she saw it, the two of them walking barefooted on the hot white sand while azure water dazzled their eyes and brilliant flowers scented the air. Romantic. Her voice was unconsciously wistful as she said, "I'm afraid we'll have to settle for the Sound."

"Cold and rocky." The crease in his cheek deepened as he smiled down at her. "Are you trying to tell me something?"

He had a sexy mouth, she thought, and her voice didn't sound quite normal when she said, "Only bringing you back to reality."

"Reality doesn't seem too bad right now."

Suddenly she was stunned by the force of her longing. She wanted him to be someone different, *her* to be someone different.

When the silence lasted too long his smile faded, but the expression in his blue eyes was warm. "Hey. It was just a compliment."

Ellen felt the heat rise in her cheeks. "I've said some pretty lousy things to you."

"Dr. Braden!" The urgent voice penetrated their invisible bubble like the sting of cold rain. The nurse had her head out the door, and her expression spoke louder than words. "Dr. Braden, you're needed immediately."

He was moving even before the nurse had finished, long strides taking him to the door. "We have to finish this discussion, Ellen," he said over his shoulder, and then he disappeared.

The glass door quivered for an instant after he vanished inside, as though a breeze whispered behind him. Ellen stood very still, clutching her purse. What did he mean? But then her mind veered.

Somebody was having a crisis, perhaps even dying. *Had* anybody ever died here? she wondered. And then, like the grip of a cold hand, she took the next step. Could it be Linda? Would they have told her if it was?

She had no choice at last but to drive away, not knowing. And as she prayed for her sister, whom she had loved and worried about for so long, it was Nick Braden she saw in her mind.

THE SHRILL of the telephone hadn't even died when Laura rolled off the couch and ran for the kitchen. "I'll get it!"

"I wanna answer!" Patrick wailed, although he hadn't moved from the couch. "No fair! My turn! I wanna answer!"

Ellen squeezed her eyes shut. "Guys, if you keep fighting about it, neither of you can answer the telephone!"

"I don't like my sister," Patrick mumbled tearfully. Ellen sighed, gave him a quick hug and followed her niece.

Laura was already planted firmly on one of the tall kitchen stools, chattering happily into the phone. "It's Grandma!" she said to Ellen, before continuing into the receiver, "Aunt Ellen keeps leaving us at some friend's house. Her name is Joanne. She's okay, I guess. She gave us hotdogs for lunch yesterday, but today Aunt Ellen made us come home and she wanted to make a *salad*. Yuck! Rabbits eat things like lettuce, not kids. So we said..."

Ellen rolled her eyes. "Let me know when it's my turn, okay?"

The little girl sniffed and turned her back on Ellen, who promptly stuck out her tongue at her niece. Immature or not, the gesture felt good.

Ten minutes later, Laura reluctantly surrendered the phone. "Grandma wants to talk to you," she said, her tone making it quite clear that she couldn't imagine why.

She eavesdropped as Ellen greeted her mother, then apparently decided that their conversation wasn't interesting enough to bother with and disappeared back into living room. A moment later Ellen heard the television.

She sighed. "There goes the TV again. But it's the only time Laura stops talking. She even sulks out loud!"

Her mother said anxiously. "You're getting along all right, aren't you? I know you've never spent much time with them, but they're really good kids. Linda isn't a bad mother."

Yeah, right, Ellen thought, but didn't say. "I'm managing. Barely. I just don't think I'm cut out to be a mother."

"Of course you are!" Mrs. Whalley said in a rallying tone. "But Laura and Patrick aren't yours. Even when you have your own, it can be hard to deal with other people's children. And they must miss their mother."

"I'm not sure," Ellen said. "Sometimes I think they do and then sometimes . . . Well, Laura is pretty mad at Linda. She says she doesn't want to visit her. But she isn't too crazy about me, either."

"Oh, Ellen," her mother said sadly. "You're making me feel so guilty. I could take care of them. Maybe I should . . ."

"No, you shouldn't," Ellen interrupted. "You know the doctor wants you to take it easy. It's not fair of Linda to keep putting you on the spot! You shouldn't have to raise her children."

"So you get stuck instead."

"We're managing," Ellen said again. "And I've refused to do anything else for Linda. But I'd be happy for a little advice from the expert."

"I'm a fine one to give any. I made too many wrong choices. It's a credit to you, not to me, that you..."

It was a familiar lament. Ellen interrupted, "Linda's problem isn't your fault." The words came automatically, but they were no sooner out than she thought of Nick Braden. Whose fault is it, then? she demanded silently. If Linda isn't responsible for her own life, who is? Her mother? Her father, who according to the Braden philosophy wasn't to blame for his own drinking? Another finger of anger curled inside her, making her forget for an instant the warmth in Nick's eyes and the gentleness of his touch.

Who, damn it?

HEALTHY, LINDA WOULD have been a pretty woman. Petite and small-boned, she had Ellen's brown eyes, huge in her pinched face, and fine, pale hair that was cut in delicate wisps above her ears and slender neck. But now she was painfully thin and her complexion had a yellowish cast. She was galvanized by a sort of frantic energy that had her pacing the room.

"Get me out of here, Ellen! Please? I can't stand it! I feel so trapped. It's not that I need to drink. I won't even have a beer! I promise." She jerked the curtain aside to look out the window at the bleak gray day, then shuddered and let it drop. "You don't have to let me out of your sight. You can frown at me all you want! I don't care. Just get me out of here!"

"Linda, it was only a week ago that you almost died!" Ellen was perched uncomfortably on the edge of one of the room's two armchairs. She had to turn her head to keep her sister in sight. "I know this must be terribly hard for you..." she began tentatively.

Linda whirled to face her. "You have no idea! No idea at all! It's..." Her lips compressed and she knotted her hands before her. The words came faster and faster until they began to run together. "I'm sick. Really sick. They've detoxed me too fast. I know they have. I had convulsions and they didn't do anything. I could have died! I don't think they care, as long as they get their money!"

"Linda..."

"Don't keep saying that! Just listen to me, will you? I know you don't approve of me, but you must care a little! Please! You don't want me to die, do you?"

Ellen kept her voice level with an effort. "Have you tried to check yourself out?"

"I don't have a car. And they took my purse. I can't even find my shoes." She looked about vaguely, as though they might appear.

"You didn't have any on when you were brought here. Do you remember that at all?"

"Of course I remember it!" Linda's hostile expression was disquietingly reminiscent of her daughter's. "I'm not crazy! I just had a little too much to drink, that's all."

Ellen seemed to hear an echo. *A little too much. That's all. Just a little too much.* The memory brought a needle of pain. "You sound just like Dad," she said flatly.

"That's ridiculous! I'm nothing like him. He was a drunk. He lost his job and everything."

It was another echo. Ellen's stepfather had never been an alcoholic, either. After all, he went to work every day like any of her friend's fathers. George Whalley just liked a few drinks when he came home. Of course, his were more vodka than mixer, and by dinnertime he was in a state of stupefaction. He invariably passed out by seven-thirty, eight o'clock. But that was normal, right? Trying desperately to pretend that it was, Ellen had learned not to bring friends home with her. Public occasions had meant an agony of humiliation for her and Linda.

Ellen was away at college, Linda a senior in high school when the end came. He had come home, aged ten years in one day. His lunch hours had become too long, his afternoon fuzziness too obvious, and he had been fired from his job at the telephone company. The pretense that made his life bearable was over. Only a few weeks later he staggered off to bed one evening at his usual time. Ellen's mother was doing the dishes, Linda her homework at the kitchen table. The crack of a gun shook the thin walls. Denial was over, reality faced.

Now Ellen stood in agitation, torn by present and past. "Linda, for God's sake . . . !"

"I do drink too much, I know I do. But I don't need this place! It's horrible!" Pleading dark eyes searched Ellen's face for sympathy. When she failed to find what she sought, Linda stifled a sob. "I miss Laura and Patrick so badly. You don't know what it's like to be a mother! I think about them at night, without me, crying . . ."

The look, the piteous tone, were all too familiar. This scene had been played out too many times. Something clamped painfully about Ellen's heart. She felt suddenly overwhelmingly sad, as though this brown-eyed, blond woman were a stranger, no longer the sister she loved.

"It won't work with me, Linda," she said, with finality that surprised even her. Purse over her shoulder, she walked past her sister to the door. Her hand on the knob, she glanced back. "Don't forget that your daughter was the one who had to call me because her mommy hadn't fed her or her brother lunch or dinner. Because her mommy was having convulsions on the bathroom floor just like her dog who'd died. All this because her mom 'just had a little too much to drink.' If you *really* love your children . . ." Ellen suddenly couldn't go on, had to blink back a sting of tears. Why was she wasting her breath? There was nothing she could say that would change Linda. She'd learned that long ago. So she finished instead, "Call when you're ready to see them."

"Ellen . . . !"

She didn't turn back, didn't even bother to close the door. Her feet carried her steadily down the hall, past the nurse's station where she nodded at the woman who had earlier escorted her to Linda's room. In the last stretch of hall she kept her eyes fixed ahead on the gray daylight framed by the glass doors. Escape.

Past and present had become one. The picture of her stepfather that Ellen carried in her head wavered and shifted, as though seen in a distorted mirror, until it became Linda's face. As though in a logical sequence, Ellen thought of Laura, small and vulnerable, sulky and fearful. Herself twenty-five years ago.

Well, nobody had saved her from years of anger and humiliation, but it wasn't too late for Laura or her younger brother. The past didn't have to replay itself, Ellen thought fiercely. Somebody had to be responsible for stopping it. Whatever Dr. Nicholas Braden said, somebody had to be responsible, period.

Despite her own bitterness, her own sense of inadequacy, Ellen seemed to be the only available candidate.

Laura and Patrick deserved—and needed—better than that. The truth was, they needed better than any of the adults in their lives seemed to be capable of giving.

CHAPTER THREE

DAMN, HE HATED TAX TIME. Accountants and their arcane rows of numbers weren't for him; he'd hated algebra even back in high school. Nick felt stifled by the last hour spent closeted with his accountant. He had come out little the wiser, but docile. He'd sign anything, he thought ruefully.

Long strides carried him into the parking lot. He needed to get the hell out of here for a couple of hours. The fresh air was seductive and he'd had all he could take of his patients. He understood their behavior all too well and empathized most of the time, but there were moments he thought he must be a masochist to have chosen to spend his life with recovering—and failing—alcoholics.

He'd had another predictable session with Linda Jarrett this morning. She had smiled and flirted and done her damnedest to convince him that *she* didn't have a drinking problem. This was all a terrible mistake. Sure. And all the while he had been comparing her to Ellen, searching for a resemblance that had proved illusory, wondering when—or if—Ellen would come to visit her sister. And whether he could find an excuse to be casually hanging around when she did.

Nick slung his sports coat over his shoulder and groped in his pocket for car keys. He idly turned his head to scan the parking lot and then stopped dead, feeling as though he'd taken a blow to the chest. Incredibly, there she was, hurrying toward her car. Today she wore a rust-colored straight skirt that ended just above the knee and had a slit in back that revealed beautiful legs. Above a short-sleeved white silk blouse was that glorious hair, primly confined in a French braid. Her walk was leggy and undeniably feminine.

As Nick veered to intercept her, thoughts of accountants and patients left his mind as though they'd never been. When she was close enough he raised his voice. "Ellen."

She turned with a curiously blind look on her face, the response automatic, but a part of her very far away. Then she blinked. "Dr. Braden. How are you?"

Close up, he was disturbed by her pallor and by the brittle control that showed in the white-knuckled grip she had on her shoulder bag. "Please, call me Nick," he said. "And I'm fine. Were you here to see Linda?"

"Yes, I just..." She stopped and swallowed. "Actually, I just walked out on her."

He grimaced. "She wanted you to break her out of here."

"How did you know?"

Taking her arm, Nick steered her out of the path of a slowly on-coming pickup that she gave no sign of noticing. He had to make himself let go of her. "I saw Linda this morning myself. If I'd known you were coming I would have suggested you put it off until another day."

"She doesn't think she's an alcoholic."

"Nobody thinks they're an alcoholic," he said dryly.

"My stepfather didn't think he was one either. Until..." She faltered.

When she didn't continue he prompted, "Until?"

Her mouth trembled. "Until he killed himself. I guess he knew then."

Her pain felt like his. Without conscious thought, Nick reached out and touched her shoulder. "I'm sorry," he said roughly. "I didn't know. Linda didn't tell me that."

"She pretends it never happened," Ellen said, her eyes, wide and vulnerable, searching his for understanding. "But she was home. So was Mom. How could a man do that to people he loved?"

Nick wished, as much as he had ever wished for anything in his life, that he *didn't* understand. That he didn't know the helplessness and despair that made death a form of peace. He felt himself withdrawing from her by shoving his hands into his pockets and hunching his shoulders. With an effort he made his voice level.

"God knows. The kindest interpretation is that he was comforted by having people he loved close by. And often a person who is suicidal thinks he's doing his family a favor by killing himself. If your stepfather faced the fact that he was an alcoholic, that he'd damaged people he loved by his drinking, he'd figure you were better off without him. Once he'd convinced himself of that, he was probably pretty single-minded. He wouldn't even think about the ugly part."

"Dad was really a very kind man." Ellen's gaze was vaguely unfocused, as though she saw back to another time and place. Nick stood quietly and let her remember. Maybe it was cathartic; maybe she needed now to face those memories.

But then she gave a soft sigh and the tension seemed to drain out of her. Her smile was rueful. "What a subject. And you were probably running away from stuff like this. I'm sorry."

Nick held up one hand in mock warning. "No more apologies. Remember?"

Her small nose crinkled. "I'll try. Am I allowed to thank you for listening?"

"Nope." He hadn't thought it over, but he knew suddenly that he didn't want to let her drive away, even though he was a fool to think anything could come of his attraction to a woman haunted by her particular ghosts. But why assume anything? If she saw the ghost of her stepfather over his shoulder, she'd politely refuse any invitation. He knew better than to get his feelings hurt. And what was that old saying? Nothing ventured, nothing gained. Recklessly he said, "You can pay me back by having lunch with me and listening to all *my* woes."

"Lunch?"

"We won't talk about Linda. We'll pretend this place doesn't exist," he promised.

Her smile became more genuine. "You have other woes?"

He grinned, feeling suddenly lighthearted. "I'm afraid the hospital does represent most of them. Forget what I said. I'll detail them all if you'll let me feed you. How's that for an inducement?"

Hesitating, Ellen had the strange feeling of being on the edge of a precipice. She knew so little about him, even whether he was married, and yet they had shared some moments of disquieting intimacy. He stood patiently waiting, straight dark hair ruffled by the breeze, blue eyes expectant. And she couldn't resist the heady impulse to take that step off the edge, even if she didn't know where it would take her.

"Why not?" she said, feeling equally reckless.

She was rewarded by the pleasure on his face. "I promise to bring you back here before your carriage turns into a pumpkin." His large warm hand touched the small of her back to steer her toward his car. "Whenever that may be."

"I really shouldn't take too long," she said, conscious of a quickening in her stomach at even such a casual touch. "Can we be back by one-thirty?"

"No problem." He stopped by a beautifully restored humpbacked Saab. "Just painted," he said, his tone offhanded but his pride apparent. "She's a classic. What do you think?"

Ellen couldn't resist sliding her fingers over the satiny coat of forest green. "It's beautiful. Did you do it yourself?"

He held the passenger side door open for her. "Not the paint job. I rebuilt the engine, though. It's a 1969. Didn't know much about cars before I started, but she runs. Goes to show you can do anything if you put your mind to it."

"An optimist," she said in surprise. "How can you be?"

He slammed the door and went around to the driver's side, levering his big frame in behind the wheel. The grin he slanted at her was wry. "How can I not be? This job can be a downer even when you expect the best. If I weren't, I couldn't take it."

She studied him curiously as he started the car, which roared to life before settling smoothly into gear. "Do you track people after they leave here?"

"We try." He looked over his shoulder and backed the quaint car out of its slot. "Part of the program is a lengthy outpatient follow-up. We encourage graduates to attend AA meetings here for a while, come back for dietary and individual counseling. A big percentage do it."

She had seen his intensity; now she understood it. "You really care, don't you?"

"I wouldn't want to do something with my life that I didn't care about," he said matter-of-factly.

Ellen looked away from his hard, masculine profile, conscious of an ache in her chest. He was so sure about everything. In contrast, she felt so unsure.

Whether his approach was right or wrong, he was trying to accomplish a worthwhile purpose. He salvaged lives. And what did she do? She compiled cost estimates, which usually had little to do with the final decisions. And she would never have a real shot at making those decisions.

"What about you?" he asked.

"Oh, I work in Finance for the Kashiwa Corporation. We design and manufacture software."

"Finance? God, don't tell me you're an accountant."

"I'm not a CPA, although I wish I were. Why?"

"I can't see you spending your life peering at a ledger."

"Actually, it's a computer nowadays," she said stiffly. "And numbers can be infinitely fascinating. They're not dry at all."

He gave her a humorous glance. "I take it you enjoy your job."

"Yes, of course!" she said strongly, wondering all the time who she was trying to convince. "It's really a wonderful company. I have a generous salary and benefits. Sometimes I have to work overtime, but I'm never pressured, which is rare in the corporate world."

This time his glance was more searching. "You didn't really answer my question. Is the job itself satisfying?"

"I enjoy accounting work, believe it or not. But at Kashiwa I'm sort of a small cog and ... Oh, any job gets boring eventually, don't you think?"

"Maybe. But when you get bored, I think it's time to make a change."

Ellen was silent for a moment. "That sounds so easy." Her job was safety, security, people she knew, a check at the end of each month. She'd be crazy to give that up. So why did she feel so restless?

Nick's glance made Ellen wonder uncomfortably whether he had read her mind. But all he said was, "Shall we forget your job along with mine? We *are* supposed to be getting away from it all, remember? Speaking of which, here we are. Unfortunately, it's not Tahiti..."

Ellen laughed. "That would have been asking for a lot, considering we only had an hour and a half to work with!"

His smile was lazily charming. "I thought you'd see reason."

As she waited for Nick to lock the car, Ellen forgot her vague discontentment with her job—with her life?—and took a deep breath of the soft spring air, now spiced with the salty tang of the Sound. The restaurant Nick had chosen was just above Everett's marina, where they could watch the gulls and the sparkling blue water and the boats bobbing at their moorings. His choice was, in its own way, as romantic as his unexpected gesture in picking a flower for her. She couldn't imagine that he made a habit of being romantic in conventional ways; he was too intense, too impatient for that. But she found herself intrigued by the paradoxes that made up the man.

On the way in he again guided her with a casual hand on her back that seemed to burn her skin, leaving its imprint even after he had stood aside to open the door. That kind of touching seemed to be natural for him, Ellen thought. She told herself sternly that she should accept it as the impersonal gesture it no doubt was, not imagine that his hand had lingered or that his thumb had moved in a gossamer caress.

The hostess led them through the quietly elegant restaurant to a seat by the window. Diamond-tipped water dazzled Ellen's eyes, interrupted only by log booms and a sandy bar that was Jetty Island, a nature preserve. The dark green bulk of Whidbey Island stretched across the horizon. Watching a gull gracefully skim an air current, Ellen suddenly longed to be out on the Sound with the wind blowing her hair.

Smiling, she turned to Nick, only to find that he was watching her across the table, his eyes disturbingly intent. Her heart seemed to jerk and her pulse accelerated. Their gazes clung for a strange, dizzy moment in which the restaurant and the other patrons faded into a meaningless blur and the clatter of cutlery and low-voiced conversations were muted. Ellen saw only the battered, strong lines of Nick's face, the light in his startlingly blue eyes, the wry curve of his mouth.

And then the moment shattered. A waitress stood beside the table, smiling at them. "Can I get you a cocktail?"

Nick responded smoothly. "Ellen?"

His expression was now inscrutable, but Ellen suddenly remembered him saying, "How could you bring yourself ever to take a drink?"

"Just a diet cola, please," she said.

"Nothing for me," Nick added.

Somehow Ellen wasn't surprised. She wondered if he ever drank alcohol. After all he had seen, he should be marching for temperance.

"Are you ready to order, then?" the waitress asked.

They both chose the crab fettucine. When the waitress had gone, Nick leaned back in his chair.

"Since we're going to forget our woes, tell me about yourself," he commanded. "How you live, what you do in your spare time."

"I think you already know more about me than I do about you," Ellen countered. "Maybe you should go first."

A twinkle showed in his eyes. "But I'm bigger and tougher than you are."

"Typical male," Ellen teased. "You always resort to brawn."

"If you've got it, flaunt it."

"Then you're wearing the wrong clothes," she pointed out. "Although maybe if you undid a few buttons, added a nice gold medallion..."

He glanced down in mock surprise at his blue oxford cloth shirt, narrow tie and navy blazer, then self-consciously tugged at the tie.

"And here I was trying to impress you."

"You have," she said, her voice suddenly a little husky.

His smile faded and the tension between them became palpable. "Good," he said softly.

Perhaps fortunately, the waitress appeared then with their salads. Picking up her fork, Ellen wondered if she had imagined the heat in his eyes.

If it had ever been there, he had himself in hand now. His attention was divided between her and the food, his tone light. "So where do you live?"

The rest of lunch passed in the kind of tentative conversation two people employ in getting to know each other. They shared a liking for Italian food and hours spent browsing in bookstores. They read murder mysteries and science fiction. They both skiied, although Ellen knew herself to be timid. She seriously doubted that Nick

Braden knew the meaning of the word. Ellen loved her houseplants; Nick told her that he was building a house.

"Now that I've conquered the internal combustion engine, I'm moving on to bigger and better things."

"You mean you've never built anything before?" she asked, appalled.

His grin flashed. "I like a challenge."

"Good heavens," Ellen said weakly. She, who was afraid to give up the known even to the extent of hunting for a more exciting job, could hardly fathom beginning such a monumental project. Why, mistakes could cost thousands!

"I can make it exactly the way that suits me," he said with obvious satisfaction. "Down to the height of the kitchen counter and the size of the front door."

"It sounds..." She paused, searching for the right word. Daunting? Scary? Definitely challenging. But also exhilarating. She didn't sew or pot or paint, so she had never shaped anything, brought it alive, with her own hands. What would it be like? She imagined a house—*her* house, and leaned forward eagerly. "Have you started?"

"The foundation is being poured this week. Last summer I bought the land, ten acres on a bluff above the Stillaguamish. You can see forever, even the Olympic Mountains on a clear day." He spoke with growing enthusiasm, his lunch forgotten as he gestured with his big hands, trying to make her see his vision. "The property is wooded, firs and a few cedars and alder. The drive slants up through the trees, and then all of a sudden you come out in the open, feeling like you're at the top of the world. I won't even be able to see another house. My place is going to have solar heating and a big wraparound deck with a smaller one upstairs off the master bedroom. I'll have a vegetable garden, of course, and fruit trees. And a dog. I haven't had a dog in years, since..." A shadow crossed his face. "Since I was married," he finished abruptly.

Ellen concentrated on stirring her coffee and tried to sound casual. "Are you divorced?"

"Almost ten years ago." He shrugged. "Sometimes it seems like another lifetime."

She wanted to know more but didn't dare ask. It really wasn't any of her business. *Yet,* a small voice whispered. She tried not to hear it. She wouldn't read too much into an impulsive lunch invitation.

A few minutes later they wound their way toward the exit, Nick pausing to greet several people on the way out. Ellen noticed other diners glancing up at him as they passed. He had a quality that was larger than life, an unconscious charisma that along with his big, muscular body and rough, compelling face drew the eye. It was no wonder that in closer quarters he stole her breath.

The casual talk during the drive back took an effort on Ellen's part. With each mile closer to the hospital, she felt the loss of their companionable, even flirtatious, byplay. Soon he would be Dr. Braden again, Ellen, the sister of a patient. She hated the sight of the parking lot, where Nick steered the old Saab into a slot marked "Director." When he turned the key off, the car choked, fell silent, then gave one last spasmodic jerk.

At the sight of the rambling brown building with its sightless double glass doors, forgotten tension began to knot again in Ellen's chest. Linda had been here a week already; in three more, she would walk out, ready to take the children back. Ellen would be free, as well, to go on with her life. She ought to be looking forward to that moment. So why did it hang instead like a heavy dark cloud above her?

She didn't wait for Nick to come around and open her door. Instead she met him behind the car. "Thank you for lunch. I really enjoyed myself."

"I did, too," he said. "I'm glad I saw you leaving."

Ellen glanced involuntarily at the hospital, then back at his face. "I am, too. I . . . I guess I needed . . ."

"It's okay," he interrupted. "That's what I'm here for."

"You must get tired of listening to sad stories." Was that why he had taken her to lunch as well? Just part of the job?

"An experience isn't any less sad just because other people have had equally hurtful ones," he said roughly. "Don't belittle yourself."

"I wasn't . . ."

He looked almost angry. "Yes, you were. Don't try to convince yourself that the way you grew up is common-place. You have every reason to hurt."

"No." The ache in her chest had returned. "I'm an adult now. It's over. My childhood wasn't any worse than a lot of other people's. I can't let it stop me forever."

Nick spoke flatly. "Hurting pushes you sometimes, instead of stopping you."

"You sound almost . . ." Ellen stopped. His face had closed and she knew suddenly that he wouldn't welcome what she had been going to say. He sounded as though he was talking about himself. Well, why was she surprised? Had she imagined that his life had been a bed of roses? All she had to do was look at his face to know other-wise. The lines that carved his cheeks were too harsh, the faint scar just above one temple that disappeared into his dark, disheveled hair too telling, the ability he had to hide his emotions too practiced.

After a moment he said, "Sorry. I seem to be waxing philosophic today. God knows why."

Obeying an impulse she didn't understand, Ellen reached out and lightly touched his arm. Under her fingertips his muscle went rigid. Her hand dropped to her side but she didn't lower her gaze. "To quote from you, I was asking for it."

He looked down at her hand, then back at her face. His eyes had darkened and they mesmerized her. The hunger she saw there was muted, kept reined by his strength of will, but its heat was enough to spark a response in her. Her heart began to hammer and her breath seemed to have stopped. She was filled with a heavy, warm stillness that left her conscious of nothing but his scorching blue gaze and the hard line of his mouth.

He took a purposeful step forward and his big hands came up to close on her shoulders. "Those damn windows," he said huskily. "This isn't the time... Oh, hell." And his head bent.

His mouth couldn't have been more than a hairsbreadth from hers when he gave a low groan and stopped. His fingers bit into her arms and he lifted his head to look down at her with eyes that smouldered. His voice was uneven. "This is crazy."

Her mouth seemed to be trembling and Ellen bit her lip to control it. "I ... I really should be ..."

He still hadn't released her. "I need a chance to see you away from this place. Will you have dinner with me? Friday, maybe? Or Saturday?"

She smiled shakily. "I'd like that."

"Good." At last his hands dropped from her arms, but reluctantly. "If we go Saturday, maybe we could drive up to my land first, weather permitting. I want to take a look at the foundation, anyway, and I'd enjoy your company."

"If the weather is nice, maybe we could take a picnic with us instead of going to a restaurant," Ellen suggested. Immediately she wondered whether she was trying to chicken out; was she afraid of the connotations attached to a romantic dinner date?

The warmth in his eyes didn't make her knees feel any stronger. "A woman after my own heart. Listen, will you be able to get a baby-sitter?"

"Baby-sitter?" she echoed. Then her eyes widened. "Oh, no, I forgot the kids."

He shrugged. "Hey, why not bring 'em along? What's a picnic without kids?"

"Do you really want them?" she asked disbelief. "I'm sure I can..."

"I really don't mind," he interrupted, then shoved his hands in his pockets and smiled down at her. "They're part of your life. I don't want to pretend otherwise."

She opened her mouth to argue, to remind him how temporarily the children would be with her, but closed it again. The truth was that although she would have liked to see Nick alone this weekend, she also would have felt guilty at leaving the children, who were already in day care all week while she worked. Now of all times in their lives they needed more than to be dumped at a baby-sitter's.

So she said very softly, "Has anybody ever told you what a nice man you are?"

His smile was wry. "I have an ulterior motive, Ellen. I'm not a saint."

"I wouldn't accuse you of such a thing. But I'll still look forward to Saturday."

"Good. Until then . . . Try to be patient with your sister, okay? This first couple of weeks is hell."

Ellen gave a tiny nod. "I'll try."

"That's all any of us can do. Including Linda."

When Ellen drove away a minute later, she carried a picture of Nick Braden with her. Not handsome, with a nose that looked as though it had been broken and too many lines on a face that showed more than his age. But he had a capacity for enthusiasm that made her own life feel empty in contrast. When had she last cared passionately about something—or somebody? When had she last taken a chance?

At a stoplight Ellen momentarily closed her eyes, her fingers curling on the steering wheel as she remembered with heartstopping vividness the instant when his mouth had been so close to hers, when she had felt the warmth of his big body and the intensity of his gaze. The memory alone was enough to make her pulse accelerate. And she knew, although it frightened her, that there was one risk, at least, that she was prepared to take.

CHAPTER FOUR

LINDA'S HANDS were shaking as she dialed the phone. Shaking, and cold. With a shiver she cradled the receiver between her shoulder and ear and then tucked her hands under her arms. God, she was sweating again. How could you sweat and be cold at the same time?

"Hello?" It was her daughter's high, eager voice, and Linda was almost crushed by the wave of painful love mixed with guilt and a reality she couldn't face.

Tears stung her eyes and her mouth trembled as she said in a rush, "Sweetheart, it's Mommy. Oh, I miss you so much! You'll come and see me, won't you? I know Aunt Ellen will bring you. Promise me you'll come soon."

The answering silence was horrible, fraught with messages that Linda couldn't quite untangle. Laura loved her, didn't she?

"Mommy?" The too slow response was small, hesitant. "Where are you, Mommy?"

"I'm in a hospital. Hasn't Aunt Ellen told you? I must have scared you when I got sick, didn't I? But I'm better now. Really. I'm ready to come home as soon as the doctor will let me."

"Aunt Ellen says Patrick and I are gonna be with her for a long time. At least until Easter, she said. She said the Easter bunny would find us here okay."

Linda struggled against the nausea that rose in her throat. Was Ellen trying to turn her own daughter against her? Swallowing hard and hugging herself, Linda glared at the teenage girl who'd come out of the rec room to hover in the hall near the telephone. She could just wait.

"Well, you won't be there until Easter," she said, with an edge in her voice she didn't like. But it hurt, having Laura sound as if she didn't care whether her mother came home or not. Linda gave her another chance. "I miss you, sweetie."

"I thought you were dead," the little girl said with curious detachment. "Except you jerked sometimes."

Tears slid down Linda's cheeks and the taste of salt in her mouth increased her nausea. "I'm sorry," she said hopelessly. "I guess I'm not a very good mommy, am I?"

This time the silence was stubborn, just like Laura. Who had she been kidding? Linda thought. Laura didn't need her. Ellen would probably be a better mother anyway.

She lifted one cold hand to wipe her wet cheeks and sniffed. She tried to sound bright and uncaring. "Be good for your Aunt Ellen now, okay? Can I talk to her?"

"Don't you want to talk to Patrick?"

She closed her eyes against another wave of despair. "Not right now, honey. I don't think I . . ." *Can bear it?* She couldn't say that. "I guess I just feel a little sad. I need to talk to your Aunt Ellen, though."

"Okay." There was a pause and Linda thought her daughter had gone away until she heard the words, almost whispered. "I love you, Mommy." And then, muffled, "Aunt Ellen! It's Mommy! She didn't want to talk to you, Patrick."

Again that dark tidal wave of pain and guilt reared above Linda, threatening to crash down. In self-defense she made herself promises, a string of them like a rosary holding a crucifix, something to ward off the unbearable.

She was detoxed now; she would no longer wake up in the morning ill, desperate for a drink. She could find that core of serenity in herself that would allow her to be patient when Patrick and Laura quarreled, when Patrick wet his bed because he'd insisted he didn't need a last visit to the bathroom, when they wouldn't stop whining. She could be there when the children needed her, not retching over the toilet. If only they would let her out of here, she was ready to be a better mother.

She was jolted by her sister's cool voice coming on the line. "How are you, Linda?"

"Better," she said. "I'm . . . I'm sorry about the other day. It's scary being locked up. I'm not used to people like some of the ones in here. I guess I was feeling frantic."

"It's all right." Ellen still sounded distant. "I understand. Did you get a chance to talk to Laura?"

"Sort of." Linda hugged herself more tightly. "It's hard, just on the phone." Through a mist of tears she stared unseeingly at the girl still waiting for the telephone. "Ellen, does Mom know?"

"Yes."

How uncompromising she could sound, this big sister who was incapable of doing wrong. Would it have hurt her not to tell Mom?

Defensively, Linda said, "I just thought, with her health, that it might have been better if you didn't say anything."

"I couldn't exactly hide Laura and Patrick."

"Oh. I guess not." Hearing that familiar note of censure, of judgment, in her sister's voice humiliated Linda.

Torn between love and resentment, she said stiffly, "Could you come and see me again? I know you can't get me out of here. I won't ask you again. I promise. But it's lonely here. I just want..." She didn't know what she wanted. Out of here? A drink? Somebody to love her enough to understand?

Sometimes, to Linda's amazement, Ellen seemed to. This was one of those times, because her voice warmed even though she sounded tired when she said, "Of course I'll come, Linda. I didn't really mean it the other day. Can I bring you anything? Books or magazines, maybe?"

"I don't think so," Linda said quickly. "All we do is go to meetings. I don't have a chance to read."

"Tomorrow, then, during my lunch hour. Is that a good time?"

"Yes." She clutched at the telephone with her ice-cold hands and made herself say it, despite the bitter taste in her mouth. "Thank you."

She hung up the telephone and slumped back in the seat. Closing her eyes, she made herself another promise. Someday she wouldn't have to thank anybody. If she offered the words at all, it would be as a gift. Not as a payment.

"DO YOU REMEMBER Johnny Benson?" Ellen asked. She had come prepared with a store of small talk. It was all that stood between her and Linda, all that warded off the awkward silence. Or, worse yet, the hurtful words that could so easily slip out, never to be recalled.

Linda's brow crinkled in puzzlement. "Johnny? I'm not sure..."

"Remember, he lived down the street from us? He was the one who used to come in and head straight for the refrigerator. Drove Mom crazy, because he never asked permission, just helped himself. He was always starving.''

A spark of interest lit her sister's dull brown eyes. "Good Lord, yes. He was horribly shy. I remember trying to flirt with him when I was about twelve. He turned beet-red. He kind of disappeared after that, didn't he?''

Ellen smiled at the memory. "He was terrified of you.''

"Whatever happened to him?''

"That's what I was going to tell you. Mom ran into his mother a couple weeks ago. He must have quit being shy, because he has *five* children!''

A tiny giggle actually escaped Linda. "Maybe he undresses in the closet and then turns out all the lights.''

"But that's not the best part! Guess what he does for a living? And if you say accountant, I'll never speak to you again.''

"Well, what else could he... I know! He's a computer programmer!''

"Nope," Ellen said in triumph. "He's an obstetrician!''

The two had a fit of giggles that sharply reminded Ellen of the pink, ruffly room she and her sister had shared years ago, of the nights when they had whispered in the darkness and giggled about boys. For just an instant it brought back closeness that the years and alcohol had stolen from them.

But, too soon, the laughter was gone. Linda began to fidget again, to glance every few minutes at the clock as if the passing of time would change anything. She began to grumble about the Alcoholics Anonymous meetings, what a waste of time they were for her. Naturally, *she* didn't need them.

"They're like some kind of revival meeting. All these people standing up and beating their chests and wailing.'' She paced restlessly, her movements sudden and jerky. ''I mean, I ask you. It's embarrassing!''

Ellen left as soon as she decently could. Beyond the double glass doors the sunshine was warm and soft on her face and she noticed with pleasure the daffodils that had already replaced the crocuses in the narrow beds beside the walkway. As always, she felt as though she were fleeing from the hospital. Exactly what she ran away from, she didn't know.

No, that was a lie. She did know. It was the past she fled, the memories that Linda's thin, sallow face and haunted eyes brought alive. Ellen was beginning to realize that she had spent too many years running away from those memories, constructing a life in which they had no place.

Her sister had no place in that life, either, but Ellen couldn't bring herself to shut her out for good, however much she sometimes longed to. Today's visit had reminded her why.

However sulky Linda still was, however hard she still denied her alcoholism, increasing soberness *had* brought changes. There had been a wistful quality about her today, a sweetness that Ellen had nearly forgotten she possessed.

As though looking at a snapshot, Ellen saw her giggling. Linda's eyes had sparkled and her nose had crinkled endearingly. For just an instant she had looked so free, so young. She might have been sixteen again, before she had taken that first drink.

Ellen stopped beside her car and groped in her purse for the keys. Her vision was blurry, the keys elusive, and it was only then that she realized she was crying. Tears slipped quietly down her cheeks leaving in their wake not wrenching sorrow, but sadness. Sadness, mostly, for the woman Linda could have been.

Ellen glanced around surreptitiously to see if anyone had seen her, but found the parking lot blessedly empty. She had always hated pity. She was especially grateful that Nick hadn't appeared today. He'd given her enough.

Driving away from the hospital, Ellen tried not to think about Nick. Tomorrow she wanted to forget what he did with his life, what he was asking of her.

How *could* she forgive Linda, let the pain and anger go? And yet, today, for that one laughing instant, she had seen the way.

In some ways Linda *hadn't* changed. It was as though she had frozen emotionally, forever a teenager. She still couldn't see ahead, imagine consequences. Whatever emotion gripped her at the moment was all-consuming. Even her taste in clothing hadn't evolved. The fluffy, pink bathrobe she'd worn today was typical. Girlish, coy. That was Linda at sixteen, and at twenty-seven.

For the first time, Ellen let herself wonder whether her sister was the only one whose emotional growth had been arrested. Had she herself stopped maturing at some point she was afraid to reach beyond? If not, why had she let herself be trapped in a dead-end job? Why had she reached thirty without ever falling in love?

And why did her feelings for Nick scare her so much?

"So, WHAT DO YOU THINK?" Nick spread his arms wide, the expansive gesture taking in the sweep of river valley at their feet, the far-off, snowcapped Olympic Mountains, and even Everett, flattened by distance into a miniature on a giant topographical map.

The view was breathtaking. It also didn't surprise Ellen. Narrow lots, closed-in views, tidy lawns—they didn't seem to go with Nick Braden. This wooded bluff did feel as if it were on the top of the world. Ellen looked down at the Stillaguamish River, high with snow-melt from the Cascade Mountains, and smiled.

"It's glorious. You *can* see forever."

Turning her head, she saw that he wasn't looking at the view, but at her. That intensity was there in his blue eyes, and it made her uncomfortable.

But then he grinned and in one exultant movement swept Patrick onto his shoulders and grabbed Laura's small hand. "Come on, gang. Let me show you the house. It's got everything!"

At the moment, "everything" consisted of a gray concrete foundation surrounded by bare dirt. Metal rods stuck up through the rough concrete, and dibs and dabs of the hardened mix sprinkled the dirt like the remains Patrick and Laura left on Ellen's kitchen floor after every meal.

"Wow." Laura scrambled up onto the gray wall. "Watch me. I can balance up here. I bet Patrick can't."

"I can, too!" her younger brother protested indignantly. "Let me down! Let me..."

Ellen stepped forward. "Laura, I don't think that's very safe. If you fell on one of those metal poles you could hurt yourself badly."

"Hey, let's start the tour." Stepping over the foundation, Nick snatched Ellen's niece off her imagined balance beam without releasing Patrick, who still sat astride his shoulders. "This," he announced grandly, depositing her on her feet, "is the bathroom."

Feeling like an ineffectual fussbudget, Ellen trailed behind.

"The bathroom?" Laura scrunched up her nose, apparently not holding any grudge because he'd interrupted her fun. She peered at a wide pipe that disappeared into the ground. "You mean that's where the poop and everything goes?"

"Yup. And there's going to be French doors here leading out onto the deck, where there'll be a hot tub. So you can sit in here and, um, poop while you admire the mountains."

"Yuck." She looked genuinely appalled. "I like *privacy* while I go."

Not that she was willing to accord it to anyone else, Ellen thought, rolling her eyes. She never went to the bathroom that Laura didn't immediately follow her, Patrick usually in tow. Maybe after the indignities of childbirth, a constant audience was something a mother easily got used to. Ellen was finding it a little harder. This time, though, she had to agree with her niece.

"All that glass would make me nervous, too," she ventured.

"Hey, who's to see?"

"Somebody in an airplane," Laura suggested quite seriously.

Ellen bit back her smile. "Right. Or a parachuter."

"Or somebody in a balloon." The little girl spread her arms as wide as they'd go. "One of those big fat ones like you can ride in at the fair."

Ellen was getting into it. "Yeah, or a hang glider."

Nick tilted back his head to exchange a glance of masculine disgust with Patrick. Suppressing his own grin, Nick said, "What you're telling me is that someday I'm going to be in the can, just sitting here, and some hang glider is going to hover out there staring in my window. Is that it?"

The smile trembled betrayingly at the corners of Ellen's mouth as she said innocently, "Well, you never know."

He actually looked thoughtful. "I'll put blinds. Just in case."

Ellen's laugh bubbled over then, and so did Nick's. Laura looked from one to the other, frowning. Eventually losing patience—or maybe feeling left out, Ellen wasn't sure which—she grabbed Nick's big hand. "Show us some more, okay?"

"More," Patrick agreed.

Nick did, from the huge living room that was going to have maple floors and a wall of windows to the open kitchen and the bedroom wing. "Master suite upstairs," he said, gesturing at the sky, the words coming quickly and with obvious pleasure. "The stairs go right here, with a skylight up above and a curved balustrade. You know, the kind you used to slide down when you were a kid. And there'll be a bookcase on the landing and room for a big stuffed chair. So, what do you think?"

Somehow, with words and gestures and sheer enthusiasm, he'd succeeded in bringing the house alive. With a sharp pang of envy, Ellen saw it around her, white walls and gleaming wood, plants and books and colorful furniture. Unexpected corners and angles, and always space. It would be an exciting house, as bold as the man who created it.

"I'm jealous," she said softly. "It's going to be wonderful. Perfect."

His mouth had a wry twist. "Never perfect," he said. "How could it be? I'm not."

They looked at each other, silent, unguarded, and Ellen's heart ached. Could he see her cowardice, thrown into relief by his confidence? No, surely not. They were only talking about a house, symbolic perhaps of his delight in challenges, but possible also because of his money. Money, she told herself, earned from the wretched. Richly earned, a small voice in her whispered.

Something of her introspective mood lingered when they found a grassy knoll to spread out their picnic. The children frolicked like colts, rolling down the grassy slope, carefree in a way she hadn't yet seen them. Perhaps it was Nick, unfettered himself, releasing the constraints that bound others. She wondered if he would have that effect on her.

He proudly spread a hideous purple-and-red flowered tablecloth atop the grass, then plopped the plastic ice chest down in the middle of it.

"So, what do you think?" he asked.

"Uh . . ."

His sidelong glance held humor. "The cloth is courtesy of my mother. She never did have any taste."

Ellen pretended to look shocked. "What a thing to say about your own mother!"

"Wait till you meet her." With a firm hand on her upper arm he drew her down beside him, instead of safely on the other side of the ice chest as she'd intended. "My dad doesn't care, because he's color-blind. Mom likes red. Dad thinks it's a nice, discreet gray. So they're both happy. I just find," his grin flashed, "*alternate* uses for Mom's presents."

Ellen threw back her head and laughed, letting it wash over her like a splash of perfume that made her skin tingle. She crossed her legs and leaned back on straight arms, tilting her chin to look at him. "Is the feast courtesy of your mother, too?"

His answer didn't come immediately. Instead, his gaze took in her smiling face, lingered on her mouth, the vulnerable line of her neck. At last he said huskily, "Nope, but if she could see you, she'd be rooting for me."

Ellen's mouth felt dry, but she didn't try to look away. Her voice was just above a whisper. "Is that a compliment?"

"Lord, yes." He startled her by reaching forward to lift her braid, which had flopped over one shoulder. He fingered it, as though taking pleasure in its strong, satiny texture, before plucking off the band that held it confined and slowly, carefully, separating the heavy copper strands.

Ellen sat frozen, robbed of breath by his touch. Her hair, tumbling now in unruly waves, felt as if it were on fire, and she knew pink must stain her cheeks. She was spellbound, hypnotized, caught in a web of his making. She watched helplessly as his eyes darkened, as he let the heavy satin of her hair slip through his fingers, as he bent his head toward her.

The spell was shattered when Patrick flung himself at Ellen, knocking her backward when her arms lifted in reflex to hug him. Laughing, she struggled out from under his solid little body.

"I think you were just sacked," Nick observed.

Giggling, Patrick scrambled away. Ellen grabbed the little boy before he could escape and rolled over to pin him. She shook her head and growled, going for his neck, then turned the assault into a kiss at the last second.

"And as for you, young lady!" Ellen let one wriggling child go to turn to her attention to Laura, who'd watched bright-eyed, unquestionably the catalyst. In a minute Ellen was chasing her blond niece around the meadow, with Patrick trying to tackle her whenever she got within reach of his shorter legs.

Nick leaned back on one elbow and watched, content but for a wisp of regret. He'd have kissed her in another ten seconds, he'd have known what that soft, pouty mouth tasted like. On the other hand, he was pretty sure a fleeting taste wouldn't have been enough, so maybe it was just as well.

He could tell when the gang started to run out of steam, but he would put money on the kids outlasting their Aunt Ellen. With those long coltish legs in black jeans above white sneakers, and a baggy jade-green sweater that disguised her breasts, she looked almost as youthful as they did, but when she veered toward him, Nick saw that he'd been right. Beneath the freckles her face was rosy and she was puffing.

With split-second timing he reached out as she passed and snagged her ankle, bringing her crashing down on top of him. He wrapped his arms around her and tried to catch his breath, but that glorious red hair tumbling over her shoulders and tickling his face didn't help. Neither did the soft breasts he could feel compressed against his chest. She crinkled her nose at him, but her warm brown eyes were laughing.

"Hey, whose side are you on, anyway? That wasn't fair!"

"This is lots more fun than tackling Patrick," he said meaningfully, then grinned at the blush that made her cheeks even hotter. Raising his voice, he called, "Hey, gang, pile on!"

"You'll be sorry..." she began, too late. He hadn't known a three-year old could hit so hard.

Nick croaked a protest as Laura launched herself in turn, but all that came out was the last of his air when she landed. He lay there gasping when Ellen rolled off.

"Serves you right," she said heartlessly. "Well, are you going to feed us or what?"

"Did you make something icky?" Laura asked, scrunching her nose.

"You know, that expression makes you look a lot like your aunt."

"That was a sneer!" Ellen protested. "I never sneer!"

Practically with the same breath Laura said, "I don't look like Aunt Ellen! I don't have those spots all over my face. Mom says they're cute, but I don't think so." Her eyes crossed as she tried to look at her nose. A note of doubt entered her voice. "I don't have spots, do I?"

"They are cute," Nick assured her. "And no, you don't. But you *do* look like your Aunt Ellen sometimes. *And* like your mom."

He felt the child's instant withdrawal, though she didn't move. It was Patrick who said, "You know Mommy?"

"Yep. She's looking forward to seeing you guys. Now," he made a production out of opening the ice chest, "here comes the good part. Liver pâté, cold chicken cordon bleu, a superb dry white wine..."

There was silence, three pairs of appalled eyes staring at him. Nick laughed. "Hey, it was a joke. Really. I mean it. We're having do-it-yourself sandwiches, and I even brought peanut butter."

Actually, the lunch he spread out on the cloth turned out to be a little fancier than the mention of peanut butter had suggested. He'd apparently gone to a deli, because he'd brought bagels, sliced turkey and Havarti cheese, and containers with fruit salad and potato salad and even carrot cake at the end.

Later, watching the kids happily munching, Ellen said quietly, "Thanks for thinking about what they'd like. You must remember being that age."

"All too well. I was one of the pickiest eaters in the world. If it was green, I didn't like it. I wouldn't even try mint ice cream. It might be veggies in disguise. I used to try to hide my broccoli or whatever under my plate. Never seemed to occur to me that Mom would find it when she cleared the table."

Ellen sighed. "You ought to see these two. They think everything I make for dinner is gross. No, I take that back. Laura thinks it's gross and Patrick takes her word for it. From the amount they eat, I keep expecting them to start getting pale and weak. But, no. As far as I can tell, they thrive on ice cream and sugar-coated cereal."

He heard the frustration in her voice, and diagnosed it correctly. She'd been saddled with two kids and she didn't know how to be a mother. He'd be willing to bet she did just fine, considering, but he also had a feeling that Ellen was a perfectionist. Scrambling to get by wouldn't be enough for her; she'd want to be an instant supermom.

"Hey." He reached out and tugged at her hair. "Don't worry. Kids don't need a whole lot to eat, you know, especially if they're not having a growing spurt. Laura and Patrick aren't wasting away."

"I guess not." She made a face. "How come you're such an expert? Do you have kids?"

Being with her sharpened that familiar regret. "No," he said. "Which is probably just as well. I'd hate to be an absentee father. I've always liked kids, though. I thought about becoming a pediatrician. Even though I didn't, we do all learn a little nutrition in med school, you know."

"Why didn't you become a pediatrician? You're so good with Laura and Patrick."

Again he hesitated, conscious of the narrow line he walked. What he believed—what he was—was repugnant to Ellen. Reminders wouldn't serve any purpose. "You might call what I do a personal crusade," he said evasively. "It's important."

She looked down at her hands, and her voice was suddenly constrained. "I can't argue with that. If you can help Linda... If you can cure her..."

"Hey." He reached out to clasp her hand. "You don't have to say it. I know how you feel."

She lifted her head and tried to smile. "You do have a way of reading my mind, don't you?"

"No." His own voice became huskier. "Not always."

Again that thread of tension bound them. Damn, she was beautiful, he thought. And he was crazy to want her as badly as he did.

Nick made himself let Ellen's hand drop, although he kept looking at her when he said, "How would you guys like to go for a walk? My neighbor is building, too. I wouldn't mind seeing how he's coming along. His house must be about done, and I'm pretty sure I saw a barn going up."

"Do you think he has horses?" Laura asked eagerly.

"I don't know if he has any there yet," Nick said, "but I imagine that's what he has in mind."

"Wow!" Laura said. "I'll bet he does. Let's go. You want to pet a horse, don't you, Patrick?"

Patrick nodded shyly, and Nick grinned and tousled his hair.

After they'd put the remains of their lunch in the car trunk, they strolled along a path through the woods that Nick knew popped out on the next property.

Long before they could see the house, they heard hammering and the whine of a saw mixed with voices. The kids bounded out of the woods, with Nick and Ellen following at a more leisurely pace.

At the edge of the clearing Ellen stopped stock-still. "Oh," she breathed in sudden delight.

Nick followed her gaze to the white-fenced pasture, behind which a couple of horses grazed on the sparse spring grass. As far as he was concerned, a horse was a horse, but it was plain that to Ellen, at least, these weren't your regulation four hooves and a tail.

She deserted him without a backward glance, and soon she was leaning on the fence with her niece and nephew, all three stroking the whiskery muzzles. Her fiery curls cascaded down her straight, slender back, and in the tight jeans her derriere was deliciously rounded. Nick took a moment to savor the view before he exchanged a wave with his neighbor working on the barn and headed up to check on the progress.

"Your family?" his middle-aged neighbor inquired, with a nod toward Ellen and the kids.

I wish. Nick was taken aback by the intensity of the thought. Shoving it back down where it had come from, he shook his head. "Just a friend and her niece and nephew she's babysitting for a few weeks. They're obviously horse lovers."

"Maybe the kids'd like to be led around on my mare. She's gentle." The man unplugged his saw, then stuck out his hand. "I don't think we got around to trading names the last time. I'm Les Richards."

Nick shook the proffered hand. "Nick Braden. The lady is Ellen Patterson. And that's Laura and Patrick."

Nick was introduced to Les's wife, Barb, who was busy directing a couple of volunteer carpenters in putting up stall partitions. Two minutes later he found himself leaning on the fence watching as Les saddled the fine-boned mare. The two horses were apparently Arabians, and Les and Ellen happily threw around talk about Egyptian Arabs versus Polish before coming to some kind of concurrence.

"You ride regularly?" Les asked as he boosted Patrick into the saddle, followed by Laura.

"Yes, I have a friend who breeds Arabs. Sweet Home Arabians, over in Stanwood. I'd love to have one of my own, but it wouldn't be any fun if I had to board it." She tickled the chestnut mare under her chin and added wistfully, "Maybe someday."

Nick couldn't help thinking about how easy it would be to clear part of his property for pasture. He even had a nice flat spot for a barn. There *was* something appealing about these horses, with their dished faces and elegant, graceful bodies. Right. Only what the hell would he do with one? he asked himself. Collect its manure for his garden?

But he liked watching Ellen's slim hand caress the mare's sleek reddish-brown coat and listening to the gentle, mesmerizing voice that had the horse's neatly pointed ears flickering her way.

It was all too easy to imagine that hand on him, that soft voice becoming dreamy for his benefit. Forgotten, he propped his elbows on the fence and let himself indulge in a little fantasy. The sweater would go first, he decided, remembering the scattering of freckles on her throat. Finding out where else she had freckles would be a pleasure. Down that narrow, slender back, maybe? What about the gentle curve of her buttocks? Those incredibly long, slim legs?

Nick swore under his breath. Those were dangerous thoughts in mixed company. Les was already completing the circuit of the paddock, leading the horse back his way. Ellen, who'd walked beside the children with a reassuring hand on Patrick's ankle, flashed a smile of pure delight at Nick. It was echoed by Laura's, and for a moment the woman and child looked uncannily alike.

Nick straightened, forcing lustful thoughts back under cover, and walked to meet them.

Les smiled at Ellen. "Like to give her a try?"

"I'd love to."

"Do we *have* to get off?" Laura pleaded.

Reaching up to grab her younger brother, Les grinned. "You can have another turn when your aunt's done, how about that?"

"Well . . ." Laura reluctantly disentangled her fingers from the pale mane. "All right," she conceded, and allowed Nick to lift her off. A minute later she and Patrick had scrambled up onto the fence to watch.

Ellen adjusted the stirrups and swung herself effortlessly onto the mare's back. Nick watched as she tried out the Arab's paces, trotting, cantering, pulling her to a sliding stop. She rode with easy grace, a part of the horse, her curls as fiery as the mare's sleek coat.

"That's a pretty sight," Les murmured. "She's a natural."

Nick didn't know about the natural part, but the pretty sight he could go along with. When at last she stopped beside them and slid off the horse's back, her cheeks were pink again and her hair wind-tossed.

"That was wonderful!" Ellen exclaimed. "She's a joy."

It wasn't the horse who was the joy in Nick's opinion. Her wariness gone, happiness shining in her eyes, Ellen damned near took his breath away. He'd known she was beautiful the first time he saw her, but now... Now he wanted her to look like this forever, wanted never to see her sad again, never to see her lift her chin in that gesture of pride that closed him out. He wanted suddenly, badly to make her happy. If only it were that simple.

Twenty minutes later, the kids satisfied, eternal gratitude to Les sworn, they headed back on the trail. In the woods the sun found its way through the still bare vine maples and the tall branches of the Douglas firs to dapple the ground. Lacy, new fronds of ferns uncurled in the deep shade and the rare white flower of a trillium peeked from behind a fallen, decaying log.

Ellen was admiring the wildflower when she realized that the children had disappeared ahead. She could hear their muffled voices, Patrick singing tunelessly and Laura calling something indistinguishable. Blurred, the voices didn't intrude on the stillness, the hush, that seemed a natural part of even this small woods.

The hair on the back of her neck prickled as Ellen turned slowly to face Nick. He was looking at her as she had somehow known he would be, his blue eyes darkened, the sensuous quirk of his mouth tempering his rough face.

"The kids..." she heard herself say, her voice not quite her own. "I should..."

His voice sounded different, too. "They'll be all right," he said gruffly, then, "I've wanted to do this all day."

All it took was his hands on her shoulders and her pulse took a dizzying leap. She shivered, more from fever than chill. The charisma she'd sensed from the beginning was a force field around him now, an electric current that scraped across her nerve endings. His gaze trapped hers as Nick drew her forward, bent his head.

There was nothing tentative about his kiss. When his mouth took hers she felt only energy and heat and hunger. He made her weak and helpless too quickly; but when she heard his groan, felt the increasing desperation in his touch, she knew power. She parted her lips, clung to him, dissolving and coming alive all at the same time.

"Aunt Ellen!"

Laura's imperious summons was unwelcome, a shocking reminder of reality. Nick's mouth stilled against Ellen's, and then with a ragged sound he broke the kiss, burying his face in her hair. His arms tightened almost convulsively before he let her go.

"Aunt Ellen, aren't you coming?"

It was all she could do to answer. "We'll ... we'll be along, Laura."

"Unfortunately," Nick said under his breath. He stepped back, breathing hard, his blue eyes hot with barely banked desire.

Ellen was shaking as she wrenched her gaze away and struggled to regain her shattered control. How could she lose so much of herself so quickly? Was that what falling in love meant?

As she turned away and began to stumble along the path, she was certain of only one thing. It was time to flee, just as she had done all her life.

CHAPTER FIVE

SHE SHOULD HAVE KNOWN that anything too good to be true probably was, Ellen thought tiredly. That day with Nick, Laura and Patrick had been so heartbreakingly normal she had convinced herself it might last. Maybe *this* was what the children would really be like, freed from their unhappiness.

Well, if so, they had become unhappy again the minute they walked in the front door of her condo. In fact, the whole wonderful day already seemed distant to Ellen, and this was only Wednesday. When she tried to picture Nick lounging on the purple-and-red tablecloth with his smile deepening the creases in his cheeks, or the children laughing as they ran across the meadow, the image shimmered like a mirage. Or a dream.

Laura had gone right back to watching television as many hours of the day as Ellen would let her. She always stared, mesmerized, with a glassy look in her eyes that told Ellen her mind was elsewhere. Her small hand no longer curled confidently in Ellen's. If Ellen even sat next to her on the couch, she stiffened, withdrew. Although she chattered constantly, it seemed almost compulsive. And she never laughed. Not like she had that day with Nick.

In Patrick the difference didn't seem quite so acute, maybe because he was always quiet. But on Saturday he, too, had laughed and frolicked and teased. Once home, he'd reverted within a day to his usual play.

Now, pretending to flip through a magazine, Ellen watched him surreptitiously. Blocks were set out on the living room carpet and Patrick was running his tanks and trucks over them, simulating terrible smash-ups that especially bothered Ellen because he added no sound track. If he'd yelled even a joyful, "Kaboom!" she would have figured it was just typical boy play. Instead, he masterminded the violence with grim intensity made the more obvious by his silence.

Overlying the sound of grinding metal and crashing blocks were the canned voices from the TV, which Laura watched expressionlessly. Coloring things were spread all over the floor in front of the couch and she had even managed to spill some glitter, but she'd lost interest once she turned the cartoons on.

Ellen realized wearily that she should have refused permission. But she'd desperately wanted the chance to clean up the kitchen and balance her checkbook in peace. The week was barely half-done, and already it seemed endless. How did parents manage? she wondered, for at least the hundredth time. Thank heavens it was the kids' bedtime.

Now she clapped and said brightly, "Okay, gang, time to turn the TV off and start picking up."

"But I want to watch the end!" Laura protested. "Please?"

"Is it almost over?"

"Well . . . Not really."

"I'm sorry. You know eight-thirty is bedtime." Ellen picked up the remote control and switched the TV off.

Laura didn't move. "Patrick's not picking up."

Ellen turned. "Hey, Patrick." When he didn't lift his head, she snapped her fingers. "Time to put the toys away! Do you need help with those blocks?"

"I don't want to pick up."

"I'm sorry. I know you were having fun, but you need to get ready for bed."

"Don't we get stories?" Laura demanded.

"If everything is put away in time."

"Can't we leave it 'til tomorrow?"

Ellen tried hard to sound patient. "No. Now let's get started or we won't have time for reading."

"It's not fair," Patrick whined. "I don't like to pick up."

No kidding. They had this conversation every single night. Slowly but surely, it was eroding Ellen's patience.

"You know what?" she said, as she started fitting the wooden blocks back in their box. "Neither do I. In fact, I don't know anybody who likes to."

When she glanced over her shoulder, she saw Laura slowly put a cap back on a marker, then toss it toward the plastic cup, missing by six inches. With great concentration, she tried throwing another one that missed, too.

Ellen gritted her teeth. "Laura, you're playing, not doing your job. Now come on."

"Mommy doesn't make me pick up," Patrick said, ramming one truck with another. "She says I'm too little."

"If you're old enough to make the mess, you're old enough to help pick it up," Ellen told him. She could hear the edge in her voice, feel the tension tighten around her forehead.

"I'm too tired. I want to go to bed."

"Me, too," Laura chimed in.

The temptation was huge. Just to have them out of the way, do it herself . . .

"No!" Ellen was startled to realize that she'd said it aloud. But she meant it. Heaven only knew how long she would have Laura and Patrick. This constant chaos would drive her nuts if they wouldn't help.

She slammed a block into the box with unnecessary force. "You guys promised! Remember, when you took the stuff out? Now I expect you to do your part!"

Patrick's face crumpled.

"Patrick!"

Tears spurted like a water faucet turned on. Before she could grab him, he ran to the hall. At the last minute he turned around and sobbed, "You hurt my feelings when you yell!"

Ellen jumped up. "Patrick! Don't you dare . . ."

Too late. The bathroom door slammed and she heard the lock click. Oh, boy. Here they went again. For a moment she closed her eyes, feeling her head throb. Now what? Pry him out?

She turned helplessly to his older sister. "Laura . . ."

"I'm not going to pick up without Patrick! It's not fair!"

She couldn't tell a six-year-old that life wasn't fair. So Ellen just sighed. "You can clean up your own mess. I'm not asking you to pick up Patrick's."

The lower lip was trembling. "You're mean! I want Mommy!"

So did Ellen. She wanted Linda to come home, take responsibility for her own children, love them the way they deserved to be loved. Because if she wouldn't—couldn't—then it was up to Ellen. And she didn't know if she was capable of giving the children what they needed.

She hid her sadness and unease. "Laura, will you come here and talk to me for a minute?"

Laura turned her face away and began to cry. "I want my mommy," she whispered. "Please? I want..."

"I know." Her chest aching, Ellen drew the child into her arms. "I know," she repeated.

THE CRIES WRENCHED her out of sleep. Disoriented, she sat bolt upright in bed, straining her ears. What had she heard? Something out of the ordinary. A car engine? The door? Footsteps?

Then it came again, muffled sobs. Remembering, she swung her legs off the bed, groped blindly for her robe. Down the hall, bare feet soundless on the carpet.

Light from streetlamps filtered through the thin curtains in the guest bedroom. Patrick was huddled with his face buried in the pillow and his knees drawn up under him; his shoulders shook with his crying. The sound was a mere thread, stifled by the pillow and his fear of the darkness. It was a miracle that she'd heard him. And another miracle that Laura, a dark mound beyond him, was sleeping right through it all.

Ellen sat on the edge of the bed and gathered the small body onto her lap. "Sshh," she murmured. "It's okay, pumpkin. I'm here. Come on, let's have a cuddle."

She carried him to the rocking chair and sat, beginning the slow, back and forth rhythm that was one of the barely remembered patterns of her own childhood. Her voice was a gentle whisper that slid easily into song.

"Sshh, love. I'll stay with you until you're ready to go to sleep. I promise. How about 'Rock a bye baby, in the tree top? When the wind blows, the cradle will rock. When the bough breaks, the cradle will fall...'" Over and over, barely murmuring, the song a muted part of the night.

Slowly he relaxed, clutched her with disarming trust. He was so small, so young. Not ready for the pain life had dealt him. It *wasn't* fair. No child his age should have to carry the weight of sadness.

As happened to her often these days, present and past overlapped, and she was both holding and being held. So afraid of the darkness. Afraid her mother wasn't strong enough, but never daring to let herself think it. Afraid to let sleep capture her, because then she was helpless.

The faint light fell softly on his tear-streaked face, on the curve of lashes and the wisps of pale hair. His breathing became regular, a sigh against her neck. He was so tender, so young, she thought again, blinking back the sting of unbidden tears. It wasn't fair.

"LET'S TALK ABOUT what we can do to keep the alcoholic from drinking." Nick crossed his arms and leaned against the wall, his gaze scanning the group.

Ellen narrowed her eyes, instantly suspicious. He'd said it so casually, so...affably. She saw none of his usual intensity. He wasn't pacing, gesturing impatiently, piercing each participant with a gaze that demanded response. He just leaned there, waiting.

From the back of the room came a hesitant response. "You mean, like if they go off the wagon once they get out of here?"

"Sure." He abandoned the wall, as though suddenly restless, and moved to the table at the front, where he perched on the edge. "Or we can talk about what you've tried in the past to keep them off the booze."

"Everything," somebody muttered, and Nick inclined his head in acknowledgement.

"Okay," he said, in that gravelly voice that was so compelling. "Let's play some games. Mary, why don't you come on up here? And, let's see, John." The young, ponytailed man and the middle-aged woman obeyed, not meeting each other's eyes. "All right, Mary. John's your husband. You know he's started drinking again. You've smelled it on his breath. Today while he was at work you searched the house and couldn't find a bottle. Hey, you've all done that, right? Now you're in the middle of making dinner and you discover that you don't have any tomato sauce after all. Guess what? John offers to go to the store for you. Generous. Let's see you take it from here."

The room was silent. Uneasy gazes moved from the charismatic doctor to the mismatched pair who stood awkwardly beside the table. Where had the tension come from? Ellen wondered. Over the two weeks they'd met, this hodgepodge of people had gotten used to each other, even become fond of each other in the odd way of people who share a misfortune. Last week's talk about nutrition had become animated, a cozy sharing of recipes and stories. But something different was going on here.

She glanced at Nick and wasn't surprised when their eyes met. She'd been wrong about his intensity; it was there, all right, only masked. And she felt, in that instant of wordless communication, that this mattered. That he wanted *her*—no, all of them, it had to be—to understand something that he couldn't explain.

He stood up again and strolled to the side of the room, leaving the pair in front alone. There was panic in the woman's eyes, but the man started gamely.

"Uh... Hey, listen, I'll go to the store. No problem. Do you need anything else?"

"No!" There was startling force in the middle-aged woman's answer, which even she heard. A flush crept up her neck and across her cheeks, and she bit her lip. "No, I'll go."

"That's dumb. You're the one who has to cook dinner. By the time you make a salad I'll be back."

Mary squeezed plump hands together in unconscious anxiety. "But it'll be so late... Maybe we should just go out to dinner instead. I have to grocery shop tomorrow anyway."

"We can't afford to do that. Anyway, why are you making such a big deal out of this? What is it, don't you trust me?"

Unwillingly gripped by the artificial tableau, Ellen couldn't tear her eyes from those hands, writhing, kneading. And yet, always, she was aware of Nick, a potent presence even when he'd directed attention away from himself. What did he want of them?

Even though she'd been thinking about him, she was startled by his voice. "Okay, cut." He walked back to the front. "Let's have comments. Was this a familiar conversation? What could Mary have done?"

There was a moment's silence, and then Ellen heard herself say it. "Nothing."

Heads swiveled, and she was conscious of heat rising in her own cheeks. "It... it doesn't work," she said lamely.

Now his blue eyes bored into hers, seeing to the terrified center of her being. "What doesn't work?" he asked.

"Trying to stop them..."

He waited.

There might as well have been no one else in the room. Somehow this had come down to the two of them. Ellen's pulse was racing and she felt dizzy.

"Okay," he said. "Let's explore a different side of this issue. You're at a party and he's gotten sloshed. He staggers against the coffee table and falls down. Everybody turns to stare. What do you say?"

"What *can* I say?" Ellen's answer held unconscious bitterness.

"Naturally, he wakes up the next morning sick as a dog. But he's already missed too much work. He'll lose his job if the boss finds out booze is the problem. He wants *you* to call in sick for him. The boss'll believe you." Nick's arms were crossed, his gaze still steady on Ellen's. "Do you do it?"

She was suffocating with anxiety, with memories. The sound of her stepfather retching in the bathroom, her mother's face pinched but her voice cheerful and slightly exasperated as she called in. That darn stomach trouble again. If I could just get him to the doctor, but he's so stubborn! Then later, the young Ellen had overheard her mother talking to her stepfather, voice pitched low but her desperation still audible. "What will we do if you lose your job?"

And then he did. The memory of the choice he had made sent a shudder through Ellen.

"Yes," she said in a stifled voice. "If we need his salary, if he needs the job..."

Nick looked—what?—disappointed? Something flickered in those blue eyes, and then he began to pace, the uncompromising force of his gaze turned from her. "What about the rest of you?"

"If the family depends on his job..."

"We have a right to protect ourselves, don't we?"

"Yeah, he's not the important one here."

"Okay." He rapped his knuckles against the tabletop. "That was a toughie. When you have to start adding the well-being of other family members into the equation, decisions are hard. But let's think about the messages we're giving him. We make excuses for him. What are we really doing?"

Mary spoke up, sounding almost angry. "Making it easy for him."

He gave her a quick thumbs-up and began to pace again, faster now, his voice forceful. "Right! But maybe we could be sneakier. What if we'd made an excuse the night before to drag him away from the party before the danger point? We know how much it takes to make him sick the next day, don't we?"

"Yes, but..." Ellen stopped.

"But?"

"We're trying to...to control him."

He balled his hand into a triumphant fist. "Got it! And what'd you say earlier?"

"It doesn't work," she repeated dully.

There was pity in his eyes, and yet also the warmth of approval. "Does making excuses for him work?"

Of all people, she should know. "No," she said, almost whispering. "No."

"Are you saying that we have to let them hit bottom?" a woman asked.

Ellen felt both safer and bereft when his gaze again left hers.

"Not exactly," he answered. "Yes, I'm saying you need to let the alcoholic suffer his own consequences. That's different than the idea of hitting bottom. That implies that his disease is far advanced, which means there is some irreparable damage to his liver and his brain cells. Actually, the sooner an alcoholic gets in treatment, the better. But when you protect him, however well-intentioned you are, the longer it's going to be before he faces his disease. If you make excuses for the boss, you'll save his job for awhile. But you're also putting off a confrontation that might tip the balance, make him get help. Do you see?"

Heads were nodding, there was a murmur. Ellen thought of her mother, of all the excuses, of the times the whole family had withdrawn to protect George Whalley from embarrassment that would have been devastating to him—and might have saved his life.

Nick began to pace again, this time between the seats. It was as though he needed to touch, to make his message more concrete than mere words could manage. Ellen almost flinched when she felt his hand on her shoulder, when he squeezed gently, and yet the warmth of his big hand was also reassuring.

"But I don't want you looking back and blaming yourself for times you did just that—protected someone you love," he continued. "The trouble with the disease of alcoholism is that it comes on slowly, and it's often years before it's recognized. The issue here is not the past. That's done, closed, over. Forget it. Think about the future. No matter how badly you want somebody to quit drinking, *you can't make him.* If you try, you'll end up feeling like a failure. Anybody want to argue with that?"

He paused at the front and raked them with that devastatingly perceptive gaze. "No? Okay. There's a side issue to all this. If you admit that you can't control the alcoholic's behavior, if you do quit trying, then what?"

Why did he always look at *her?* But Ellen couldn't help but see what he was driving at, though she didn't like it, didn't want to believe it.

"Then you're not responsible for him," she said slowly. "You don't need to feel guilty because of what he does, or blame yourself."

"Right," he said again, flashing a quick smile that deepened the crease in that harsh cheek, inexplicably warming her. "You're responsible for your own behavior, for how you *react* to his; but not for his."

There was silence, and then he smiled and sat on the edge of the table again. "Okay, folks. Think about it. We'll talk more about this issue next week. By the way, can you wait a minute, Ellen?"

In the shuffle of voices and chairs being pushed back, Ellen, too, stood, then hesitated. Nick was surrounded, but in only a few minutes he'd answered questions and ushered the last family members out. Then he turned to Ellen. "Thanks for waiting."

"I brought your books back." She nodded at the pile she'd deposited on the table.

"What'd you think?"

"They were . . . interesting," she said.

As though hearing her restraint, he said quizzically, "Did tonight's session upset you?"

Her fingers bit into the soft leather of her purse. "Upset? Why should I be?"

A small frown furrowed his brow. "Okay. I won't push. Can I suggest something, though?"

She made herself relax and smiled ruefully. "I'm sorry. Of course you can."

"Go to an Al-Anon meeting."

"A what?"

"It's AA's unofficial family group. For people whose lives have been affected by an alcoholic, present or past. I think you'd find it . . ." he seemed to search for a word, shrugged, "liberating."

"I don't live with Linda. Her problems don't really affect me."

"But your stepfather's did." He reached out, touched her cheek. "Try it."

Her smile trembled only a little. "I'll like it?"

"Yeah." Again that smile quirked, softening his rugged face. "Speaking of liking, could I talk you into a night on the town Friday?"

"Is there such a thing in Everett?"

The smile widened. "Actually, I had the big city in mind. One of my favorite comedians is at the Comedy Club in Pioneer Square. We could have dinner first, a moonlit walk on the waterfront... What do you say?"

Her own smile was uncomplicated, heartfelt. "I'd love it."

WOULD ELLEN BRING the children? Restless, impatient, Linda paced across the lobby and peered out at the parking lot. She sat down but found herself too anxious and jumped up again. How she missed Laura and Patrick. She hadn't known how bad it would be until they were taken away from her.

She picked up a magazine from a small side table, glanced at it without interest and tossed it aside. Her reflected image in the glass doors caught her eye and she paused. Really, she didn't look too bad. Maybe a little skinny and waif-like, but then that had always been half her charm. Men liked petite women. Dr. Braden—no, Nick, she liked to think of him as Nick—was so big, so husky, that the contrast was especially exciting. He had such fire, such power, but with her he was always gentle. That turned her on.

She saw Ellen's charcoal-gray Accord the minute it swung in from the street. Her heart sank when she saw nobody beside Ellen, and then leaped into her throat again when she caught a glimpse of the top of a blond head. She ached to run outside, cursed the stupid rules that wouldn't let her. It was torture to watch from behind the glass as Ellen unbuckled Laura and helped Patrick out of his car seat, then took both children's hands to walk across the parking lot. Linda had never felt so caged.

The minute the door opened she crouched and held out her arms. She was hardly even conscious of the dampness on her cheeks.

"Oh, sweeties."

"Mommy?" Laura hung back, looking wary, even doubting. Patrick, though, didn't hesitate. He flung himself into her waiting arms and clutched her with all his strength. Thank God for the uncomplicated love of a toddler.

Over his head she met Laura's dubious gaze.

"You don't look sick," her daughter said accusingly. "How come you're in the hospital if you're not sick?"

Ellen stood silently back, refusing to help Linda out. Linda was their mother, not Ellen. This was her job.

As gently as she could, Linda said, "I've been sick, honey. I'm getting better now. But it's slow. You know how it is when you've had the flu, and you try to jump up and play too soon?" Laura's head bobbed and Linda continued, "Well, if I leave too soon, while I'm still feeling sick, it's going to be hard for me not to drink. I need to get strong before I can go home. But I miss you guys." She squeezed Patrick, blinked back the tears. "I miss you so much."

Linda was surprised by Ellen's smile. It contained the approval that she had always longed for from her big sister, but which came so seldom. So why did she feel the bite of anger? In a rare moment of insight, she realized that Ellen's approval now was only the flip side of her usual disdain. After all, Ellen was perfect and Linda was the screwup. Right? Nothing changed.

No, not true. One thing had. Now she was a mother, and she wanted better for her kids. For them, she couldn't screw up.

Biting her lip, she straightened and held out a hand to Laura. "There's a rec room down the hall that has some toys. I think there's even some books. Maybe I could read you guys a story."

Laura hesitated for a bare instant and Linda held her breath. Then she slipped her small hand into her mother's. "Okay," she agreed, and Linda exhaled on a wave of bittersweet pleasure.

Ellen followed them down the hall, feeling curiously detached, an observer, not a participant. In the otherwise deserted rec room Linda did read Laura and Patrick a story, then sat cross-legged on the floor and helped set up a wooden train set. Completely absorbed in her children, she looked childlike herself beside them. Arms and legs akimbo, she hugged, tickled and giggled, tossing only an occasional comment at Ellen.

Unfortunately, most of them had to do with Dr. Braden.

"He says to call him Nick. He's spending a lot of extra time with me. I guess he can tell I've got more potential than most of these people. It's not like I have any secrets from him, right? He knows I can make it. I think he expects to keep seeing me even after I leave here."

True or false? It shouldn't have mattered, but Ellen felt her detachment slip a notch. She was uncomfortable with Linda's small secretive smiles and the way her voice softened on Nick's name. Did he have this effect on all women?

Linda went on with a shrug, "We have these stupid meetings where people cry and dump out all their problems. I mean, I have more dignity than that. That's why Nick respects me. He can talk to me like an equal. Sometimes I can feel this spark."

"I'm sure he's wonderful," Ellen agreed stiffly. "But I hope you don't expect too much from him. It's yourself you have to think about, and getting well for Laura and Patrick's sake."

"What's the matter, don't you believe he'd be interested in me?"

"I didn't say that..." Scary thought. Was she crazy to date a man with his kind of sexual charisma? And how could she tell Linda, 'Oh, by the way, I'm having dinner with Nick tomorrow night'? Feeling clumsy, she said, "I just . . . I don't want you to *depend* on someone else. Because then if you're disappointed . . ."

A flash of pure anger crossed her sister's delicate face. "You're jealous, aren't you? What's the matter, can't you handle turning thirty and not having a husband?"

"Don't be ridiculous! It's *you* I'm thinking about."

"Oh, sure. My guardian angel. Doesn't the saintly stuff get old sometimes?"

Ellen was suddenly sick to her stomach. She stood up, aware of the children raising their heads. "I think we'd better go. Next time I'll drop the children off for a couple of hours if it's allowed. I'm sure you need time alone with them."

"I don't want to go," Laura protested.

"Don't leave!" Panic made Linda look even younger and so terribly vulnerable. "Come on. I didn't mean it!

You know that. I'm just sort of mixed up right now, that's all. Please, Ellen.''

''It's okay,'' Ellen said uncomfortably. She made herself sit down. ''We do have to go pretty soon, though.''

''Just don't listen to me when I talk like that, okay?''

Easier said than done. She'd always known Linda felt resentment, but this was the first time it had been said aloud. She couldn't even blame her sister. Ellen had always been the good one, the reliable one. The family had needed her as a facade. Without her, the whole world might have known how messed up they were. Well, Linda wasn't the only one who'd sometimes resented Ellen's role. She had, too.

Ironically, Ellen was far from sure that her automatic response today had been motivated by her usual sense of responsibility. Nick had complicated things. Maybe Linda hadn't been so far off, after all.

Because Ellen knew the answer, even before she asked herself the question. *Was* she jealous, even of her own sister who needed Nick so badly?

CHAPTER SIX

"THANK GOD WE DIDN'T sit in front," Ellen muttered.

"Try thanking *me*," Nick murmured in her ear. "I had a feeling you wouldn't like being a sitting duck."

Before them, under the spotlight, the comedienne paced across the small stage with the nervous energy all funny people seemed to share. Turning back the way she'd come, the woman stepped deftly over the trailing microphone cord.

"Everybody got a good look at that cake, didn't they? It's tall enough, or maybe I should say erect enough? Hey, hold it up. No, not you. We know your hands are already busy under the table."

The young couple in front both blushed a furious crimson, while the friends who were presumably responsible for the pornographic cake doubled over with laughter. Ellen felt sorry for them. The cake was funny, though, even imaginative. She'd blushed herself when a waiter ceremoniously presented it to the couple and beside her, Nick choked.

The woman on the stage gave a quick, engaging grin. "We've tortured these poor people enough, don't you think?"

Half the crowd in the dim, smoky room yelled, "No!"

She reeled back in mock dismay, then said, "Since we can't get our minds out of the bedroom—or maybe I should say toilet—I'll give you one more song lyric.

Come on, I want a show of hands. How many of you always thought Creedence Clearwater Revival's song was 'There's a bathroom on the right'?''

A startled giggle rose in Ellen's throat. The rock group had been popular when she was in high school, and for years she had thought that's how the song went. Until, that is, she made a fool out of herself singing it aloud, and discovered the truth: ''There's a bad moon on the rise.''

Over the laughs, the comedienne said into the microphone, ''Seriously, folks, thanks for coming.'' She smiled at the young couple. ''And thanks to all the good sports among you. Hey, I'll even thank the bad sports!'' She stepped back and waved. ''See ya.''

Ellen came to herself with reluctance. It had felt good to let go and laugh with pure enjoyment. There was a pleasant feeling of anonymity in the cavernous, dark room, a delicious shock at the ruthlessness implicit in many of the jokes. The give-and-take between the comedians and the crowd had generated real electricity, the jolt of personality and wit.

She felt a loss when Nick withdrew the arm he had casually slung around her shoulders. He stretched, groaned, then smiled at her.

''Hungry?''

''Starved,'' she admitted. They had nibbled on a tray of vegetables and chicken wings, and she had forgotten the passing of time, but now she realized it was almost nine o'clock. They'd decided to take in the first show and save dinner until afterwards, when they wouldn't have to hurry. ''Where are we going?'' she asked.

''If you like Italian, Trattoria Mitchelli. It's not fancy, but the food is great.''

''I love Italian.''

"Great." He held out her coat. "You up to that moonlit walk? It means a couple of extra blocks."

"Sure." She slipped her arms into the sleeves, then, with Nick close behind, edged into the noisy crowd exiting the Comedy Club.

Outside, she felt Nick's hand on the small of her back, steering her toward the waterfront. Parking in the popular Pioneer Square area of Seattle was at a premium, so they'd had to settle for a lot some blocks away. Ellen liked walking, though, and now she blissfully drew in a deep breath of salt-scented air. Giving Nick a sidelong, saucy smile, she said, "I don't see the moon."

"Complaints, complaints." Nick drew her hand into the crook of his arm and slowed his long strides to match hers. "Modest man that I am, I have to admit the weather is beyond my control."

"Are you sure?" she teased. Suddenly a shimmer of silver showed around the edges of a dark cloud. The next instant, the half moon sailed regally out.

"My mother taught me never to brag," Nick said, straight-faced.

They were laughing when they reached the lighted windows of the Elliott Bay Bookstore. "It's open until eleven," Ellen said in surprise.

"They can afford extra hours on what I spend there," Nick said wryly. His gaze as well as hers was drawn to the books artfully displayed in the window.

"Oh, Ellis Peters' new Brother Cadfael mystery." Ellen stopped. "Maybe we should ... No, I'm hungry."

"Then let's continue on to the restaurant. We can come back here after dinner."

"That sounds wonderful," she agreed.

When they reached the waterfront a cross-Sound ferry was just leaving the dock, its decks brightly lit and the horn giving a deep, resonant farewell. A huge cargo ship, strung with tiny white lights, moved majestically across the path of the ferry, leaving a dark wake that lapped against the bulkheads. The sounds and smells of the waterfront were tangled and evocative: soft laughter and the delicious fragrance of cooking that spilled from restaurants, a metallic clang from the bowels of a berthed ship and the pungent aroma of fish and creosote.

They walked silently now, Ellen very conscious of Nick's sheer size and of the powerful muscles flexing in his arm as he tugged her closer. Until he stood up, she sometimes forgot how large he was. He looked more like a linebacker for the Seahawks than a distinguished doctor, she thought. Somehow, here in the midst of the city, surrounded by people, she could let herself enjoy that heady awareness without feeling threatened by it.

Her complacence wavered, though, when she glanced up to see that he was watching not the moon-silvered Puget Sound, but her. She felt the sudden tension in the muscles beneath her fingertips, saw that the lazy contentment on his face had metamorphosed to something far more disquieting. They passed through a streamer of light from a doorway and back into the night shadows beyond. When Nick's strides slowed and then stopped, Ellen's heart skipped a beat.

"You're beautiful, do you know that?" he said, catching her by the shoulders.

In the darkness she couldn't read his face, but the rough hunger in his voice was enough. Too much. She struggled against the sting of tears, determined to pass the moment off lightly. "With freckles and carrot-colored hair? I'm afraid not."

His big calloused hand cupped her cheek, slid around to the back of her head to tangle in her hair. There was no amusement in his voice, only the huskiness that was her undoing. "Your hair is the color of fire, and you know damn well that most men would be glad to risk getting burned by it. And as for those freckles ..." His other hand lifted her chin, so that she had no choice but to meet his shadowed gaze. His voice had lowered to a soft growl. "They're like a sprinkling of cookie crumbs. Very tempting."

He'd stolen her breath again. She was paralyzed by a wave of undiluted longing. How did he do this to her? And so easily! He made her want too much; not just his kiss or even the tender-rough touch of his hands on her body. He made her want the morning after, flowers and intimacy. He made her want to be able to respond wildly, without inhibition. He made her want ...

The feather-light, achingly gentle feel of his mouth on hers drowned her thoughts and fears. She had never been kissed that a part of her had not stood aside and coolly watched, coolly observed that she should be feeling more. Now, spent with laughter and unexpectedly captured by a gruff voice that had torn her defenses, Ellen only felt. The staccato of his heart under her palms, the sharp edge to the teeth that nipped at her full lower lip, the hungry pressure of his mouth and the restless warmth of the big hand that slid down her neck, over her shoulder and wrapped her rib-cage tantalizingly close to her breast.

The sound of heels clicking on the sidewalk, a laugh, penetrated their sensual cocoon. Nick lifted his head, took a deep, rasping breath, and smiled with clear, sensual intent. "I'm already a little singed around the edges," he murmured.

Incapable of self-propelled movement, Ellen docilely allowed him to turn her, tuck her hand under his arm, and lead her along the sidewalk. Dazedly she thought about the kiss and her own uninhibited response. She had thought letting go of her fears would free her. Why was she so sure now that she'd been wrong, that her life had only been complicated?

She was still functioning on automatic when they walked into the restaurant. It didn't help when Nick glanced down at her and she saw the glint in his blue eyes. Obviously there had been nothing casual about that kiss where he was concerned, either. It stood between them now, a wall. Or was it a bridge? She was grateful when the ordinary took over in the form of a smiling hostess who seated them at a small table crowded among too many others.

Giving her order to the young waiter with spiked black hair and a long earring dangling from one ear, Ellen began to relax. The chatter around them was soothing, Nick's rueful smile disarming.

"You can't say I'm not a romantic," he said suddenly.

Her own smile trembled betrayingly at the corners of her mouth. "A romantic? After moonlight and a flower to put in my hair? How could I accuse you of such a thing?"

"Oh, I don't know." He reached for a roll, but his gaze didn't leave hers. "Half the time I seem to be battering at your psyche. That can make a man unpopular."

Ellen took a sip of the white wine that she had half-defiantly ordered. Over the fragile rim of the glass she smiled. "I'll bet every one of your patients loves you."

"Right. When they don't hate me."

"Your approval means a great deal to Linda."

"Hey, I'm like God in there." He was definitely serious now. "It's a little scary sometimes. Fortunately the effect wears off real quick when they walk out the front door. And I fail often enough to keep all that power from going to my head."

"It really matters to you," she said again, knowing the answer but wanting reassurance. Not for Linda, she realized, but for herself. She needed to know that it was possible to do something with your life that held meaning, that was worth the risk. She needed to know that *she* could make more of her life.

"Yeah." A hint of the intensity that he showed at the hospital crept into his voice. "As you've probably gathered by now, I think the traditional ways of looking at alcoholism—and 'treating' it, if you can call it that—are way off base. Those methods and attitudes have hurt more lives than they've helped. I'm going to change that."

"Just with your treatment center?" Ellen asked curiously.

"No. I do research, give talks." He shrugged a little sheepishly. "I even have a book coming out this fall."

"Which you wrote in your spare time."

His smile was rueful. "To tell you the truth, it was an ordeal. You ever heard that quote about how 'writing is easy—you just sit in front of your typewriter until drops of blood appear on your forehead?' Yeah, laugh all you want, but it's damn close to the truth. I'm a scientist, not a writer. I swear I wrote the thing one painful word at a time. I'd vow never again, but I know myself better than that. When the time comes that I have something to say..." He shrugged. "What the hell. I like challenges."

"I admire you for that," Ellen admitted. "I'm afraid I have more of a tendency to avoid them."

She both resented and was grateful for the compassion in his eyes. "That's not uncommon for a child of an alcoholic," he said. "Assuming it's true, you can do something about it. Try Al-Anon, Ellen. I think it's important for you. I have a suspicion that you're misjudging yourself, though. You took on Patrick and Laura, didn't you? Aren't they a challenge? And, hey, you're here tonight."

Ellen had to laugh. "You see yourself as a challenge?"

There was a brief interlude when the waitress brought their salads. As they picked up their forks, Ellen thought the subject had been dropped, but she should have known better. Nick shook some Gorgonzola on his salad and then said bluntly, "I think I scare you a little. Maybe with good reason."

She made herself tell the truth. "It's me I'm scared of, not you."

It was a shock to meet Nick's gaze again, to feel it penetrating her facade. "Why? What scares you?"

"I . . ." How to find words for that vague, formless feeling of anxiety? "I don't know," she said helplessly.

He searched her face for an uncomfortable instant before he said, "We're getting too serious here, anyway. Tell me the story of your life instead. Start anywhere. What time of day you were born. If I were into astrology, I could predict your future."

Grateful for his light tone, she said, "You don't believe in the stars?"

"Oh, I don't know. Luck seems to go in streaks, totally unpredictably. Maybe the stars are the explanation."

Ellen wondered whether her own were positive or negative at the moment. She'd have said all bad, except that Linda's latest crisis had also brought Nick into her life.

Watching her, Nick thought how amazingly readable her face was. A little frown puckered her brow, and then the shadow seemed to pass and she crinkled her nose at him in that impish way she had. In another woman, he'd have thought it calculated, but Ellen seemed honestly unaware of her beauty. Incredible. With that sultry mouth and matte cream complexion dusted with freckles, she could have been a movie star. Although maybe, having tasted that mouth, he was a little prejudiced.

"Well, let's see," she began. "It was a dark and stormy night..."

"And your mother had you in the car on the way to the hospital?"

"Don't spoil my story," she said sternly. "Actually, Mom swears she was in labor for three days. That might be a *slight* exaggeration... No, seriously, my life was perfectly uneventful. My parents were divorced when I was so young I don't even remember my father. After a while I forgot that my stepdad wasn't really my father. It didn't matter, I guess. He treated me like I was his. He was a good man, except for his drinking." Ellen was silent for a moment, looking pensive. "Actually, I don't think he drank that heavily when I was really young. We had fun. We went camping a lot and he taught us how to fish. I remember how happy Mom always seemed. Strange, I haven't thought about those early years in a long time. Mostly I remember..." She stopped abruptly. "Well, never mind."

Nick didn't need the blank filled in. He could have done that from his own life.

"We did a lot of camping when I was a kid, too," he said. "Boy did I get sick of taking that tent up and down, waiting while that damn gas stove took twenty minutes even to boil water. What I'd have given to stay in a hotel room, eat in a restaurant. But, like most people, we couldn't afford it, and my parents really loved to travel. Nowadays they stay at those Elderhostels. They take fascinating trips. And me? I go camping. What else?''

She chuckled, a low delicious ripple. ''The question is, are we growing up, or are we recreating our parents' mistakes?''

Nick deepened his voice, swept his hands out in a grand gesture. ''It's tradition!'' he proclaimed.

Ellen laughed again, her soft brown eyes sparkling, and he felt that now-familiar pang. He wanted to protect and cherish her until that laugh came as easily as her gentler smile, until her ghosts were chased away. It was unnerving to feel so much, so quickly. Especially since he was far from certain that he was capable of defeating her personal ghosts.

Over rigatoni tossed with a spicy, cheesy Bolognese sauce, they continued to talk about the past, always the safer, distant one. It was easier, somehow, to remember through children's eyes.

''Mom made the most beautiful quilts,'' Nick said. ''Still does, for that matter. When I was a kid she made one for my bedroom that was pieced together from old clothes of mine. I remember how comforting that was. There was my favorite shirt, even a bit of the blanket I loved when I was a toddler. That quilt got washed so many times it finally wasn't much more than a rag, and Mom made me a glorious one that's on my bed now. It doesn't have the memories, though.''

Memories. Awakened, they had the golden patina of a very old picture. The remembered emotions were gentle, buffered by time. And so many of those memories were good ones.

Nick saw Ellen realize that as she talked. It was as though she had locked the good away with the bad, determined never to look back. Doing so now, she was discovering which memories had brightened with time, which had faded. He was pretty sure that Ellen was surprised at the result.

As she looked down the years, she smiled reminiscently. "My dad—Linda's father—made furniture. He quit later, when his hands got shaky. He was such a perfectionist, I don't think he could bear to do less than the best. I've got a storage chest he made. We kept toys in it when we were kids. He used to wince when we flung things at it, but he never said a word. Scars and all, it's still beautiful. He made it out of cherry, and it feels like satin. I keep blankets in it now."

They ate for a moment in comfortable silence, then Ellen said suddenly, "I wish I had a hobby like that. Something that gave me pleasure and left a legacy. Dad tried to teach me to work with wood, but I was too young and impatient. By the time I was old enough, he wasn't doing much anymore. Mom sewed, and I do, too, but it's not the same. Twenty years from now, nobody is going to run their hand lovingly over the machine stitches on the sweatpants I just made."

"I know what you mean," Nick agreed. "I suppose that's what I'm trying to do in building the house. A hint of immortality? Sobering thought. Speaking of which," he signaled the waitress, "shall we head back to the bookstore? Now there's immortality."

"Next year, your own piece of it will be there," Ellen reminded him.

"Nah." He tossed some bills on the small tray the waitress presented, then stood to hold Ellen's coat for her. "Twenty years from now every word I wrote will be outdated. I'll be an old fogey."

"Not at all," she said soberly, but with a smile quivering at the corners of her mouth. "You'll have changed with the times. You'll have a teenager who is embarrassed because dad is such a radical."

"Right." Nick grinned at her. "How about you? What are you going to be twenty years from now?"

Her smile flickered and died. "I don't know," she said, and he could have kicked himself for dimming her happiness.

The walk back toward Elliott Bay Bookstore and their car was different from the romantic stroll to the restaurant. Passing the old brick square that had given the area its name, they stuck to First Avenue this time. Window-shopping had to satisfy them, since the chic stores that sold everything from handcrafted wood furniture to beautiful English woolens were closed and only dimly lit. In a strange juxtaposition, next door to expensive shops were missions where the hungry were fed, a remnant of the time when Yesler Avenue had been Seattle's skid road. Winos slouched in barred doorways, watching blearily as Ellen and Nick passed.

"Got some change?"

Nick groped in his pocket and thrust a couple of dollars at the grizzle-faced man with the sad eyes. Dirty and inadequately dressed for the chill spring night, he met Nick's pity with indifference. For a bottle he'd sell his soul; maybe already had. There but for the grace of God, Nick thought somberly. He saw the way Ellen looked at the man, compassion mixed with revulsion, or perhaps even fear.

Inside the store it took Nick a minute to shake off his grim reflections. A bookstore, though, he couldn't resist. Elliott Bay consisted of room upon room of books, a warren of shelves and balconies and nooks. Cases were crammed full, tables heaping, every spare foot used. There was something about books, the weight and the color and the crisp bindings, even the smell of the ink when he cracked a new one open, that had always captivated Nick. Checking books out of the library had never been good enough; he liked to own them. Discovering that Ellen shared his passion put the cap on the evening.

They talked about favorite mysteries, children's books they remembered, travel stories that made them want to start packing.

Ellen loved to read historical accounts of travel. "Especially the women's," she said, sliding her fingers lovingly over the bindings of travel books jammed onto the shelves.

On the small balcony that held the section, there was scarcely room for her or Nick to turn around. So close to Ellen, he found his attention straying to the tiny wisps of hair that curled above her forehead, to the faint scent of lilacs that clung to her.

"They were so extraordinary," she added, her tone one of wonderment. "To set out alone, parasol in hand, determined to experience the world. It must have taken courage for a Victorian woman just to leave her bustle off, never mind heading into the African jungle with only native guides! Imagine!"

"It's hard," he agreed. "But there have always been extraordinary individuals, women and men. Those women aren't so different from a Jane Goodall, for example. I'm not so sure it's much easier today for a woman to be a maverick. Don't you find that even in business a woman has to fight harder to succeed?"

"I suppose so," she said thoughtfully. "I don't think there's a single woman in a real decision-making position at Kashiwa. Oh, there are some managers, but when the serious huddle is called, they're not in it."

"Then what they need is one of these intrepid explorers. Damn the torpedoes!"

"Uh...I think you're mixing your metaphors a little."

"Well, hell, maybe the women should file a lawsuit instead. That's the modern way, right?"

"Mmm hmm." Abstractedly Ellen added a couple of books to her pile. Then she made a face. "My arms are starting to ache. How about you?"

"I've got my quota," Nick agreed.

They were still happily talking about books, with a few detours on lawsuits, modern mores and exotic corners of the world, when Nick turned into her driveway forty-five minutes later.

"Can I drive your baby-sitter home for you?" he asked.

Her smile was fleeting. "Chivalry lives on! But no, thanks. Lisa lives just a couple of doors down."

"Good." He turned the ignition off, and in the sudden night silence laid his arm across the back of her seat. He felt her stiffen, saw the wariness in her nervous glance. Was it just him? he wondered. Or was it men in general? Either way, she had chosen with apparent delight to go out with him. And when he'd kissed her, she had responded.

The memory of Ellen's mouth softening and parting for his stirred Nick, and he let his hand slide beneath the heavy silk of her hair to the delicate nape of her neck. He heard the quick breath she drew, felt her pulse take a leap under his fingertips. When she turned to look at him, her eyes were wide, although in the faint illumination from the porch light they were deep, mysterious pools of darkness. Her mouth, a gentle curve, had already parted, and that full lower lip trembled slightly. On a rush of potent longing, Nick bent his head and captured her enticing mouth. She tasted of Italian cooking and tangy wine, with a hint of sweetness that was all her own.

Passion swept over him like an avalanche, roaring in his ears. He pulled her into his arms, deepened the kiss, plunged his tongue into her mouth as an age-old harbinger of things to come. She melted, accepted his hunger, kissed him back. Her arms twined about his neck, and he reveled in her gasp as his hand found her breast. Just like that, the avalanche buried him, smothered him with its power. The hint of softness, the peak against his palm, was not enough. He devoured her mouth and pressed her back against the seat as his hand slipped inside the low neckline of her dress. Above the lace of her bra, her breast was full, the swell a perfect match to his hand. Nick groaned, wanting to rip her dress off, taste the sugar-sprinkling of freckles and her taut nipple. How he wanted her!

When her hands pressed against his chest and she pulled her mouth from his, Nick was momentarily disoriented. What was wrong? She felt it, too, didn't she? With wrenching reluctance, he opened space between them, until the only contact was his hands on her shoulders.

"I . . . I'd better go."

Go? Oh, Lord. There was a baby-sitter, kids. He'd forgotten them, forgotten the world. With sudden anxiety he wondered if he had frightened Ellen. But he hadn't imagined her response, had he?

He searched her face, took in the flush that crept up her cheeks, the tightly compressed mouth, the shadowed eyes that examined him in turn. She looked...shaken. And no wonder, if the earth had moved for her as it had for him.

"I..." She stopped, nibbled at her lip again. "I'm sorry, I..."

"Don't apologize," he said roughly. "I'm the one who should be sorry."

"Don't be," she said. "It was..." She hesitated again, and then to his astonishment smiled, a delicate, delicious bloom of joy. "It was wonderful," she finished softly, and leaned forward to kiss him on the cheek. The caress was the brush of a moth's wings, velvet gentle, impossibly sensual. And then she was gone.

Stunned, he watched her hurry up the walk, head bent as she fumbled in her purse. A moment later, her front door cracked open and she disappeared. In the darkness Nick gripped the steering wheel and just sat there.

He was in love. Desperately, frighteningly in love with a woman who despised alcoholics.

CHAPTER SEVEN

"NEED THOSE D22 estimates ASAP. Before quitting to-day!"

Ellen sighed when she saw the note left on her desk. Was it supposed to be news? The estimates were *always* needed instantly. Why, when they were invariably ignored, she hadn't figured out.

Unfortunately, she still lacked figures from a couple of engineers, which meant she couldn't finish compiling the latest report. Sighing again, she dropped her purse in a drawer, kicked it shut and reached for the phone. "Steve Dixon, please."

Twenty minutes later Ellen had promises, for what they'd be worth. She glanced at her terminal, where columns of numbers glowed, then turned away to stare through the barely cracked blinds at the parking lot. She wanted to be out there, walking toward her car, free for the rest of the day.

More and more often she felt like this. The job that had once been, if not stimulating, at least satisfying, was now stifling. The tastefully neutral blinds meant to screen out the sunlight had begun to look like bars. And whose fault was that? she wondered.

Her own, for letting herself get stuck here? Or Nick Braden's, for making her want something more? Probably all of the above, she admitted. There was no doubt that Nick had strengthened this restlessness, although he was only a part of the changes that had shaken her life.

There were the kids, of course. They'd dribbled toothpaste all over the bathroom, torn apart her living room, spilled potato chips in her kitchen cupboards. They'd made her mad, made her laugh, brought tears to her eyes. They had made her *feel*.

And Linda. Each of her sister's crises had torn one more thin layer off Ellen's bandaged wounds. Each one had brought her closer to actually having to look at herself, to see what the years had wrought. She was open now, raw, and she hated it. But just lately she had begun to wonder. Had it been necessary so that she could now begin to heal?

It was funny, because she'd been kidding herself that she attended those sessions at the clinic for the children's sake. Even for Linda's. Well, maybe that was partly true, but mostly she went for herself. *She* was the one who needed that understanding—who needed to know what had gone wrong and who was to blame. Who needed to let go of her own guilt at failing to keep her fragile family safe.

All of which had absolutely nothing to do with her job, Ellen thought, grimacing as she glanced back at the computer terminal. She *liked* numbers. So what was her problem?

It wasn't hard to figure out the answer to that. She liked numbers that *meant* something. These didn't. And she was pretty sure she couldn't face these day in and day out for the rest of her life.

Before she could think it through, talk herself out of it, Ellen reached for the phone book. University of Washington. Admissions—new graduate students. 555-5929. She punched the buttons quickly, waited for that pleasant, anonymous voice. She just wanted information, that was all. Finding out what she had to do to apply couldn't hurt, could it? It wasn't as though she had to follow through.

"THIS WAS A GOOD IDEA," Ellen said, scanning the menu.

"Um, that fettucini looks wonderful," her mother said. "Probably a week's worth of fat. I'd hate to have my doctor see me, but I'm tempted to splurge."

"We don't do this very often," Ellen said. "Not often enough."

She was surprised to realize that she meant it. She and her mother hadn't been close in years, although they were when she was growing up. Then they had been a united front, in silent collusion to hide George Whalley's drinking, to pretend as much for themselves as for outsiders that they were a normal family. Stripped of that function, they seemed to have nothing left to hang a relationship on. They talked on the telephone regularly, went shopping together, had Thanksgiving and Christmas as a family, but real friendship had eluded them.

They gave their orders to the waitress and then looked at each other. The small silence was uncomfortable, a truth that needed to be veiled with chatter.

"Could I have the kids Thursday night?" Mrs. Whalley asked. "I'm afraid they'd tire me out for much longer than that, but you could use a break and I'd love to spend some time with them."

"You're sure? We're doing fine. I don't want you to strain yourself," Ellen said. The conventional disclaimers slid off her tongue smoothly, but this was the first time in a long while that she had really studied her mother, seen how pale she was, how tired her eyes were.

It was scary, the idea of losing her like a huge gulf that had suddenly opened at Ellen's feet. Why had she let the years go by without grasping the love her mother had always offered?

Ellen was still grappling with the question when her mother asked suddenly, "How does Linda look? I've talked to her, of course, but it's not the same. Maybe I should go. Staying away seems so..."

"No," Ellen said instantly, forcefully, her instinct shaping her answer. What was right for other people, she didn't know. But Linda was too dependent on her mother; she had to gain the strength to stand alone. "You know it won't stop there," Ellen said, softening her tone. "You'll want to do more for her."

"Surely I can just visit. Linda needs to know that she's still loved."

"How many times over the years have you visited her in treatment? Driven her there, taken the kids, picked her up? You've done too much. You're not helping her."

"What do you suggest I do, cut her off?"

"I suggest you let her face her own consequences." She knew where she had heard that, where the words had come from. It didn't matter. They were real, they felt right. "You're only hurting Linda by protecting her," Ellen finished.

Her mother flinched, then turned her head to stare out the window. In the bright light her faint wrinkles were thrown into sharp relief and her bones seemed more prominent. Again Ellen felt that tug of fear. Her mother looked...old. Weary. Sad.

"I'm sorry," Ellen said on a rush of remorse. She reached across the table and took the thin hand in her own, squeezing gently. "I know it's hard. And of course you couldn't let Laura and Patrick suffer because of

Linda's drinking. It's just that. . ." She hesitated, trying to think of a kind way of touching upon the past.

There were tears in her mother's eyes when she met Ellen's gaze. "I suppose you think I protected your step-father, too."

In all the intervening years, they had never talked about him. Now Ellen shied away from Mrs. Whalley's bluntness, from the painful truth. "I didn't say that."

"But you think it. Don't you?"

"I . . . Yes. Yes, I do."

The waitress who appeared with their salads seemed not to notice the thick silence. "Enjoy your lunch," she said cheerily.

Ellen's response was automatic. "Thank you."

When the waitress walked away, neither Ellen nor her mother reached for their forks. "I've been going to the family sessions at the clinic," Ellen said at last. "Nick—Dr. Braden, that is—said once that the longer you pro-tect an alcoholic, the longer it will be before he faces his disease and gets help. I think all of us protected Dad un-til it was too late. Maybe if he'd lost his job, or gotten picked up for a DWI, or even been allowed to embarrass himself, he'd have admitted how out of control his drinking was."

"It was *us* he embarrassed," her mother said with sudden passion.

"But we weren't the ones who were drunk. It wasn't us people were looking at."

Mrs. Whalley's face twisted. "I had no right to put such a burden on you. I know it wasn't fair. It was just . . . too much for me, and you seemed so mature . . ." She stopped again, drew a shuddering breath, and met her daughter's eyes. "I'm sorry, Ellen. If I could do it over again . . ."

Ellen felt the sting of tears. "It's okay, Mom."

"No. No, it's not okay. I was the adult. I should have..."

It was what Ellen had thought a thousand times. Her mother should have taken charge, not let herself and her children be drowned in George Whalley's painful addiction. But in her resentment she had let herself forget that choices were never simple, that it couldn't have been easy for her mother either.

"Did you ever think about leaving him?" she asked, wondering why she never had before.

"A million times." Her mother looked down at the table, where she twiddled with a fork. "But I didn't have any real job skills. How would I have supported the three of us? He wasn't a bad father, you know. He was so proud of you two. It would have destroyed him if we'd left. Despite everything, I loved him. I couldn't do that to him. I'm not telling you this to excuse myself. I just would like you to understand."

"I never really have," Ellen said quietly. "I've had a lot of anger."

"I know." Her mother tried to smile, failed. "I could see it. I guess we should have talked about this years ago."

Seared by almost forgotten pain, choked with love, Ellen managed a wavering smile. "I think you're right. But it's never too late."

Mrs. Whalley just looked at her. "Isn't it?"

"AHA! SORRY!" Ellen exclaimed triumphantly, picking up Laura's game piece and plopping it back in her beginning square before she put her own bright red man in the spot Laura's had occupied. "I've got you now!"

"Oh, pooh. You're mean!" Her niece's small brow furrowed with concentration as she picked up a card. "Two! See, you didn't even slow me down!"

When the telephone rang, Ellen said, "Hey, Patrick, do you want to get that?"

He stuck out his tongue at his sister and ran for the phone. Picking it up, he said, "Hi, what's your name?" A pause. "Are you the Nick who took us to ride the horse?"

Ellen scrambled up. "I'd better get that. Don't you dare peek, Laura!"

Patrick handed her the receiver. "Can he take us to ride the horse again?"

"Honey, it wasn't his horse." She put the receiver to her ear. "Hi. Nick?"

"I'm glad those kids aren't yours. I'd be shoveling manure before I knew it."

What was he implying? That he would do anything to please her? She pictured him so easily, his face roughly carved and strongly masculine. The froth of excitement she felt was as heady as the wine she'd sipped when she was with him.

"Maybe we'll convert you," she teased. "Horses are noble animals, you know."

"They attract flies."

"Flowers attract bees."

He just laughed, a rusty sound that she loved. "Flowers are closer to what I have in mind. Would you and the kids like to take in the Tulip Festival this week? Ever seen the fields?"

"Every year," she said. "That sounds wonderful. Are you sure . . . ?"

"What? That I want you? Or the kids?"

"The kids."

Nick sounded amused. "Why not? Half the population of Washington will be wandering around the tulip fields. I can't kiss you in front of them, anyway. So what's two more?"

Laughing, blushing, she found herself agreeing to take a day off work so they wouldn't have to compete with impossible crowds. A moment later she hung up the telephone and wandered back to the game.

"Nick's going to take us to see the tulips this Thursday."

Laura scrunched up her nose. "That sounds boring."

"We'll have fun. I promise. Now, it's my turn, isn't it?"

Promises, promises, she thought. She made herself lots of them, lived in terror that she couldn't make them come true. This one, though, she had confidence in.

"IT LOOKS LIKE a rainbow," Ellen said softly, with awe she felt afresh each year.

The fields stretched from each side of the road like gaily colored squares on a quilt, brilliant red and yellow, purple and rose. Outside of Holland, Skagit Valley, sixty miles north of Seattle, was the center of the flower bulb industry, the source for most of the major nurseries. Glancing over her shoulder, Ellen saw that even the children were captivated; wide-eyed, they stared out the car windows at the bright tapestry of flowers.

"Here we are," Nick said. "Roozengaarde is my favorite." Slowing to follow the long line of cars into a roped-off, bark-covered parking lot, he muttered, "Obviously I'm not alone. Where the hell do all these people come from on a working day?"

Ellen hid her smile at his disgruntlement. "They're all taking a day off, just like we are. Enjoying the sunshine, the slower pace of life..."

His mouth quirked. "Are you implying that I'm harried and impatient?"

"Heavens no!" she said airily. "Just reminding you that you're the one who knew ahead of time that half the population of the state would be here. Remember?"

"Yeah. I remember." His voice was low; a sexy growl. "So why is it that I wish we were all alone?"

Warmth heated Ellen's cheeks. "Maybe because I wish we were alone, too," she said, too quietly for Laura and Patrick to hear.

Nick gave her a look from those intense blue eyes that made heat curl in her stomach. He had to turn away as the car bounced into a pothole, and Ellen struggled to regain her composure. She managed, barely in time, before the car lurched to a stop in a row of others on the rough field.

Without looking at her, Nick turned the engine off and announced, "Here we are, gang."

As Ellen gathered herself, the children spilled out, talking excitedly. Ellen hurried after them and latched firmly onto Patrick's small hand. "Now remember, you can't pick the flowers and you have to stay on the grass. Okay?"

"You've already said that a million times." Laura sounded impatient. "Don't you trust us?"

"Yes, of course I do." *No, I don't.* It was all too easy to picture Laura clutching a ragged, illicitly gathered bouquet of tulips or Patrick, who still had a toddler's clumsiness, stumbling into a cluster of crisp narcissus.

Nick had either imagined much the same calamities or read her mind, because when they reached the garden, he scooped Patrick up onto his shoulders. He grinned up at the boy. "We wouldn't want someone to pick you by accident, would we?"

Patrick giggled, until Laura pinched at his toes and said, "Yeah, I can pick you."

Her brother wriggled and kicked at her hand. "Stop it!" he wailed.

Ellen grabbed her niece's hand. "You can tell he doesn't like that."

The six-year-old mumbled something rude under her breath, but forgot her disgruntlement at the sight of the incredible array of flowers.

"Can you buy some, Aunt Ellen?"

"Maybe a bouquet," Ellen said. "That's the only trouble with a condo. I don't really have room to garden. Are you going to put some bulbs in this fall, Nick?"

"Sure. By next spring when they come up, I ought to be moved in. Help me pick some out."

They wandered down the path that zigzagged between display beds of tulips and hyacinths and daffodils in every color imaginable. The rich scent of the hyacinths perfumed the air, and the proud heads of the many-colored tulips were irresistible.

"Oh, look at this one," Ellen exclaimed. The petals were washed with mixed reds and yellows like paints being swirled together. "Gudoshink," she read from the small sign. "It's gorgeous."

They had been handed an order form listing hundreds of varieties of spring flowers, from Darwin hybrid tulips to the ruffled Parrot ones, from the tiny wood hyacinths to the huge nodding heads of fritillaria. Ellen put a check, the first of many, beside the Gudoshink, but she knew the truth. She wanted them all.

By the time they emerged at the hub, where a huge swath of grass sloped toward the fields they'd seen from the car, Ellen's eyes were dazzled and she'd forgotten the first tulips in the magic of the later ones. Out on the grass families picnicked while their children chased each other and took turns rolling down the incline. Nick set Patrick down and watched as brother and sister joined a group who were chasing a hapless butterfly. Glad she had worn jeans, Ellen sat cross-legged on the grass, close enough to a bed of tiny yellow daffodils to smell their sweet scent.

She inhaled and turned her head to smile at Nick, who lounged beside her, leaning back on his elbows. Straight dark hair brushed his collar and flopped over his forehead. "This is heaven," she said, not sure whether she was talking about the day or the flowers or him.

"Close," he agreed, and a flash of hunger in his eyes told her what he meant. For just an instant, tension shivered between them and she thought he meant to kiss her despite the crowds, but then his mouth twisted into a rueful smile.

"Grand Central Station. Me and my bright ideas."

"It was a wonderful idea," Ellen said softly. "Right this minute, I'm perfectly happy."

"Then so am I," he said, his tone odd. Their gazes held for another second, until he looked away, as if deliberately breaking the spell, to watch a small, homemade kite wobble into the sky behind a running boy.

Following his gaze without really seeing boy or kite, Ellen realized suddenly that she'd meant it. She *was* happy. Actively, joyfully, gloriously happy. Her body tingled with it, her mouth curved, her toes curled. Even the ends of her hair felt alive, as if the severely tamed waves had fizzed like a can of pop given a few shakes.

How bland her normal state of contentment was! she thought in wonder. *This* was the way life ought to feel.

The rest of the day was equally enchanted. They enjoyed the sunshine, talking lazily, and on the way back to the car Nick bought a huge bouquet of daffodils for Ellen and a single tulip for each child.

"And you're not a romantic?" Ellen murmured.

Nick gave her a wry smile. "Just don't let my staff know."

"They think you're such an ogre," she teased.

The route away from the nursery took them past more fields of flowers, huge old Victorian houses turned into bed-and-breakfasts, and at last to the small town of La Conner. Mobbed during the Tulip Festival, it nestled between a channel of water and a steep hillside to which old houses clung precariously. A tall red bridge soared over the slough and fishing boats glided serenely past, sending small waves to lap against the pilings. Nick bought them huge sandwiches to go from the bakery and they found a picnic table on a dock where they could watch the water.

Done eating first, Laura and Patrick followed an ant's slow, erratic progress across the wooden boards of the dock, then hung on to the railing to watch a twenty-foot-long sailboat tie up at a lower, floating pier.

"That's the way to travel," Nick said in admiration. "Now if I were a real romantic, I'd take you sailing for the weekend in the San Juans."

"Would you actually know how to steer the thing?"

"Oh, I'd figure it out," he said blithely.

"Sort of like building a house?"

"Right." He was laughing at her. "Learn as you go."

She rolled her eyes. "At least your house is on solid ground."

"Can't you swim?"

"Not when the water is sixty degrees," Ellen informed him. "I believe in comfort."

They lapsed into peaceful silence, watching the kids and listening to the voices of tourists who wandered through the small shops that lined the street behind them. Ellen surprised herself by asking suddenly, "Have you ever owned a house before? I mean...well, I know you don't have kids, but I thought..." Cursing her awkwardness, she stopped. Subtle, really subtle.

She saw no perceptible change in his expression, and yet his answer was almost too casual.

"When I was married?" He shrugged. "We didn't get that far. One or the other of us was a student for the whole eight years we lasted together. We were too broke even to think about buying a house. Anyway, with me in medical school, we figured we'd have it all someday."

Troubled by the poignancy of his last comment, Ellen looked away. "Do you ever see your ex-wife? Or wonder about her?"

Nick leaned back against the picnic table and clasped his hands behind his head. "I haven't seen Marie in, oh, it must be five years. I think about her sometimes, but our parting was pretty bitter. That gets in the way. Anyway, I know damn well Marie wouldn't want to see me."

Ellen sat in silence for a moment, trying to figure out why she was pushing this. But it seemed to matter. She sensed that she and Nick were on the brink of something important, and she needed to know that his past was just that—settled, behind him. And so she let herself push just a little harder.

"What happened to your marriage?"

He gave her a look she couldn't interpret, one she tried to meet calmly. Then he sat up straighter and began to gather their lunch garbage. "I was under a lot of strain in med school. That came out in ways Marie couldn't deal with. I don't blame her. I was hell to live with." Nick seemed deliberately to lighten his tone. "Hey, I'm an ogre, remember?"

She managed a smile, knowing a warning when she heard one. "Right. Hey, Laura, Patrick, time to go."

Nick tossed their empty wrappers and paper cups in a garbage can, and they took their time heading back to the car, glancing in a couple of shops on the way. Nick bought a handsomely framed copy of this year's Tulip Festival poster, an abstract wash of vivid colors.

"Nice against a white wall," he said with satisfaction.

For the children, the magic Nick seemed to work on them lasted long enough to get them through the hour drive to their grandmother's without bickering. Ellen's mother lived only a few blocks off the freeway in Marysville, and Nick had offered to take them on the way home, saving Ellen the trip.

When Nick's car pulled into the driveway, Mrs. Whalley hurried out of the small rambler.

"Grandma!" Laura scrambled out of her seat belt and the car to fling herself in her grandmother's arms.

The answering hug was enthusiastic, although Ellen was again struck by how fragile her mother looked, like fine porcelain that would break too easily. "What a lovely flower!" Mrs. Whalley exclaimed.

"I have one, too, Grandma!"

"Why, yours is beautiful, too." She smiled at her small grandson, who Nick was helping out. "We'll put them in water as soon as we get in." Her smile and voice changed. "And you must be Dr. Braden. Linda and Ellen have both talked about you. It's a pleasure to meet you."

"And for me to meet you." He engulfed her fragile hand in his huge one. Beside him, Mrs. Whalley seemed to shrink. It wasn't just his size, but his life force, the energy that his big frame fairly crackled with.

Ellen's mother must have been aware of the contrast, too, because even her smile appeared wan. "I'm so grateful . . . I know you're helping Linda . . ."

"I'm doing my best."

He couldn't bring himself to tell a lie, Ellen thought, bothered by his choice of words. She waited, though, until they had finished the pleasantries, unloaded the children's bags of clothes and toys and departed.

"I haven't asked you recently how you think Linda is doing."

He glanced at her. "What do *you* think?"

"I think . . ." Ellen didn't see the passing landscape or cars. She struggled to frame her uneasiness with words. "I think Linda is still convinced that she's special, that she doesn't really have a problem."

"Denial. Yeah, that's my feeling, too. Complete humility is tough. She hasn't achieved it yet."

"Are you saying . . . ?"

His voice was rough. "That I don't think she'll make it? I don't know. I don't have a crystal ball, thank God."

Ellen looked at him quizzically. "Thank God?"

"I don't want to give up on anyone. If I knew they were going to walk out the door and straight to a bar, I might. But what they learn this time might help them make it next time. Do you see what I mean?"

"I see." She reached out to lightly touch his hand, resting on the gear shift. "I don't know how you can have such patience and hope."

She felt the instant tension as his hand tightened on the gear stick. He sounded inexplicably angry. "Damn it,

Ellen, I've told you before. I'm no saint. I lose my temper and there are times I couldn't care less, patients I want just to slam the door on. I need you to see me the way I am. I want honesty from you."

"I'm giving you honesty," she said. "You're talking as though you want me to dislike you! I don't understand."

Nick's chest rose and fell with a harsh breath and she saw him momentarily close his eyes. "Yeah, you're right," he said. "I'm being a jerk. I guess I'm having a hard time believing you're really attracted to me. A part of me is afraid it's not me you want. I'm not some noble doctor from a TV show, Ellen. Of all people, you should know that!"

She didn't know that she could equal his kind of honesty, but the ache in her chest made her try.

"I don't want Dr. Kildare. I want you. I'm a little scared by how much."

There was a brief silence. Then a muscle twitched in his jaw and he said roughly, "Couldn't you have waited to say that until we were home?"

"You asked."

"So I did." He shot her a look that was half amused, half desperate. "Do you have any idea how badly I want to kiss you?"

Ellen felt dizzy, unable to think clearly. "I'm...looking forward to it myself," she admitted.

He groaned, and the Saab shot toward the freeway exit as though it were pretending to be a Corvette. Ellen clung to the edge of the seat as Nick swerved across lanes, gunned around corners. She watched his hands, big and blunt-fingered, and wondered how they would feel against her skin. Would he be clumsy, deft, gentle? She hadn't lied when she told him she was scared. But the heat that curled in her stomach, the anticipation that sang through her veins, were just as real, just as compelling. This was her own small leap of faith, surely a part of love.

But when he turned into her driveway and silenced the Saab's engine, Ellen couldn't look at him. Not until those blunt fingers lifted her chin, so that she had to meet his eyes.

He frowned as he searched her face, but when she touched her tongue nervously to her lips, his gaze lingered on her mouth with such possessive intent that her own doubts were swept away by intoxicating need.

When he spoke, his voice was thick, uneven. "Tell me I'm not imagining things. You did issue an invitation?"

Here it was, the moment of truth. Ellen didn't even hesitate. She stepped off the precipice. "Yes," she said. "Yes, it was an invitation."

And then his mouth met hers, and she didn't even feel herself falling.

CHAPTER EIGHT

"MAYBE WE'D BETTER get in the house before it's too late." Nick's gravelly voice rasped against her ear, blending with the rough feel of his jaw under her palm.

Dazed, Ellen repeated, "Too late?" Then said, blushing, "Oh. Yes." She tried to duck her head and grope for her purse. "I have to find my keys."

The big hand lifted her chin again, and her breath almost stopped when she saw the raw need on his face. "Quickly," he said. "Otherwise I'm ready to break the door down."

She wanted him to kiss her again. Instead, she blindly fumbled inside her overstuffed purse. From long familiarity her fingers identified her wallet, address book, breath mints. She almost gasped with relief when she encountered the jagged edge of a key.

"Here they are."

Without a word Nick was out of the car, circling it to hold open the passenger door. As she slipped by him, clutching her purse, and led the way up the walk to the front door, Ellen tried to think, but her mind blurred. She could feel him behind her, making the air prickle with static electricity.

She knew deep inside that making love with Nick would be nothing like her previous experiences with sex. For her the physical intimacy had never been quite enjoyable enough to balance the loss of dignity, of self.

Knowing that Nick wouldn't let her hold back anything of herself made Ellen a little afraid.

And yet her blood still sang with joy, and warmth swelled inside her like a hot air balloon rising into the sky. She wanted him so badly; she wanted to know what it could be like. What *life* could be like, for someone brave enough to risk being hurt.

Her key scraped against the lock and the door swung smoothly open. Following on her heels, Nick kicked it shut behind him. When his hands closed on her slender shoulders, her purse dropped from suddenly nerveless fingers and thudded to the floor. He lifted her heavy hair from her neck and his mouth brushed softly over the sensitive nape. Tremors raced up her spine and she felt boneless, quiescent, a mass of conflicting sensations.

"Turn around," he said hoarsely, sliding his fingers into her curls. "I want you to look at me."

Slowly Ellen obeyed, not knowing what to expect. A triumphant male on the brink of overpowering and conquering? Her mouth was dry and her heart thudded hard when she met his gaze. Instantly shaken, she recognized an echo of her own uncertainty. Leashed tension evident in every line of his body, he seemed to be waiting, asking for something from her. The hand in her hair didn't move, his intense gaze didn't waver. What did he want from her?

Honesty. She heard it as though he'd spoken aloud. *I want honesty from you.*

She had been waiting to be swept away, for him to take her despite her fears. That was cowardly, Ellen knew suddenly. She had to be honest about her own needs.

It was like opening a door, letting sunlight wash over her. She smiled and slid her hands up around his neck. On tiptoe she kissed him, timidly but with reckless intent. One instant his mouth was motionless under hers, the next a deep shudder racked him and her tentative offering was accepted with fierce pleasure.

With his tongue he tasted her mouth, teasing her own with sensual promise; with his teeth he roused a sharp response. Passion rocked through her like deep bass notes, primitive and powerful. Ellen was shocked, with some distant part of her, to realize how powerful *she* felt. The low groan that welled from him, the heartbeat that ricocheted against her restless hand, fueled her fragile courage.

And yet it also weakened her. She was melting, shivering, her uniqueness becoming lost in something more elemental. She was hardly aware when he swung her into his arms and carried her toward the hall.

"Which door?" he asked, in a voice so ragged as to be unrecognizable.

She swallowed and said, "That one," knowing she didn't sound like herself either.

Beside the spool bed with its soft yellow comforter, he made a gritty sound of satisfaction as he let her slide down his body. Like a stab of excitement, she felt his arousal. The hem of her thin T-shirt caught on one of his buttons so that the buckle of his jeans pressed into her bare skin. Each sensation was separate, exquisite, making her long for more. She leaned against him, loving the feel of her breasts flattening against his broad, muscular chest.

Nick's laugh sounded as though it had been torn from him, and he muttered, "Do you know what you're doing to me?"

"Mmm hmm," she murmured dreamily, as she began unbuttoning his shirt where it was coming loose from his pants.

"Dear Lord," he said roughly, and in one quick move pulled her T-shirt over her head and tossed it aside. His chest rose and fell hard under her hands, and his own were unsteady as he struggled with the catch of her bra. When he succeeded and slid the straps from her shoulders, Ellen shivered with pleasure.

Desire coiled tightly in her stomach, a spiral of heat. The sight of his large brown hands engulfing the creamy, gentle curves of her breasts, sampling their weight, was unexpectedly erotic. That aching need inside her turned into a knife edge of urgency. And when his mouth followed where his hands had led, when his teeth grazed her nipple and his tongue tasted, the knife turned.

Her head fell back and she heard a soft whimper she didn't realize was her own. Her blood roared through her veins, thundered in her ears. She was lost in its turbulence, knowing only that she wanted him over her, in her, dominating, overpowering, taking.

"Please," she whispered.

He gave another choked laugh and kissed her again as he eased her back onto the bed. He was heavy on top of her, his bulky shoulders shutting out the room. Rolling to the side, he slowly unzipped her pants and eased them off. When his fingers slid inside her panties to find the hidden warmth she had never known contained such explosive possibilities, Ellen moaned. But when Nick's other hand gripped hers and guided it to the bulge in the front of his jeans, for a fraction of a second she stiffened and resisted. He instantly stilled against her, then lifted himself on his elbow to look at her.

"Am I pushing you?"

There was strain in the set of his jaw and his eyes smouldered molten blue, but his mouth was tender. Even such a small, instinctive reaction as hers, he had honored.

If it was possible to blush under the circumstances, she did. "No. I . . . I just haven't done this very often before."

Still he hesitated. "You're sure?"

"Now I am," she said very softly, and let her gaze hold his as she reached out to unbutton the fly of his jeans. She felt as though her fingers were being singed by the contact and that made her clumsy, but any embarrassment fled in the face of the white-hot desire that flared in his eyes.

When at last he moved away from her to get rid of his jeans, Ellen looked at him, big, solidly built, aggressively masculine. As he turned back to her, muscles shifted smoothly under his skin, and she wonderingly reached out to touch his chest. When her hand slid up to cover his heart, his breathing stopped and their gazes locked. Just for that fraction of a second they were motionless, vulnerable. His heartbeat was heavy under her hand, his skin warm and sleek. Like a prism, time seemed to distort and fragment, as though this were only one tiny moment of the many possible. And even that shifted and was gone when he bent his head and reclaimed her mouth with a kiss that shattered her defenses.

From then on Ellen only felt, as he caressed and coaxed and demanded, murmuring endearments in a hoarse voice that was unbearably sexy, until she grew frantic. When at last he entered her, Ellen's body arched convulsively to meet him. Even then he went slowly, allowing her time to adjust to him, keeping his weight on his elbows so that he didn't crush her. Above her, his face was transformed, taut with passion and burnished with a a sheen of sweat that dampened the unruly lock of dark hair hanging over his forehead.

The moment shimmered, a mirage, unreal and piercingly sweet. With a cry Ellen wrapped her legs around him, and when he began to move she clutched at his powerful, muscled back. That was all it took for his control to snap, for the rhythm to become wild and intoxicating. He buried himself deeply inside her and groaned against her throat at the same instant that pleasure exploded within her, shuddering even to her toes and fingertips.

In the still aftermath, Nick rolled to one side, taking her with him, so that she half lay across him, head pillowed on his shoulder. Muscles bunched under her head as his arms tightened about her. The silence was dreamlike, a sweetness made tangible by the big hand that gently stroked her back. A part of Ellen wanted to think, to worry, to wonder. But thoughts refused to form. She was floating, filled with quiet joy.

When Nick spoke, his voice was husky, a rumble that vibrated against her chest. "Now *that*," he said, "was heaven."

KNOWING SHE WAS forgotten, Ellen stood in the doorway of her sister's room and watched her greet Laura and Patrick.

Words were tumbling out of Laura. "Aunt Ellen helped us boil eggs and we brought the dye and everything. I want to put glitter on mine. Patrick says *he* wants..."

"Let me tell her!" Patrick protested, his face crumbling. "You always want to tell everybody everything! I want..."

"Hey." Linda gave him a quick hug and turned him on her lap to smile beguilingly into his eyes. "We have all day. You can tell me everything. You both can. I promise. Okay?"

His mutinous expression melted. "Okay. I love you, Mommy."

"I love you, too, Mommy," Laura said, tugging at Linda's other arm.

"And I love both of you." The smile she gave her children was soft, her arms around them strong.

Ellen felt her heart squeeze painfully. Could she possibly be jealous? Ridiculous. Ellen said, "I've got to go now. Have a good visit, guys."

Patrick, quiet and sensitive, climbed down from Linda's lap to give Ellen a hug. She closed her eyes and kissed the top of his head. The silky hair tickled her nose and she let him go reluctantly, feeling as though she were saying goodbye for much longer than a few hours.

"Goodbye." Laura barely gave Ellen a glance before pointedly turning to Linda. "Can we color the Easter eggs now?"

"Sure." The smile that lit Linda's small, elfin face seemed to complete the circle that left Ellen out.

Ridiculous, Ellen thought again. It was right that the children should love their mother more than their aunt. She'd let being their savior go to her head, that was the only reason she felt this tug. She was just disconcerted by how easily they'd turned back to their mother.

Or maybe she and Nick and the children had felt too much like a family.

Again she forced a smile. "It'll be four or five o'clock, I guess. Is that okay?"

Linda had been whispering in her son's ear, making him giggle. "Sure," she said, looking vaguely surprised that Ellen was still there. "Are you doing anything special?"

She didn't sound as though she cared. But if Ellen didn't tell her, the kids would. "Actually," Ellen said, trying to sound casual, "I'm going out with your Dr. Braden. Nick and I have been dating the last couple of weeks."

Linda straightened, her expression changing. Patrick squirmed under hands that must have tightened on him. "I don't believe you."

"He's nice," Laura contributed helpfully. "He bought me and Patrick flowers."

"Why didn't you tell me?" Linda's voice crackled like thin ice.

Because I didn't want to hurt you. Or was that the truth? Sometimes Ellen wondered if she really cared any more, if she hadn't avoided telling her sister about Nick only because she didn't want to deal with the tantrum she had known Linda would throw.

"I've had...mixed feelings about going out with him," she said. It was an honest answer that was at least partly the truth.

"You must have been laughing at me."

Out of the corner of her eye, Ellen saw Laura step back, her gaze moving anxiously from her mother's face to her aunt's. "Don't be silly," Ellen began.

"Were you planning to steal my kids, too?"

"Linda, this isn't the time or place..."

"No? What is?"

Before Ellen could respond, a deep voice came from behind her. "I thought I'd find you here." Nick touched her shoulder lightly, gave her a quick smile, before crouching down to the children's level. "Hey, guys. You gonna have fun with your mom today?"

Patrick flung himself at Nick and even Laura smiled shakily, although she still looked wary. Linda's narrowed gaze moved from the precise spot on Ellen's shoulder where he had laid his hand to the sight of her children so obviously attracted to him. Her lips began to smile prettily, but Ellen hadn't missed her smouldering eyes.

"Nick," Linda said sweetly. "I hear you've already gotten to know my children."

"Yeah, and they pack a mean wallop." He cuffed Patrick on the shoulder and grinned at Laura. "They flattened me."

"That was nice of you." Linda still smiled. "They haven't had a man to roughhouse with in a long while."

"We had a good time." With a last squeeze he deposited Patrick on his mother's lap and glanced at Ellen. "Ready? We'll be off then. See you, all."

Linda sat frozen on the bed, staring after them. Ellen could feel her sister's gaze long after she was out of sight. It left Ellen with a vague sense of guilt that she tried to quash. Why should she feel guilty? Linda had brought her problems on herself.

Nick didn't try to start a conversation until they were in the car. But once out on the road, he glanced at her shrewdly. "You look upset. Is it Linda?"

"Oh, sort of." Ellen leaned back against the headrest and sighed, feeling drained. "We were good friends when we were children, but since her drinking became a problem there's always been tension between us. Some of which is my fault, as you pointed out."

"Wait a minute, that's not what I..."

She smiled wryly at him. "No, you were right. I *was* judging her, and it must have showed. Besides, I'd be surprised if Linda doesn't hate me. Even as a teenager, she was in trouble a lot. Me, I was always the good one. I was afraid to get in trouble."

As usual, his rough-textured voice was compassionate. "Playing those kind of roles is pretty common, you know. What I'll bet your sister doesn't know is that yours was as stressful for you as hers was for her."

"How did you know?" she asked in surprise, then stopped herself. "Never mind. I forget that you're the expert. Anyway, that's all that was going on today. Except . . ." she hesitated.

"Except?"

She wanted to say it aloud, exorcise herself. "I actually felt jealous of Linda, when the kids were so happy to see her. It made me think."

"Feeling like that doesn't have to be complicated," he said.

"No, I know that, but it brought back some memories. I've been thinking about the past a lot lately." Ellen was vaguely aware of the tile and carpet store ahead, of the Saab's turn signal being on. They were almost there, but it seemed important that she finish what she had begun. "In our family I wasn't just the good one. I was the one who always smoothed everything over. I tried so hard to make our family seem normal." She shook her head, remembering.

"The peacekeeper," he said softly.

She tried the word, nodded. "That was me. I was the peacekeeper." She half laughed. "That sounds more important than I was. Like the priestess at the gates or something. Anyway, today when I felt jealous, I wondered if it was because Laura and Patrick don't really need me, not the way I'm used to feeling needed. Do you see what I mean? Linda's a good mother when she's sober. And I wondered if... oh, if I wanted to be the only one who could make everything right for the kids."

Put that way, it sounded petty. Linda had so little, Ellen thought. Had she wanted to take even her children from her?

Outside the tile store, Nick parked the car and turned off the engine. Then he laid one arm across the back of her seat and studied her troubled expression. He had a feeling it was more his fault than her sister's that Ellen felt compelled to analyze herself. He'd been so sure that taking a long, hard look at buried emotions would be good for her. Now it scared him, because he was afraid that she would be ready soon to turn the white light of her scrutiny on him—and on why she was attracted to him.

"Hey." He gave her braid a gentle tug. "We all have feelings like that. Yours come from the best of motives. You want to protect the kids. What's wrong with that?"

Her brow furrowed in a way that made him want to smooth it with his lips. "I don't think it's that simple," she said doubtfully.

"Is anything ever?"

She blinked as though in surprise, frowned again, then smiled a little sadly. "Probably not. But I guess I needed reminding."

"And I need to kiss you."

This time it was her nose that crinkled as her smile became more uncomplicated. "You need...?"

"Mmm hmm." He bent his head slowly, traced the full curve of her mouth with one fingertip. "How about you?" he murmured.

"I..." Her tongue skimmed nervously over her lips as wide brown eyes searched his face for... what? "Yes, please," she said huskily.

"Your mother taught you to ask very nicely," Nick said, and kissed her. She responded like every man's dream, soft and receptive with a tart taste as potent as smooth whiskey. He had a feeling she would be as addictive, too.

When he reluctantly ended the kiss, she smiled a little mischievously. "Satisfied?"

"What do you think?" he said. Her chuckle followed him as they got out of the car.

Inside they wandered through the carpet section first, feeling the samples that went from velvet soft to nubby.

"What colors do you like?" Ellen asked.

"You know, I'm not sure," he admitted. He hadn't known it was possible to make carpet in so many colors and textures. "I want the walls white, so the rooms don't feel cluttered, but I hadn't gotten as far as picturing the floors. That's why I brought you."

"What if I have terrible taste?"

"Then I'm in big trouble," he said, meaning it in more ways than one.

She looked startled and turned quickly away. "How about pink?" she asked, he hoped tongue-in-cheek. A minute's flipping through a heavy pile of plush carpets revealed one that might be okay in an eight-year-old girl's room, along with posters of unicorns and princesses.

"Uh, I had something more like brown in mind."

"Brown?" He could tell she was teasing now. "That's boring."

He cleared his throat and tugged at the collar of his khaki shirt, which happened to be paired with brown cords. "Actually," he said apologetically, "I kind of like it."

Ellen's eyes danced. "I *was* kidding. Really. Although you ought to at least look at some of these other colors." She uncovered a peacock blue in a soft, uneven texture that made him think of the Sound on a bright, breezy day. "What about your furniture?" she asked.

He tried without an awful lot of success to picture the living room of his apartment. He hadn't bothered trying to make it feel like home. He'd saved his energy for the clinic and now the house he was building. "Pretty ordinary," he admitted. "I'll probably buy a new couch and stuff."

"Wow. You can do anything you want, then." She grabbed Nick's hand. "Come on, let's just look today. Maybe something will really grab you."

"What about you?" he asked, following. "What colors do you like?" When had he become so sure that the house had to suit her, too?

"Umm..." She tilted her head to one side and looked thoughtful as she ran her hands over an unbelievably luxuriant plush. "Peach and yellow and blue. Or for the floor maybe a foresty green like this."

He touched it, too, and surprised himself. "Yeah, that'd be nice. I like it."

He also liked it when she laughed at him. "We don't dare let a saleswoman get her hands on you," she teased. "What's that old cliché? A babe in the woods?"

His own mouth quirked in a rueful smile. "More like a peasant in the czar's palace. To tell you the truth, I thought all carpet was tan or gray or something."

"Who picked out the colors for your clinic?"

"A decorator."

"You really do need help, don't you?"

"I'm all yours," he said, earning another wary glance.

Two hours and three stores later, Nick hated all carpet. He was ready to hire another decorator—or give Ellen a free hand, if she would take it.

"Let's have lunch," he suggested. "How about the Red Robin? No." He heard his own voice change. "I have a better idea. You can come home with me and take a look at my furniture."

Amusement trembled in her voice. "You mean the ordinary stuff you're going to replace?"

"Yeah, that's it." He grinned ruefully. So much for subtlety. "Actually, I'm not sure you can see it under... Well, you may have noticed by this time that I'm not exactly..."

"Neat?"

"Right. I have a cleaning woman, but she won't pick up after me. She just, uh, moves the piles around."

"Oh, I see." The laughter was in her eyes now, although she was trying to suppress it. "And does your kitchen have piles, too?"

Lord, had he left dirty dishes in the sink that morning? Probably. "Maybe we'd better make it the Red Robin after all."

"No," she said firmly. The soft glow in her eyes didn't quite match the smile. "I'd like to see your place. Really."

His hand closed tightly around hers, and he had to clear his throat before he could speak. "You're on," he said roughly, and released her to start the engine.

Nick's apartment was in North Everett just off Marine View Drive, with a sweeping view of the bay. Ellen climbed out of the car and stood admiring the bobbing sails of two boats out on the Sound.

"Another couple of years and the only view I'll have will be of aircraft carriers," he grumbled, sorting his keys for the right one. He could still hardly believe that Congress had actually okayed a ludicrous amount of money to build a new navy base in Everett at the same time as others around the country were being mothballed. Talk about a pork barrel.

"Is that why you're moving?"

"One of the reasons." With the door open, he gestured for her to precede him. Behind her, he nervously scanned the living room, really seeing it for the first time in a long while. He couldn't help comparing the tan carpet and brown tweed couch to the rich colors and textures they'd spent the morning looking at.

"You were right about brown," he had to admit. "Except for your eyes. There's nothing dull about them."

She flashed him a distracted smile. "One thing you need in your new house are bookshelves. Lots of them."

He rarely even noticed the piles of books on end tables and coffee tables, sliding off the couch and occupying a couple of dining room chairs. "I know where everything is," he said defensively.

She chuckled and slipped a hand under his arm. "What was it your mother said? If your head wasn't attached . . . ?"

"Cruel," he complained, and gently drew her into his arms. Looking into those limpid brown eyes, he said, "Are you hungry?"

"That depends what you're offering."

"Peanut butter or cheese sandwich."

She wrinkled her nose. "You don't cook either?"

Nick slid off the band that confined her hair and began combing the braid out with his fingers. "Waste of time," he said. "That's what restaurants are for."

"Oh." She gave her head a shake, until the fiery curls tumbled in provocative disarray over her shoulders. "Well, tell me. Is the bed covered with books, too?"

He bent his head until his mouth was a hairbreadth from hers. "Probably."

Ellen stood on tiptoe to press tiny kisses along his lower lip. "If we push them off," she whispered, "you won't be able to find anything."

"I'll be able to find you," he pointed out, and pulled her up tightly against him, giving an involuntary groan at the feel of her. She fit like a dream, unbelievably soft in the right places and fragile in the rest. Next to her, he felt huge and clumsy, almost afraid to touch her.

"I'm glad I'm not fifteen," he muttered, sliding a finger down the delicate curve of her cheek.

"What?" Her dreamy expression became confused.

"At that age I stammered. I tripped over my own feet. You'd have been way out of my league. Hell, you're the kind of woman who gives a teenage boy wet dreams."

Pink washed over Ellen's cheeks like a watercolor, but she also began to laugh. "Well, that's not the most graceful compliment I've ever had, but . . . it *was* a compliment?'

"Oh, yes." He grinned at her. "I don't understand why some man hasn't snatched you up a long time ago."

"Dragged me by the hair? Thrown me across his horse? Haven't we regressed a few hundred years here?"

"No." He let his hunger show. "We baser creatures still like to indulge in the fantasy that being bigger and stronger means something."

"Oh, really." She moved intimately against him, her smile seductive, her voice a purr. "Well, indulge away. Within reason," she added, her nose having a small crinkle that betrayed her amusement.

That did it. Nick clenched his teeth on a wave of raw need. "You're asking for trouble," he growled.

"And it's so much fun," she breathed.

This time he didn't bother with words. He grabbed her, slung her over his shoulder and headed for the bedroom.

THE SWING SET and seesaw out in back of the clinic were a godsend.

"Push me again, Mommy," Patrick demanded.

"Watch me pump," Laura said.

"You're doing great," Linda responded automatically. "Here we go, Patrick." She lifted him and gave a big push. The giggle that was her reward was a rich one. She wanted it to be enough. Her kids *were* enough . . .

No, they weren't. The churning knot inside told her the truth.

It wasn't fair, she thought for the hundredth time that day. Ellen already had everything. Why did she have to want Nick Braden too? Or did she really want him? Resentment burned in Linda's throat. Had Ellen just wanted to cut her out?

What an irony. Miss Temperance, with her holier-than-thou zeal, and Dr. Nick Braden. God, it was almost funny. She gave Patrick another push, hard enough that he protested.

"Mommy, I'm not *on!*"

"Uh oh." Linda mastered herself, reached out to slow him down and helped him settle his small bottom more securely on the rubber seat. "Okay, here we go again!"

"Hi!" Ellen came around the side of the building. Linda turned and suddenly felt sick. Ellen hadn't looked like anything special that morning, wearing jeans and a turtleneck with her hair in a braid that didn't do anything for her. Well, now that hair was a wild mop around a face that positively glowed. Her cheeks were pink, her eyes soft and dreamy, her lips red. And Linda knew why.

Her own face tightened and she said sharply, "Did you have fun?"

Ellen's smile was a slap in the face. "Mmm hmm. How about you guys?"

"I'm getting bored," Laura announced, scraping her feet in the bark to stop her swing. "Can we go home now?"

A hand tightened on Linda's heart and she wanted to hurt somebody. "Go get your stuff," she said, and grabbed the chain on Patrick's swing to stop him.

She watched her daughter disappear around the corner and picked up Patrick. The arms that closed around her neck were a salve, but not enough.

"I wouldn't get too involved with him if I were you," she said, trying for a disinterested tone.

It was some satisfaction to see Ellen's glow fading. "Linda, I really don't think..."

"You'll never be able to understand him." She walked toward her sister, letting the bitterness seep out. "Not like I can. I mean, going through this is pretty basic, right?"

Ellen's eyes looked very dark, her face suddenly pale. "Going through... What do you mean?"

Linda stopped, hating herself. "You didn't know...?"

"Know what?" her sister snapped.

"That he's an alcoholic, of course."

CHAPTER NINE

LINDA WAS TELLING the truth.

Ellen couldn't even pretend that it wasn't so. The cold hand that wrapped around her heart wouldn't let her. Nor would the look on her sister's face, half triumphant, half pitying.

He's an alcoholic, of course. The clues had been there, but she hadn't wanted to see them. There were things Nick had said, small, unimportant. Odd reactions. Hints of pain, compassion that hadn't been distant enough. What had he told her about his marriage? That the strain he'd been under in medical school had made him hell to live with? She knew all about that hell.

Dear God. She stood there stricken, but without tears; she felt sick, angry, wounded. *Why hadn't he told her?*

"Ellen?" Linda took another step toward her. The sun was bright behind her, the shadows from the swing set like bars on the grass. Her voice sounded as though it were coming from far away. "Are you all right? You look...funny."

"I'm okay." The hurt part inside Ellen curled into a ball and wept. Somehow she still said, almost dispassionately, "I just...I didn't know. But we haven't been dating that long." Only long enough to lose her heart.

Consternation chased the spite from Linda's face. "You mean, he never told you?"

Like an automaton, Ellen shook her head.

"Oh, God." Linda seemed to struggle with what she had done. Then at last, fiercely, she said, "That bastard."

That was when the tears stung Ellen's eyes. Linda might have wanted to hurt her, but only in the pinprick way of siblings. If Ellen had doubted whether her sister still loved her, she no longer did. If only for a moment, this was the old Linda, who defended without question, just as Ellen always had in return.

She wanted to cry on Linda's shoulder. But Patrick's wide blue eyes were anxious as they moved from his aunt's face to his mother's and back again. And the windows behind her were silent watchers. Was Nick's office on this side of the building? She couldn't remember, couldn't think, but even the possibility stiffened her back.

"I'd better get the kids home," she said, quite steadily. Or did she mean run and hide? "I'm glad you told me. Thank you."

Linda's arms tightened around her son and she bowed her head, muffling the words against his silky head. "I thought you knew," she said softly. "I was just... rubbing it in. I shouldn't have said it. I wanted to hurt you, because I was jealous. You looked so happy. I'm sorry, Ellen."

"No, it's okay." It was, at least that part. She took Patrick from Linda, then gave her a quick hug. "Really."

"I *am* sorry."

"I know."

So little, and yet the years were erased as though they'd never been. Why did one kind of love have to be the price for another? she wondered in anguish.

Pride carried her through the trip home, the mechanical preparation of dinner, the ritual of stories and songs and goodnight kisses. Afterward she cleaned up the kitchen, straightened the living room, made Laura's lunch for tomorrow. She even managed a conversation with her friend, Joanne, who always called once a week or so. This last month she'd been a godsend, generous with baby-sitting and advice. Only at the end did Ellen falter, when Joanne asked how things were going with Nick.

"I . . . I don't know if I'll keep seeing him. But I guess I'm not ready to talk about it."

"You know where to come when you are," Joanne said quietly, and they ended the call.

All the while Ellen felt stiff, rusty, like a machine whose parts were wearing out. Turning off the lights behind her, she headed wearily for bed, but sleep was beyond her. Instead she lay staring into the darkness, asking herself the same questions, over and over.

Had Nick cared so little for her? Had he never intended a future, where he couldn't hide his alcoholism from her? But it was so hard to believe. Like clear overlays she kept seeing his rough-hewn face: smiling, frowning, intense, passionate. Was it all a lie? How could such tenderness and such deceitfulness exist in the same man?

And why was she hiding here in the darkness like a wounded animal? Any woman with dignity and self-respect would have marched into his office and confronted him. But, no. She didn't have even the courage for that. Loathing herself, she rolled over and buried her face in the pillow.

Maybe it was the faint lilac scent of her sheets that brought a sudden memory. It was of herself, just that morning. She had showered, made her bed, plumping this pillow and smoothing the covers, then started to dress while she thought about the day ahead. She hadn't gotten further than her jeans and a bra when she had been startled by a wave of happiness so sweet, so rich, that on impulse she had curved her arms above her head in a ballerina's pose and pirouetted. As she twirled she had caught a glimpse of her face in the mirror, transformed.

Now she was in the dark, alone again, and her face contorted against the pillow in a silent cry. How had so much happiness turned so quickly to pain?

ONLY AS HE KNOCKED on her front door did it occur to Nick that Ellen might have gone to church. The footsteps inside were silent, so Nick was taken off guard when the door suddenly opened.

"Yes?" she began, then stopped. "Oh. Nick." She sounded anything but pleased to see him. Dismayed might be closer to it.

"Is this a bad time?" he asked, feeling his anticipation knot. "Are Laura and Patrick wearing you out?"

"No, they're playing with a neighbor's kids. I... I just wasn't expecting you. But... Well, you might as well come in." She opened the door farther, and for the first time the morning light fell on her face, harshly exposing the dark circles beneath her eyes and the translucence of her skin. Her feet were bare and she wore jeans and a sacky sweatshirt. Ellen held herself proudly, but she looked exhausted. Defeated.

Frowning, Nick stopped just over the doorstep and reached out to caress her cheek. "Ellen, what's wrong?"

She jerked back from his touch.

Nick froze, then let his hand drop to his side. "Ellen...?"

"Why didn't you tell me?" The words were said quietly, but he could hear her raw anger and something else. Pain?

He felt as if a chunk of cement had dropped into his stomach. "Tell you what?" he asked, and with sickening certainty knew the answer.

"That you're an alcoholic." Ellen still stood with the door open, clutching the knob as though it held her up.

"I did tell you." He tried to say it calmly. "I tell the whole damn world regularly."

"You knew how I felt."

"And you knew I was an alcoholic."

"No." She evaded his gaze. "No, I didn't. I would never have gone out with you if I'd known."

"Damn it, Ellen," he said, his frustration mixed with the fear that made his voice too loud, "I started that first family orientation with the history of my life. You were there that day. I know you were!"

She closed her eyes and leaned her forehead against the door. "I was late."

It was that simple. Three little words that spelled the beginning and the end. She hadn't gone out with him despite his alcoholism as he'd imagined, smiled at him and kissed him and looked at him with heart-stopping, dreamy-eyed passion despite it. He had been right to be afraid.

And wrong to let what he was turn into a lie. He'd known they would have to talk about his past someday. Why hadn't he gotten it over with? Maybe he could have saved them both before it was too late.

"God." He, too, closed his eyes and turned away. When he opened them, he was facing the wall, looking right at a picture. It was a studio portrait, black-and-white and a little yellowed by age, simply framed: a moment stolen from time, too honest to be denied. There was a younger version of Ellen's mother, pretty but somehow anxious. The man with his arm around her had kind eyes and a face so ordinary Nick had seen it a thousand times. He didn't look as though he could possibly be the stone at the center of the spreading ripples that had devastated so many lives. In front of him the man's hand rested on the blond head of the young girl who smiled at the camera with hopeful innocence not yet lost.

And then there was Ellen. Maybe nine or ten years old, she was skinny and almost homely at that age. Her freckles were more noticeable on her thin face, her hair lighter but no more disciplined. She stood just a little apart from her parents and sister, as though distancing herself emotionally. Her expression was guarded, her posture unnaturally stiff. She had not been a happy child, he saw; at least not when this picture was snapped.

"I'm sorry," he said roughly, turning back to face her. "I thought you knew. Yeah, I was a coward to avoid talking about it, but... Oh, hell. I wanted you to think of me as a man, not an alcoholic."

Her eyes were bottomless pools of pain. "But you are an alcoholic."

What could he say? "I haven't had a drink in ten years."

Ellen closed her eyes again, drew in a ragged breath. "I don't know if I want to talk about this any more, Nick."

"You don't want to talk about it?" He was suddenly angry, incredulous, his fear transformed. "That's it? Ellen, for God's sake, I can't change the past!"

Again she wouldn't look at him. "You knew how I'd feel."

"It doesn't have to be important." He sounded as desperate as he felt. "Damn it, don't let your stepfather cripple you!"

He'd gotten to her, because she flinched, although she also lifted her chin and met his gaze with eyes in which he read no hope. "Don't ask the impossible, Nick."

He wanted to shake her, to somehow make her acknowledge him, but it was as though he were already no more than a memory, a ghost she looked right through.

"I am asking," he said from between clenched teeth. "It's not impossible! I love you, Ellen!"

She did more than flinch this time; she actually took a step back and hunched her shoulders. Shaking her head quickly, she said, "No. I need to think, Nick. Please! Don't push me."

"Damn it! I am who I am. Look at me!" He was terrified, his fingers slipping from their last purchase. "At least look at me!"

Ellen pulled in further, wouldn't meet his eyes. "Please, Nick..."

He took one long stride and grabbed her by the shoulders. His voice scraped his throat, as raw as the wound she had opened. "You want to pretend I don't even exist, isn't that right? Well, I do, and this is real. You *can't* deny it." With that he bent his head and savagely took her mouth, demanding a response for which he was afraid to beg.

Ellen stood immobile under the assault for a moment, and then she melted. Her hands fluttered to his chest and then slid up to clasp him around the neck. She began to kiss him back almost feverishly. Nick groaned and pulled her tightly against him, his pleasure and fear mixed so inextricably that he could no longer distinguish what he felt. He could only kiss her, taste her sweetness, greedily drown in the intoxicating essence of the woman he wasn't sure he could live without.

But when the sweetness became salty, he knew hopelessness. It wasn't in him to drink her tears and still demand more. Wordlessly, he released her. Nick looked for a long moment, seeing her full mouth swollen from his kiss, the dazed, hurting eyes, the tear-streaked cheeks, and hated himself for what he had done to her.

The kindest thing he could do was walk away. Abruptly, blindly, he did just that. All he could see was her face. He would carry that image with him forever.

IF HE HAD JUST TOLD HER, maybe it would have been different. Maybe she could have accepted it... Ellen buried her face in her hands. How could she lie to herself? If she had known, she would never have gone that day when he had asked her to lunch. He would have stayed Dr. Braden to her, and she wouldn't hurt right now.

She also wouldn't have felt the things he had made her feel. Would that have been better? He had helped her break out of a cocoon, unfurl her wings. Would she rather be back, safe behind the walls of her own making that had protected her from feeling too much?

In despair she scrubbed the tears from her cheeks, pushed her tumbled hair back from her face and stood up. As though by instinct, she walked quietly into the dark hall and stood in the doorway of the children's bedroom, listening to them breathe. There was a cough, a soft sigh, the rustle of bedclothes. Peaceful.

At Laura's age Ellen had had trouble sleeping. She used to lay stiffly awake, staring at the darkness, waiting for something scary. She never knew what. It didn't take the form of a bogey man that a parent could soothe away, it was fear itself. Amorphous, vague, a part of the night, leaving with morning but always waiting. She had been waiting for it all of her life.

Enough! she thought suddenly, turning to go back to the brightly lit living room. She had let her fears shape her life, until she was afraid even of the man she loved. Nick wasn't anything like her stepfather; he was a strong man who hadn't had a drink in ten years. Surely, surely he would never have one again! Surely his feelings for her were enough.

It was only nine o'clock, not too late to call. Ellen sank into the chair beside the phone and blew her nose before she dialed. She was a mess, but Nick wouldn't care.

The phone rang and she listened with trepidation for his voice. But it rang again, and again. On the seventh ring she hung up, her eagerness seeping away like water on dry earth. Where was he?

On one level she was relieved. Maybe she shouldn't have called at all, at least not yet. She should think about this longer. After all, Nick's alcoholism wasn't the only issue; the fact that he hadn't talked about it made her even warier. He'd seen her at her most vulnerable, but what did she really know about him? Very little, when she got right down to it. He had scars he hadn't showed her, and wasn't that what love was all about?

Ellen made herself start her bedtime preparation. She felt so tired; it was an effort to brush her teeth, swallow her vitamins. A few minutes later, in her nightgown, she stared at herself in the bathroom mirror. With her face scrubbed pink so that her freckles stood out and her hair tidily confined by a braid, she looked so young. So vulnerable. Nothing of the sophisticated face she presented to the world was visible now. Now Ellen saw the child inside.

She tried to smile at herself, but her lips trembled. On a rush of impatience Ellen turned away. She was flipping back her covers when the doorbell rang.

For just an instant she froze. Who could possibly want her at this time of night? Unless ... Had something happened to her mother? To Linda? Heart beating hard, she struggled into her robe as she hurried to the front door.

"Who is it?" she called, hand on the chain.

"Nick."

Ellen's heart lurched and panic engulfed her. She wasn't ready for this! But if it was too late to recapture the determination that had made her call him earlier, it was also too late to pretend she wasn't home.

She took a deep breath and unlocked the door, holding it open.

Hands shoved in his pockets, he wore a heavy sweater that added to his bulk. The porch light laid shadows beneath his blunt cheekbones and leeched the intense color from his eyes. Even so his face had that rough charisma that had first attracted her.

"I guess I shouldn't have come so late," Nick said, his gaze moving from her face to the open V of her bathrobe.

Self-consciously Ellen clutched the peach-colored robe together at her neck. "No, that's all right," she said. "The kids are asleep, but... Well, come in."

"Are you sure?" He sounded as awkward as she felt.

"Yes, of course." She stood back. "I tried to call you earlier."

Nick stepped past her and she closed the door. Once inside, he just stood there, making no move to go farther.

"I was at an AA meeting."

"Oh." Whatever she'd imagined, that wasn't it. "I suppose you run them."

"I'm just a participant." His eyes met hers squarely. "It's my way of not forgetting."

"Oh," she said again. They looked at each other in silence until she hurriedly filled it. "Shall we sit down? Can I get you some coffee or something?"

"Thanks, but I don't think so." Nick's face was carved with lines of weariness and strain. "I just came to apologize. I was angry this morning. I didn't want to leave it that way. You have a right to feel the way you do. I'm the one who was wrong, not you."

"No, I wasn't fair." Her cheeks warmed. "I should *admire* you for quitting, and for what you've done with your life, not...not treat you like a leper or something!"

"I'm an alcoholic," he said quietly. "Neither of us can forget that."

"But you were right. It doesn't have to matter! If you've made it ten years, you'll never drink again. Do you even remember what it felt like to want it?"

"I remember." Muscles flexed in his jaw. "I can't lie to you, Ellen. There are still moments when I'd give anything..." He bit it off.

"But you don't think you'd actually..."

"I can't promise." She saw the agony in his eyes before he swung away from her and began to rub the back of his neck. "It's a day at a time. With an alcoholic, there are no promises."

She looked uncertainly at his broad back. "Why not? I don't understand. Surely you trust yourself!"

He turned abruptly to face her. "Why should I? I destroyed my life once! Why not again?"

Ellen's uncertainty had become sickening fear. "You said you love me."

"I do love you! God, I love you!"

"Then...then why...?"

"It's a disease," he said. "Haven't I taught you that much?"

"But one you've controlled!" Her fingers were painfully tight as she clutched at the neckline of her robe.

His shoulders were rigid, the lines in his forehead deeply carved. "What is it you want me to say, Ellen? That I'll never hurt you? Can anybody promise that?"

She refused to let herself cry. "Most people do, when they love each other. Isn't that what a marriage vow is?"

"No!" He struggled to moderate his voice. "No. You promise to give it your damnedest. But sometimes that isn't enough. All the love in the world can't make it enough. I won't make promises I might not be able to keep."

She'd thought his confidence was rock solid, dependable enough to shore up her own. She had been wrong.

"Then I'm not sure..." Her voice wavered and she swallowed hard. "I'm not sure it's enough."

Nick's eyes closed and a muscle in one cheek spasmed. When he opened his eyes and looked at her, Ellen saw despair. "Do you love me?" he challenged.

Seared to her core, Ellen cried, "Yes. Yes! But what difference does it make?"

He sounded as though he tasted the same ashes. "Not much, if you can't give me your faith, too."

"Faith?" she repeated incredulously, her voice rising. "How can I have faith in you, if you don't have any in yourself?"

"The same way I believe in you, even though you don't seem to believe in yourself."

"No!" Incredibly, she was angry. "We're not talking about the same thing! My stepfather ruined lives. Maybe he had a disease, I don't know. But I do know he could have changed if he had loved us enough. Now I'm supposed to risk everything for a man who isn't sure *he* loves me enough? I...I just don't know, Nick. I have to think. I..."

Ellen's lungs didn't seem to have enough air to finish. Her heart was constricted. But what was said was said, and she couldn't take it back.

For a moment Nick just stood there looking baffled, hands dangling uselessly at his sides, a big man diminished by his helplessness. His mouth twisted, and then he said, "I love you enough not to lie to you."

Her eyes seemed to be burning. Just above a whisper, she said, "Maybe I would have liked you to pretend."

He lifted his hands in a hopeless gesture, then let them fall. "Will you give me a chance?"

"I..." her gaze fell. "I don't know. I have to think," she repeated.

His face looked strained, he hesitated as though wanting to say more, then abruptly turned and left.

Ellen watched him leave, wanting to call him back, tell him she didn't mean it, didn't need time. But she was frozen inside and out. Even when the door closed behind him, she didn't move. She had lost her heart, and more. Nick had taught her to believe, to dream, and then he had stolen those dreams.

At last, listening to the silence inside her, Ellen slowly fastened the chain on her door and locked the dead bolt. Perhaps at last she had discovered what shape her fear would take. It was herself she saw—alone.

CHAPTER TEN

LIKE BARE BONES, the framed-in walls of Nick's house rose angular and white in the moonlight, a ribcage reaching around what would be the heart of the house. Nick sat on the uneven foundation, back against a stud, and looked across the dark valley toward the distant glow of Everett. The few night sounds were muted: a dog barking, a car engine.

He had driven straight here from Ellen's, needing the peace this place had always given him, the reassurance of a dream gaining substance. But the magic wasn't here tonight; there was only rough concrete, the smell of wood shavings, and the rocky ground that was going to make gardening hell.

With a groan he leaned his head back against the two-by-four. He shouldn't have pushed her. He should have given her space, let her think it through. Instead he'd wanted—demanded!—trust. It was easy to forget she'd only known him for three weeks. To top it off, in those three weeks he had lied to her, if only by omission. And *then* he expected her wholehearted faith?

Right. Why hadn't he asked for a pod of Orca whales gift-wrapped for his birthday while he was at it?

Gritting his teeth, Nick picked up a good-sized stone and flung it as hard as he could into the darkness. The rattle when it struck didn't satisfy him. Restlessly he stood, swinging himself up on the cement footing by grabbing a stud.

Inside, beams marked the floor. Plywood would go down any day now. Soon the walls would be enclosed and the place would actually look like a house. Sometimes it felt like a living being to him, something he shaped with his own hands, something that grew in unexpected ways. But tonight... He looked bleakly around. Tonight it was a skeleton, brutally stripped of the flesh and life his imagination usually supplied. At best it was a sculpture, one of those abstract modern ones of rusty metal that said God knew what, and would never add beauty to its surroundings.

Yeah, and he should have gone home to bed, not taken a half-hour drive to a construction site at midnight, expecting to find some kind of salvation. He laughed without humor and headed for the kitchen door, managing to stub his toe on a pipe sticking up.

On the drive home his thoughts were as dark as the night around him. It had been years since he had relived the nightmare of being a drunk, the marriage he had shattered. He told the story often in orientations and counseling sessions, but matter-of-factly. Over those years he'd become practiced at it, smooth. Maybe even superficial.

It had been just as many years since he'd wished he were someone different. *Something* different. Not an alcoholic. There were times he'd even convinced himself that his disease was a blessing, that silver lining his mother used to go on about. He had learned humility; Lord, had he learned humility. And maybe because of his own downfall he had done something useful with his life, something that needed doing and was meant to be.

Years. He never questioned anymore that what he believed and taught and lived was true. What was it Ellen had said that day? *You're very anxious to excuse the alcoholic, aren't you?* And something about reaching the conclusion that suited him best. Could it be? He'd countered that the research results were persuasive. He was responsible for some of those results. *Had* what he wanted to be true prejudiced the conclusions?

Maybe alcoholics *were* selfish; maybe they were weak. Maybe he couldn't handle stress. Lord knew medical school had provided plenty of that. So he'd gotten drunk a lot. By luck he hadn't killed a patient with the hands that shook the next morning. The only thing that had died was Marie's love. *Could* he have quit sooner if he had loved her more? he wondered.

In front of his apartment Nick parked his car. Once he had silenced the engine and turned off the headlights, he wearily closed his eyes and leaned his head against forearms crossed on the steering wheel.

Disease or weakness, would he be able to fight it for the rest of his life? Or, given a chance, would he only destroy Ellen's love the way he had destroyed Marie's?

"HAVE A GOOD TIME, GUYS."

Grandma was going to take Laura and Patrick to dinner at McDonald's, then to visit their mom. They had progressed to Ellen's driveway, laden with enough toys and coloring supplies to last a week. It had taken Ellen an hour to get the kids ready.

Now she gave Laura one last hug and stopped to kiss Patrick's round cheek. "Say hi to your mom."

"I wish we had more toys there," Laura said discontentedly.

"More toys?" Ellen laughed. "If you were carrying any more your arms would fall right off!"

"Yeah, but they're old toys. They're boring."

"Oh, I see. What you really wish is that your mom would have a surprise for you."

Patrick's small face brightened. "Do you think she will?"

Ellen glanced at her mother, who nodded infinitesimally. Ellen pretended to look thoughtful. "Who knows?"

"Wow, that'd be rad!" Laura bounded across the driveway and slung the bulging daypack into her grandmother's car. "Come on, Patrick! I wonder what Mom's going to get us?" Patrick had barely pulled his feet in when Laura slammed the car door. Ellen winced.

Mrs. Whalley just looked puzzled. *"Rad?"*

"Far out," Ellen translated. "Groovy, fantastic."

"Oh. She sounds like a teenager."

"I think they're growing up a little faster these days," Ellen agreed. Especially when they had to, she thought. On the heels of that, she said, "Are you sure you want to do this, Mom?"

"Positive," her mother said firmly. "I should support Linda when she's doing something right. She sounds like she's honestly trying. It upsets me more to worry about her than it does to see her. Besides, you can use a break."

"You always say that. Anyway, I haven't seen the kids all day. I only got home from work an hour ago!"

"Maybe *you* should go out to dinner. Or are you planning to?"

Ellen translated that without any trouble, either. "You mean, do I have a date? The answer is no, thank heavens. I'm going to go put my feet up and eat all the goodies I've hidden from the kids and watch something really stupid on TV. Which shouldn't be hard to find.''

Her mother pretended to be busy digging keys out of her perfectly organized purse. Her casual tone didn't fool Ellen. ''I thought you and that nice Dr. Braden were seeing so much of each other. You could just call and invite him over for dessert.''

''What, Oreo cookies?'' She had a feeling her flipness didn't fool her mother, either. She sighed. ''I need some time to think. I won't be seeing him for a little bit.''

''Oh, Ellen, why?'' Mrs. Whalley sounded honestly dismayed.

There was no point in lying. ''Did Linda tell you that he's a recovered alcoholic?''

''The *Herald* did a feature on him a year or so ago. I remember that he'd had a drinking problem. Wasn't it a long time ago?''

''Ten years, he says.''

The car quivered and a brief wail was quickly shut off. Ellen's mother cast her shining Buick a nervous glance over her shoulder. ''Oh, dear, I'd better go. They've been so patient.''

Thank you, Laura. . ''Have fun, Mom. Really.''

Mrs. Whalley's smile was astonishingly serene. ''I will. But, Ellen . . .'' It sounded like an afterthought.

''Yes?''

Her mother surprised her. ''Don't let your memories keep you from happiness.''

''It's more likely they're keeping me from making a big mistake,'' she said tartly.

''If you love him . . .''

This time Ellen lifted her chin in a gesture of pride and lied without hesitation. ''I don't know that I do.''

"Love means taking the bad with the good." Mrs. Whalley got in the car and rolled down her window, adding, "Sometimes you have to trust in fate."

"And if it fails you?"

"Then you've given the most that your heart will allow."

With remembered bitterness Ellen said, "What about other people's hearts?"

Her mother understood her, all right. The delicate tracery of wrinkles around her mouth crumpled a little more. But her voice was strong. "Then maybe you have to help them understand human weakness."

The window slid soundlessly up, leaving Ellen without a chance to retort. Frustrated, she watched as the Buick backed out of the driveway.

She wouldn't let her mother confuse her. What sounded like wisdom was just a rationale. Who would want to admit that she had failed her children?

So why did it strike home so deeply? *Human weakness. Giving the most that your heart will allow.* Was she capable of that? Ellen wondered with inexplicable sadness, before she cut the thought off.

Refusing to give that sadness any more room to flower, Ellen retreated to her condo. She had gotten so used to clutter and the chatter of high voices eager to tell her about their day that for a moment she was struck by the stillness, the silence. It was lonely. Depressing.

"Peaceful," she said aloud, firmly, and tried not to notice that her voice had echoed. She felt so hollow, the echo might have been inside her.

LINDA FIDGETED in her seat. What was with Nick, anyway? She didn't think he'd even heard what she had just said.

She saw him alone a couple of times a week, just to talk. She did most of the talking, but he had a way of edging her toward realizing something about herself that left her not knowing whether *she* had figured it out, or whether he had. He didn't act like a judge, more like he was in it with her. One thing that made her comfortable was that he was usually physical. Always moving. Pacing, maybe, or just sitting on the edge of his desk, swinging his leg. He touched easily, too, something she really liked. That was when she had thought it meant something special, though. His big hand on her arm had made her shiver. Yeah, and all the time he had been seeing her sister.

"What do you think the big pressures in your life are going to be?" he asked. He just sat there behind his desk, stolid, expressionless. No rueful smile that said, I know it's a bitch, but you can do it. Instead he was frowning, like God looking down on her, except then he glanced out the window and she wasn't sure she had anything to do with it.

"Well . . ." she fumbled a little. "I guess the kids. It's not easy being a single parent. Patrick wants attention all the time, and Laura talks and talks. Well, you know them. I mean, if Tom were still around it might be different, but he never bothers to visit." *Sympathize, damn it!*

His voice was distant. "Ellen says you're a good mother."

She felt a squeeze of real pain and looked down at her hands. "I don't know. Good mothers don't get drunk when their kids need them."

"Good mothers die of cancer."

"Yeah, well, that makes the audience cry. Puking in your toilet isn't the same."

His mouth twisted and Linda thought in surprise, he hurts, too. *Why?* The silence stretched a little too long before Nick said with an obvious effort, "What about your ex-husband? Could you encourage him to take more interest in the kids?"

The pain in her stomach curdled, like cream gone bad. "He wasn't there when I needed him. Why would I want him to take more interest?"

"Because it would let the pressure off you?"

"He's a trucker, on the road all the time. He doesn't even send checks sometimes. I wouldn't trust him with the kids."

"You think he'd be careless?"

Her chin came up and she said truculently, "Probably. Anyway, I think he'd bad-mouth me to them. What do you expect? There's a reason we're not married anymore."

Nick's air of abstraction vanished. Suddenly his eyes were clear and very perceptive. "Did your drinking have anything to do with the breakup of your marriage?"

"No! It was a long time ago." She tried to sit still under his gaze, but realized she was fidgeting. At last she gave a defiant shrug. "Oh, probably. I mean, he didn't like it. Sometimes I just drank to make him mad. You know all the crap you promise each other when you get married. Well, you've been through it. Tom and I were going to have so much fun!" Her tone mocked it. "I guess we did have fun for a while, until I got pregnant. But that stupid trucking job, he was gone for days, weeks sometimes! And I was supposed to stay at home and have babies? When he was there, which was practically never, he was tired and he didn't want to go out. He wanted to sit and watch the tube and eat home cooking! What did he think I'd been eating while he was gone? I just . . ."

She'd wanted to dance and laugh and feel pretty. Not *homey*.

She felt so petty. She *loved* her kids. But she'd needed somebody else, and Tom was never there for her. When she drank she felt better. She was more fun for the kids, more patient. Only she couldn't quit.

As if she were outside herself, Linda suddenly realized that she was sweating. She wanted a drink. Just one. Fire down her throat, relief flooding her. Please, just one. Her innards were being squeezed by a need so fierce she'd have done anything for a drink. Begged, stolen, abandoned her kids. No, she'd never do that! Except she had in a way, hadn't she?

"I don't want to talk about Tom," she said abruptly, blinking to clear her eyes of the haze that kept her from seeing right. "He doesn't have anything to do with this. Our marriage was just a mistake. Half of them are supposed to be, aren't they?"

"Maybe." His voice was strangely rough and he looked away again, toward the window. "But maybe getting married isn't the part that's the mistake."

She was dying, just sitting here. Linda jumped up and headed for the door. At the last second she stopped. "What are you saying?" she said angrily. "That I should still be waiting at home for him to drop by every couple of weeks?"

"No." Nick didn't even stand up with her, just looked at her with that frown back in his eyes. "I don't know what I'm saying, Linda. Sorry, I guess I'm not my best today. Maybe we can take this up next time."

She nodded jerkily and started to open the door. Something made her stop and turn to face him. "I told Ellen you were an alcoholic," Linda said flatly. "She didn't know."

They weren't doctor and patient anymore. He rubbed tiredly at his face. "Yeah, so I found out."

"Ellen told me she wasn't seeing you any more. I didn't mean to wreck anything. It was just...a comment." *Yeah, sure.*

"It's not your fault, Linda." His chair squeaked when he tilted it back and tried a smile that didn't quite cut it. "Maybe your sister and I weren't meant to be. She's... pretty bitter about your father."

Linda chewed on her lower lip. Fidgeting again. "Yeah, I know. It's sort of weird, because she really loved him. And I used to think he loved her more than he did me. Funny, isn't it? I mean, I'm the one who was his natural daughter. But I think about him a lot and...well, it wasn't his fault. I'll bet he felt as lousy as I do. He loved us. I know he did. I wish he'd hung around, even though I know..."

How he felt. It hung between them, that knowledge that they shared.

Linda gave another jerky shrug. "Anyway, Ellen's the lucky one, except she's not really, because she can't forgive him."

Strange, she'd never put her finger on it before. Linda turned it over in her mind. Yeah, that was it, all right.

Nick sat staring at her, but not as if he really saw her. She wondered where she'd ever gotten the idea that he cared especially about her. It hurt to admit that she was just another patient to him. She wanted to blame somebody. Him. Ellen. Herself. But somehow it wouldn't quite come. She just felt sad.

That was life anyway, right? And, hey, there was too much blame going around. She didn't need to add to it.

"Uh, my mom and the kids are coming for a visit. I'd...well, I'd better go."

Those blue eyes tried to focus on her. "Oh. Sure. Thanks for..."

What? Screwing up his life? "I'm sorry," she said again, and slipped out of his office. She was halfway down the hall before she realized that the craving had left her. She'd quit sweating, quit shaking. She'd lived. All she really wanted right now was to hug her kids. To hug them and never let them go.

AT HER BREAK Ellen slit open the big white envelope from the University of Washington. The pamphlet that spilled out onto her desk blotter was glossy, edged with the University's purple and gold trademark colors. Opening it, she found pictures of old, ivy-covered buildings and huge maple trees, of the fountain and the modern red-brick library, of the stadium and computers and books and a lively classroom discussion. It was as tantalizing as a travel poster of a Tahitian beach; and as distant and impossible. Her stab of longing was sharp, and with clumsy hands Ellen stuffed pamphlet and application back in the envelope.

The whole idea was ridiculous. She had a good job here. She'd be nuts to throw it over! And for what? To pretend she was nineteen, beginning life again?

The big envelope thumped when it hit the bottom of her metal wastebasket. She could see the white corner sticking out as she switched on her computer terminal and went determinedly back to work. One small part of her stayed aware of that corner for the rest of the morning, until she picked up a couple of folders and left for a meeting.

"FINE PRESENTATION, Ellen." Pete Bronowski, vice-president of Research and Development, gave her an approving smile. "I have to admit those numbers are a surprise. They just may change the way I look at this software package. We'd really have to push those sales up to justify these kind of costs. I'm not sure that potential is there."

Ironically, the particular software under discussion was a sophisticated program for cost analysis, more effective, Ellen thought, than the one she'd used to shoot it down. Except she'd be surprised if she *had* shot it down. If the estimates didn't match what the executives wanted to hear, they were usually discounted.

This time, though, Pete Bronowski was snapping some tough questions at the engineer who'd been pushing this project, and George Grun, Ellen's boss, gave her a wink and a thumbs up. A few minutes later, when the meeting broke up, George surprised her.

"Why don't you join us for lunch, Ellen?"

"Good idea." Pete, a tall rangy man with graying hair who had a silver golf tee as a tie pin, took her arm and steered her toward the door. "Arnie's sound good?"

She couldn't help feeling flattered by being included, although she also told herself she was being gullible. They weren't promoting her to management; they were only rewarding her with a gold star for effort, or maybe using the corporate lunch as a tool to build morale.

Still, the conversation was stimulating, ranging from the effect a new law before the state legislature would have on Kashiwa Corporation to the software package they were still considering.

The leisurely lunch consumed a huge chunk of the afternoon. Ellen arrived back at her desk to realize that it was almost time to go home, thank heavens. She poked her purse back in her drawer and glanced through the messages left on her desk. Tossing them in her wastebasket, she caught sight of the big white envelope with the torn top. She sat and stared at it, feeling unsettled.

She managed to wrench her attention away and accomplish a little work, although her concentration remained frayed at the edges. Did the lunch invitation mean anything? Had they been hinting at a promotion? And was that what she wanted?

Ellen gave up at last, a few minutes early. She'd collected her purse and was halfway out of the building when she stopped. By morning her wastebasket would have been emptied. The envelope would be gone. She couldn't imagine changing her mind, but... Oh, it wouldn't hurt to tuck the information away.

Ellen hurried back, ignoring curious glances. Snatching the big envelope from the basket, she thrust it out of sight under her blotter. This time when she left, she didn't look back.

WHEN THE PHONE began to ring, Ellen's hand jerked, splattering her apron with spaghetti sauce. Damn. What was she so jumpy for, anyway? Nick wouldn't be calling. Sure as shooting, it would be Linda or her mother or Joanne or...

She realized suddenly that the ringing had stopped and Laura's voice was prattling away in the living room. Laura was probably already telling somebody—Nick?— how grumpy Aunt Ellen was and how gross last night's dinner had been.

Ellen abandoned her sauce and bolted for the living room.

"Aunt Ellen says Richard chases me because he likes me," Laura happily confided into the phone. "I think I love him. But Aunt Ellen says I'll like lots of boys before

I grow up. She says when I *really* love someone I'll know it."

Ellen snatched the receiver away and covered it with her hand. "Who is it?" she mouthed.

Laura's face darkened. "I wasn't done!"

"Is it Grandma?"

"No! It's Nick! And I wanted to tell him . . ."

Lifting the receiver gingerly, Ellen said into it, "Hello?"

"Hello, Ellen." His voice was as deep and gravelly as she remembered it, as impossibly reassuring. The sound was enough, despite everything, to make her pulse take a dizzying, glorious leap.

Tears stung her eyes. "Hi, Nick."

"I just called to see how it's going."

"Fine," she lied.

"Ellen." He exhaled and his voice changed, became rougher. "I won't push you. I just needed to tell you that . . . Oh, hell. I miss you."

The truth spilled out before she could stop it. "I miss you, too."

The pause was long, scary. She wanted to see his face. At last he said gruffly, "It doesn't have to be this way."

"Just for a little while," she said in a choked whisper. "Just give me a chance to think."

"I wish I knew *what* you were thinking."

Ellen answered indirectly. "I remember at one of the meetings you suggested Al-Anon."

"If you go," he said, "will you call and tell me about it?"

"I'd like to do that," she said, her voice tear-softened.

Again there was a silence before he said huskily, "Don't forget that I love you," and then he was gone.

Ellen slowly hung up. Blinking the tears away, she realized that the children were staring at her. Laura's hand clasped Patrick's smaller one.

Naturally, it was Laura who said apprehensively, "What's wrong, Aunt Ellen? Did Mommy die or something?"

"No. Oh, no." Ellen swiped at her wet cheeks with the apron. "Nothing's wrong. Really. I'm just turning into a watering spout."

"What's that?"

"It means I'm being silly." She crossed the room to give them a hug. "And it's too complicated to explain. Now go wash your hands. Dinner will be ready in a few minutes."

In the kitchen she dumped spaghetti into the furiously boiling water and lowered the heat before turning on the burner under the broccoli that sat waiting in the steamer. The table was already set. She had a minute.

No excuses. Reluctantly Ellen reached for the sheet of paper Nick had given her weeks ago with the Al-Anon information number on it, written in his strong hand. Except that she'd wasted this much time, maybe she should wait until tomorrow, not bother somebody in the evening . . .

But on the echo of Nick's last words, she was already dialing. *I love you.* If there was any way at all to make that be enough, she had to take it.

CHAPTER ELEVEN

"GOD, I CAN HARDLY WAIT to get out of here." Linda paced almost as restlessly as she had in the beginning. The difference was that she had become a pretty woman again. There was color in her cheeks and her brown eyes sparkled, while the pacing was impatient rather than frenetic. "Only a few more days. I can't decide what I should do first. Go to the mall? Eat out? What I'd give for a Big Mac. And Laura and Patrick would like that. Unless you or Mom have taken them."

"I don't like hamburgers, remember?"

"Still?" She laughed. "Now I sound like Dad. How could I have forgotten? It used to drive him nuts! We always had to find a place that had something besides hamburgers. Oh, well, definitely a Big Mac, then. Except I'm getting fat." Linda pinched at nonexistent flab around her waistline. "My clothes won't fit. Maybe it should be the mall. I suppose I'll go back to work Monday. I have to wear something decent looking, don't I?"

Ellen watched her sister from the room's one armchair. "Have you talked to your boss?" she said with restraint. Maybe it was natural that Linda was so eager to get out of here, back to real life. But shouldn't she be thinking about what it would take to stay sober?

"Jerome understands," her sister said self-righteously. "He said he admires me for voluntarily getting help."

Voluntary, hell, Ellen thought, but didn't say.

"He says they're anxious to have me back. I do a good job, you know."

"Haven't you missed work an awful lot lately?"

Linda twirled to face her. "Well, now they know why, don't they?"

Ellen bit her lip. She always felt so old-maidish around her sister, stiff and prudish and sanctimonious. She seemed suddenly to hear Linda's childish voice as she raced to their mother. "Ellen's being bossy!" She guessed she was still being bossy.

She couldn't help but think about the Al-Anon meeting she had attended the night before. They had talked about love with detachment. About not trying to take responsibility for another's life. It had sounded so easy, freeing somebody you loved so that she made her own decisions and faced the consequences. The people there had sounded like Nick, only he hadn't put it quite the same way. *Could* she let Linda go? Love her with detachment?

"I'm glad your boss is being supportive," she said neutrally.

Linda scrunched up her nose, reminding Ellen sharply of Laura. "Oh, well, he's not a bad guy.

Actually, Linda's boss, an insurance agent, had been extraordinarily patient with his secretary. Ellen knew how much work Linda must have missed before the latest crisis. Hard as the road ahead of her would be, it would have been rougher yet if she didn't have a job waiting.

"You look great," Ellen said suddenly. "I'd forgotten . . ." She stopped, realizing how untactful the rest of her thought would have been, but Linda had apparently heard only the beginning.

"Do you think so?" She twirled to a stop in front of the wall-hung mirror and raked her fingers through her fine bangs. "My hair is a disaster! I wonder if I can get Larry to fit me in right away? Maybe I'll call him today. Just think! Only four more days! Thank heavens!"

"Only four more days," Ellen echoed. She felt very near dread at the thought. Had she become so attached to Laura and Patrick that quickly? Or was it more complicated, as she was coming to discover most of her feelings were?

"I'd better get going," she said, standing. "I need to pick the kids up." She tried to sound casual. "Do you know whether Nick is still around?"

Linda frowned. "You said you weren't seeing him."

Ellen wasn't exactly anxious to discuss Nick, especially with Linda of all people, so she said evasively, "I just...needed a chance to think. He understands." Now she sounded like her sister.

"I think you're crazy, do you know that?" Linda said, catching her by surprise. "I'd take him in a minute, if I had the chance. And here you're being so timid! It's weird."

"What's weird?" Ellen asked unwillingly.

"I always thought my big sister was so brave and determined! Did you know how much I admired you?" Linda looked at her with something close to pity. "And here you're just as scared as I am."

She'd struck a nerve. "Shouldn't I be?" Ellen said sharply. "I don't want to go through what Mom did."

"Oh, come on." Linda tossed it off carelessly. "Nick's nothing like Dad."

Funny, Ellen thought, she had never actually compared them before. And when she did... "Actually, I think they're a lot alike," she said slowly. "Maybe what I mean is, Dad could have been like Nick if he'd..." *Quit drinking.* It hung in the air between them.

"But Dad didn't," Linda said with finality. "Nick did."

Was that what it came down to? The one strong, the other weak? So simple?

A few minutes later she found herself outside Nick's office. She wanted badly to chicken out. Strangely, it was Linda who'd strengthened her resolve. *I always thought my big sister was so brave and determined.* Ellen bit her lip and knocked.

"Come in."

Just the sound of his voice was enough to make her heart flip over. She felt sick; confused, joyful, panicky. Taking a deep breath, she opened the door.

He sat writing at the desk, head bent, just as he had been the first time she came here. Now, though, she knew the texture of the dark hair that fell over his brow, the gentleness of the big hands that dwarfed the pen. Heaps of paperwork and folders were still in danger of sliding off his desk and books were still shoved willy-nilly into the bookcase. The only thing different was the vase of multicolored tulips that was incongruously set amidst the clutter on his desk.

When Nick lifted his head, she saw the shock in his eyes; and then his gaze followed hers to the flowers.

"They reminded me of you," he said simply.

Dear heaven. How was she supposed to resist him? Her feet rooted just inside the door, she asked, "Am I interrupting you?"

He still hadn't moved, just sat looking at her. "You know better than that."

Ellen clung to the strap of her purse as though it were a lifeline. "I was just visiting Linda and I thought...well, that I'd say hello."

His mouth curved slightly. "Hello."

"May I sit down?"

"Let me clear..." At last he moved to rise, but succeeded only in upsetting one of the piles, which began an inexorable collapse toward the edge of the desk. Nick had to lunge to catch it, shoving the folders back into place. He sank back into his chair and met her gaze again, his sheepish. "Uh...is there any place bare enough to sit?"

Amusement made her lips quiver and momentarily replaced some of her more tumultuous emotions. "I think I can manage."

She transferred a heap from one chair to the other, then perched on the edge. For just a moment she let herself really study Nick.

The harsh lines that carved his cheeks seemed deeper today, his mouth compressed. She could see the years and the pain on his face, the wariness in his eyes. Ellen looked, and remembered different expressions: hunger and laughter and tenderness. Was she as crazy as Linda thought her? she wondered achingly.

To silence her own thoughts, she rushed into speech. "I went to an Al-Anon meeting last night. I wanted to tell you since..." Ellen stopped abruptly. Why *had* it seemed important that she tell him about it?

Something flickered in his eyes, but all he said was, "And?"

She hesitated, then said honestly, "And I don't know. I'm not sure what I expected, but..." She hesitated, remembering the rule about confidentiality. "I guess I shouldn't talk about it."

"Ellen, if you need to talk, it's okay. Just don't tell me names or the kind of details that might make me recognize someone."

"I'm confused," Ellen admitted on a sigh, then told him about the meeting, held in a church basement. The people had been amazingly honest, talking frankly about their individual ways of coping with alcoholic spouses and children. "But I felt like half of them were fantasizing," she finished in bewilderment. "Like this one woman who was apparently going to stay married to an alcoholic husband, but she was proud of herself because she was refusing to help him drink. Just because she refused to buy him beer at the store, it was all supposed to be okay. But nobody called her on it! All they did was applaud."

"Maybe this is her compromise."

"Is that what Al-Anon encourages? Compromise?"

A glint of humor showed in Nick's eyes. "You don't have to say it as though it's a dirty word."

Ellen felt herself blush. "But don't you think it's wrong? I remember you talking about how no alcoholic ever wakes up in the morning and says, 'This would be a good day to quit,' that if you *make* them go into treatment, then they have a chance. Just letting this person you love go his own merry way, without even trying..." She lifted her hands and let them drop. "That seems wrong to me."

She sounded almost naive, but Nick knew that her lack of understanding stemmed from something more complex than mere innocence. He guessed that she didn't want to understand what would make someone compromise, because that was the path her mother had chosen. For Ellen, understanding would have to bring forgiveness, and she wasn't ready—maybe never would be—to forgive her mother.

He began carefully, "What's the alternative for a woman like the one you were talking about? What if she's never had a career, there's no money in the bank? It's easy to say she should walk out, but to what? Poverty? Loneliness?''

He thought Ellen paled, but she argued immediately, "If she really loves him, though, shouldn't she force him . . . ?''

He could read between the lines. They were no longer talking about the woman from the meeting, he suspected, if they ever had been. "How?" Nick said bluntly.

Crinkles appeared between her brows and she said uncertainly, "Well, like you said, a threat of losing his job, or *her*, or . . . or his children . . . ''

Nick shrugged. "Well and good, but what if she's already tried that? What if he did go into treatment, and then went off the wagon? Let's face it, repeated a couple of times, threats lose some of their punch. Or what if her husband called her bluff? And if leaving him was unimaginable to her, that's what her threat was. A bluff.''

Ellen stared at him, her eyes somehow unfocused. "I wonder . . . ''

Her words trailed off and she sat frowning, distracted. Remembering, he felt sure. But what?

"What do you wonder?" he probed softly.

She blinked, then focused on his face. What he saw made love clutch with sharp claws at his chest.

"I wonder if my mother tried to bluff," Ellen answered, just as softly.

"Ask her."

She smiled sadly. "Do you know, until this last month Mom and I had never talked about Dad's drinking? It was just . . . sort of taboo. Like this pact we'd made or something. I always thought Mom was ashamed.''

"What about you?"

Ellen shifted uneasily in her seat. "Hey, what is this, a counseling session?''

Nick let out some of his tension in a wry grin. "Sorry. Occupational hazard, I guess. You're in that chair, it must mean you want to be psychoanalyzed."

"Maybe I do." Even though she was blushing, Ellen met his gaze with a determination that he admired. "I'm asking an awful lot of you, aren't I, Nick?"

"No," he said quietly. "You're giving me a chance." When she didn't immediately respond, his stomach knotted. "You are, aren't you?"

For the first time, she looked away. "I'm...I'm trying. I know it's not fair to you. But I'm doing my best."

"That's all I ask." Sitting here with the desk between them, trying to look calm, was killing him. He'd never felt such a purely primitive desire to grab a woman and dominate her physically. If he could just kiss her, *make* her respond, admit that she wanted him...

But she'd already done that. She had even said she loved him. And it wasn't enough.

He realized his fingers were clenched on the arms of the chair and uncurled them, one at a time. They ached, he'd been holding on so hard.

Ellen's eyes met his again with painful honesty. "I'm sorry, Nick," she said.

"No." His mouth twisted, but he shook his head. "You have to be sure, Ellen. I don't want any less. Not this time."

"Was your divorce so hard?" she asked tentatively.

"It was pretty bitter." Understatement. "Marie never understood that I couldn't handle alcohol, that I was really out of control. She'd beg and I'd promise and then I'd break that promise, like all the others. I was supposed to prove I loved her by not drinking. She could have asked me for anything else. That was the one thing I couldn't give her."

"So that's why..."

"Yeah. It's easy to make promises. Keeping them is something else."

Ellen studied him, concentration furrowing her forehead. "But you did love her, didn't you?"

He gave a brusque shrug. "I guess that depends on your definition of love. You're the one who said that you don't hurt someone you love. Marie sure as hell didn't think I loved her."

"But you did quit."

He had a feeling this discussion wasn't aiding his courtship. "Too late," he said, shrugging. "Marie didn't trust me. Why should she have?"

Ellen's face was too mobile to hide her thoughts. He saw the moment her brown eyes widened in comprehension. "You don't still blame yourself, do you?"

He hesitated for a fatal second. "Of course not," he said brusquely.

"It's true. Despite everything you tell other alcoholics, you think it was your fault, that you *could* have stopped!"

Nick felt like she'd turned over a rock, and he was what had crawled out from under it. "You trying to ruin my career?" he asked flippantly.

"How can you say the things you do?" She sounded genuinely distressed. "Don't you believe what you're always preaching?"

"This place succeeds for people because I listen to what the research ..."

"Research?" She shook her head hard. "Nick, I don't care what you think. I want to know how you *feel*."

Unable to stay still, he shoved his chair back and stood. "I don't preach anything I don't believe. What the hell are you saying, this whole place is a lie? Is that what you think of me?"

She watched him steadily, her brow crinkled. "What I think," she said, "is that your head believes being a drunk wasn't your fault. But your heart doesn't believe it, does it, Nick? Deep inside, you still blame yourself."

God, was that pity he saw in her eyes? "All right, damn it!" He braced himself stiff-armed on the desk and spoke through gritted teeth. "Yeah, you'll be pleased to know that sometimes I wonder. Why me? Simple genetics? Or weakness? And why didn't I have the guts to stop? I sold my soul for the stuff. Do you know what that feels like? Having no soul? Existing like an animal? Do you know what the hell that feels like?"

"No." Her eyes were wide and dark, unfathomable, in a face that was suddenly too pale. "Why don't you tell me?"

He bowed his head, almost feeling it hit a brick wall, and closed his eyes. "Because you'd never understand."

"Try me."

He made himself lift his head and look at her, a man condemned. "Why didn't you understand your stepfather?"

"I was only a child!"

"I haven't had a drink in ten years."

"What are you saying? That I should pretend you *aren't* an alcoholic?"

"That's our only hope, isn't it?"

"No. Oh, Nick." She raked her fingers through the heavy mass of her hair and lifted it back from her face. "Our only hope is you trusting yourself."

He could only shake his head, surprised by the cynicism that burned in his belly. "Don't put this on me, Ellen. You're the one who hasn't let the past go. Mine or yours."

She stood there for a moment, those little crinkles on her brow wrenching at his heart. Her dark eyes searched his face, and then she said, "Are you so sure *you* have?"

"It was a long time ago."

"Then talk to me. Let me understand."

What did she want to hear? The degradation? The helplessness that still sometimes brought him awake sweating in the middle of the night? She was asking too much.

He shrugged. "What is there to say? You lived with an alcoholic. You've seen it all."

He knew immediately that he'd made a mistake. A big one. She'd lived with an alcoholic, all right, and loved another one, her sister. Ellen had heard evasion too many times.

Clear-eyed, she looked at him, then shook her head. "You know something, Nick? Sometimes I feel like one of your patients. You know everything about me, all the ways I've been hurt and the things that still hurt me. But I don't know much about you. At least, not what counts." Grabbing her purse, she headed for the door.

Fear suddenly swelled in him until he felt sick with it. "Wait!"

Ellen stopped with her back to him. "For what?"

"I love you." He circled the desk, but didn't dare touch her. "That hurts."

She stiffened, then slowly turned to face him. Her expression was stark, her voice husky. "It hurts me, too."

"I'll talk to you. I'll tell you anything."

"But you don't want to."

Nick closed his eyes and wearily rubbed his forehead. "It's hard for me. Do you *like* to think about your years of living with a drunk?"

Ellen swallowed. "You know I don't."

"If I dump it all on you, that's all you'll see when you look at me. That's not me anymore."

"I wish I could be sure," she said, almost inaudibly.

"So what do we do, wait another ten years?" The words grated in his throat.

She spoke with painful softness. "Do I sound that unreasonable to you?"

"No." Unable to resist, Nick touched her chin, lifting it so that her wide, vulnerable eyes met his. "We're flip sides of a coin, Ellen. I understand better than you know."

"Does that do us any good?"

"Probably not," he said ruefully. "But talking would. About something else. Will you sit down for a few minutes? Let me pour you a cup of coffee?"

An attempt at a smile wavered on her full mouth. "I'd like a cup of coffee."

Some emotion halfway between elation and relief kicked in his chest. "One cup of coffee coming up."

He made a production out of pouring from his coffeepot, just as she did of stirring in a sprinkling of sugar. Silence lumbered between them, leaving Nick's mind blank. What *could* they talk about?

"Your house," Ellen said suddenly, sounding equally desperate. "How's your house coming along?"

Nick had trouble even picturing it. Ellen was too vivid sitting here across from him. He guessed she'd come from work, although today she didn't look obviously a businesswoman. Her skirt was softly gathered, a peach and rust print that might have been South American. The peach blouse revealed a creamy throat and was the perfect foil for the fire of her hair, loose about her shoulders. He'd forgotten how beautiful she was, how quickly she stirred him. How the hell was he supposed to look at her and picture the sticks and stones of a house that had come to mean nothing if Ellen wasn't there to share it?

But he desperately wanted her to stay, even if he had to make meaningless conversation to ensure it. So Nick groped for a memory of the last time he'd been up to his cliff top.

"It's framed in," he said. "I've got plywood up, roofing stuff being delivered. The windows came the other day. It might look real when they're in."

She set her cup down on the edge of the desk and leaned forward with eagerness that suddenly looked genuine. "I saw a picture the other day, of somebody's garden. There was a whole meadow of lavender, all soft gray and purple. I thought about your house. A border of lavender would be beautiful, right on the edge of the cliff."

"I like it." He didn't want to tell her he didn't know what lavender looked like. "To tell you the truth, I haven't gotten so far as to imagine the yard. All I know about gardening is that I have to dump water in the pot of that monstrosity every once in a while."

Ellen's gaze followed his to the philodendron that occupied one corner of his office. She smiled then, and he rejoiced even as he ached.

"Just don't pick out all brown plants."

Looking into her eyes, he said huskily, "It's one of my favorite colors."

Pink washed her cheeks. "I know." But then her gaze shied from his and she reached for her purse. "I . . . I'd better go."

Nick wanted to argue, but didn't dare. Just because she'd offered an inch didn't entitle him to the mile. And so he stood, too, and walked around the desk to escort her out.

"You don't have to go with me." Ellen paused in his doorway, as brilliant and fragile as autumn leaves. "Goodbye, Nick."

The last thing he expected was the fleeting kiss she rose on tiptoe to give him. Her lips were as soft and sweet as melted chocolate, the finality of her goodbye as scalding. When she whirled and fled, he was left flat-footed.

CHAPTER TWELVE

ELLEN HADN'T SEEN Linda's ex-husband in so long, for a moment she didn't recognize the strangely familiar man standing on her doorstep.

"Tom?"

The brown-haired man with quiet gray eyes smiled hesitantly. "Uh, how are you, Ellen?"

"I'm...I'm fine." She realized with sudden horror the position she was in. Nosy to a fault, the kids were bound to pop out of the living room any minute when she didn't promptly reappear. What would Linda expect of her? She knew that her sister made it hard for Tom to see the kids when he was late with a child support check. Linda claimed that was her only weapon. While Ellen thought quickly, she stepped out on the porch and pulled the door almost closed behind her. "Actually," she admitted, "I'm surprised to see you."

He pushed his hands into his pockets. "I've tried to call Linda day and night for the last week. I even checked with the phone company and they still listed the number as hers. I just wanted to see the kids. Has she moved? Or..." There was tension in his voice, although his lip curled. "Is it one of her usual disasters?"

Despite his contempt, Ellen could tell that he was worried. He had a right to be; Laura and Patrick *were* his children. And as far as Ellen knew, despite Linda's machinations, the court order allowed him reasonable visitations. "Linda is in an alcohol treatment center," she said.

Tom snorted. "For what good that'll do. Who is she trying to impress this time?"

Maybe Ellen shouldn't have been surprised by his bitterness, but she was. He had just drifted away from the marriage, his long hauls getting longer, until one time he didn't come home at all, apparently not caring enough about Linda—or his kids—to be there when they needed him.

"There isn't anybody to impress," Ellen said coolly. "Linda got sick. She'd have died without treatment."

Grimacing, he leaned against the neat white porch railing, in his jeans and flannel shirt looking ordinary, not exciting, but somehow solid. "It's not the first time she's had to dry out."

"No, but I think it's really making a difference this time." Who was she trying to convince? Lamely, Ellen added, "She's more like her old self."

His laugh was caustic. "Which old self? The one who liked to party? The 'devoted mother' who got smashed while she whipped up chocolate chip cookies? Or has she regressed to childhood?"

"Didn't you ever love her?"

His eyes were stormy, his jaw set. "Yeah, she was a lot of fun when she was eighteen. My mistake was expecting her to grow up."

"Maybe if you hadn't been gone three-quarters of the time..."

"Aunt Ellen?" The inquisitive voice came from behind her. "How come you're outside?"

Tom stiffened. "Is that...?"

Ellen took a deep breath and nodded, grabbing the knob so that Laura couldn't push the door open. "Just a minute, honey," she called over her shoulder, then met Tom's eyes. "Laura and Patrick are here with me. Would you like to come in?"

"Here?" For an instant his face came alive, then was quickly shuttered. "I haven't seen them in months. Should you warn them, or...?"

"Why? You're their father."

Again a hint of bitterness. "Not a very good one."

Whose fault was that? Ellen thought tartly. But something vulnerable in his expression stopped the words. Obviously, he did love his children—and right now, even a so-so parent was better than none at all.

"Aunt Ellen?" Laura tugged at the door. "Who are you talking to? Patrick has to go potty. He's been waiting and waiting. I don't want to help him. He always sprays all over the toilet seat. It's gross. Can you come?"

"I'll be right there." Feeling harried, but conscious of the difficulty for both father and children, she turned back to Tom and said urgently, "This has been a hard time for them. Don't expect..."

Patrick began to wail. Almost, but not quite, to the bathroom, Ellen diagnosed. She and Tom exchanged a hunted look. With Laura's silent presence just on the other side of the door, any effort to prepare Tom for his children's anger was clearly hopeless. "Never mind," she said, shaking her head. Despite his expression of panic, she stepped back and swung the door open. "Laura, look who's here!"

"Daddy?" At first tentative, her voice changed. "Daddy!" She flung herself into his arms.

Tom swung his daughter up and held her tightly, cheek against the top of her head. His eyes closed, but not before Ellen had seen the anguish in them.

Patrick's wails grew, and Ellen left father and daughter to their reunion.

"Your dad's here," she told the child, helping him out of wet pants and underwear and using them to mop up the pool outside the bathroom door. "Let's get you cleaned up."

His arms clamped around her neck. "I don't want to go with him. I want you, Aunt Ellen."

Ellen unglued his damp body from her favorite T-shirt. "He's just here to see you, sweetie."

Patrick looked doubtful. "Just to visit?"

She sank back on her heels. "Just to visit. I promise."

His thoughtful frown sat comically on the round, childish face. "Okay, I guess. Can I wear my turtle underwear?"

This time Ellen hugged him. Carefully. "You bet," she agreed.

Scrubbed and dressed, Patrick clung to Ellen's hand as they headed for the living room. Sitting on the couch with her father, Laura was chattering away.

"Aunt Ellen takes us to her friend's house sometimes. Her name's Joanne and she's fun. She has a swing set and she pushes us on it all the time. Aunt Ellen never wants to go to the playground. She's always *busy*." Laura's disdain was obvious.

Ellen rolled her eyes. "Come on, I must have pushed Patrick on the swing for two hours this weekend."

"Well, you don't want to go very often." Laura gave an emphatic bounce.

Over Laura's head, Tom met Ellen's gaze with silent humor. Then he looked at his son, squeezed against Ellen's side.

"Patrick," he said softly, and Ellen saw again that same pain, quickly hidden by a smile. "Wow, I like your hat."

Patrick had insisted on the baseball cap, pulled low over his eyes. Now he peeked from under the brim at his father. "You do?"

"Yeah, it makes you look grown-up. In fact, you *are* grown-up. No more diapers?"

"They're for babies." Patrick ducked his head. "Sometimes I have accidents."

"Who doesn't? I backed into a post and dented the fender on my rig just the other day."

"Really?"

He nodded solemnly. "I can take you guys for a ride in it tomorrow, if that's okay with your Aunt Ellen?"

"Wow, that'd be cool!" Laura agreed. "We can go, can't we?"

"Of course you can," Ellen said. Despite a small pang, she smiled at Tom. "Patrick loves trucks."

He looked at his son. "You liked your Christmas present, then?"

"You gave me the black truck?" Patrick asked suspiciously.

"Yep. It looks just like mine."

"It was my best present." Patrick shyly left Ellen's side and approached his father, ready to bolt at any unexpected moves.

"Patrick doesn't remember you very well," Laura said. "You don't visit us very often."

Ellen figured that one was up to him to explain. "I'm going to clean up the kitchen," she said loudly, and escaped.

There really wasn't much to clean, and as she wiped the counter, glancing out the window at the pocket backyard, she wondered. Why, when Tom obviously loved his children so much, did he visit them so seldom?

TOM WAS STILL THERE that evening to inexpertly tuck the children into bed. When he reappeared in the living room, he said awkwardly, "I guess I'd better go."

"Can't you stay for a few minutes? I was just going to have a cup of coffee."

"Uh . . . Sure, why not?"

After he had followed her into the kitchen, Ellen handed him a mug and watched while he stirred some milk in. "Have you been here all week?"

"No, I only drove up yesterday, after I couldn't reach Linda and I called here a couple of times and just got your answering machine. I guess I should have tried your mother, but I didn't know how she felt about me. I figured she was on Linda's side."

"We've never heard your side," Ellen said, surprising herself. She'd never thought he *had* a side, but his behavior with the kids didn't jibe with Linda's stories of his indifference. "Not that it's really any of my business," she added. "But... Well, if you'd like to talk, I wouldn't mind listening."

And listen she did, over the coffee that she hadn't really wanted and which would undoubtedly keep her awake later.

His grew cold. "God, it was hard to leave," he said finally. He sat at one end of the couch and Ellen at the other. "But I couldn't stand it any more. She's killing herself, and she didn't want to hear about it. What was I supposed to do, sit there and watch?"

"But the kids . . ."

"You think that was easy?" Tom groaned and rubbed the heel of one hand tiredly against his forehead. "I would have quit my job if I'd thought Linda would hurt Laura or Patrick, but she loved them, I knew she did. And she had you and her mom. I don't know what else I could have done, anyway. The only work I've ever done is drive a truck. How could I take the kids?"

"But if you'd visited more often . . ." Ellen said.

He gave a bitter laugh and leaned back against the couch. "I tried. Believe me, I tried! Some of it was my own fault. I mean, I expected the kids to be glad to see Daddy, and instead I had to start all over every time. Like I was a total stranger. Maybe I could have handled that, but half the time Linda had some excuse so I couldn't see them. She was real inventive. Maybe I should have gone back to court or something, I don't know. But it started to seem like I wasn't really part of their lives, anyway. I didn't feel like they needed me."

Ellen's throat was tight with tears, and her voice was a little husky when she said, "I think they need you. Linda does love them, but . . . Well, you can see, she's not exactly reliable."

"You're telling me." He raked his fingers through shortish brown hair and sighed. "When's she getting out?"

"Saturday. Are you going to stay around to talk to her?"

"I don't know." Tom sat in silence for a moment. "What's the point?"

"You don't think she'll make it." It wasn't a question.

He laughed again without any more humor. "Are you kidding? What's this? The fifth time? Sixth? Does she even try?"

There wasn't much use in arguing. Linda had yet even to admit that she was an alcoholic, far less express any determination to conquer her problem.

"But she *is* different this time." Ellen was thinking aloud. "I'm not sure how. Maybe more honest with herself? I just wish..." She stopped.

"You wish?"

"That she wasn't getting out so soon." There. She'd said it. Would he recognize the selfish underpinnings, the part of Ellen that was afraid to rediscover loneliness?

But he only took a gulp of cold coffee and said, "What difference would another week or two make?"

"Probably none." Ellen leaned her head wearily against the softly cushioned back of the couch. "I just don't think she's ready."

"You ever known an alcoholic who was ready?"

"That's what Nick... Dr. Braden says."

"Who's he?" Tom asked.

"He heads the treatment center she's in. He believes that alcoholism is a disease, that there's something different about an alcoholic's body."

"So what's the cure?" Tom asked sardonically.

There was the catch, the part Ellen couldn't accept. "There isn't one," she said starkly. "Nick says that alcoholics can control the disease, like a diabetic does, but it'll be with them the rest of their lives. He's a recovered alcoholic himself."

"Yeah, well, he's a doctor. He's probably got a fancy house and more money than he knows what to do with. *He* had something to quit for. What's in it for Linda?"

"What do you mean? She has the kids and a decent job and..."

"Come on, her boss wouldn't fire her if she passed out over the typewriter. He's got the hots for her." His mouth twisted. "Maybe he's even gotten somewhere now, I don't know."

Linda *had* dated her boss a few times, Ellen knew. Telling Tom so didn't strike her as tactful.

"I think he's been getting impatient with her," she said instead.

"Oh, I doubt that." His sarcasm was hard to miss. "Worried about her, maybe. After all, she's a poor struggling woman, having to raise her children alone after she was deserted by her husband. He probably feels like a real philanthropist, keeping her on."

"You don't like him."

"I never did." He lapsed into silence again. When he spoke again, he wasn't looking at Ellen. "God, I sound like I'm jealous. Who the hell am I to be jealous? At least her boss is still there for her. I'm not."

"Nick would say that someone like her boss is helping her to keep drinking. She *has* to have a job. If he'd said quit or else . . ."

"Yeah, well, I said 'or else' and it didn't work. A husband, a job, who cares? She'd rather be on the street than quit drinking."

"I'm not so sure," Ellen said thoughtfully. "Linda has an awfully practical streak. I remember when she was a kid, she was so cute with those big brown eyes, and then she could sound so cold-blooded."

"Yeah." He smiled, if wryly. "I know what you mean. Well, listen. I'd better get out of here. You have to go to work tomorrow, don't you? Is it okay if I take the kids instead of them going to the baby-sitter?"

"Sure." Ellen stood with him. "I'm glad you came. I just wish . . ." She let the words die. What was the point in wishing for miracles?

Their eyes met and he shrugged. "Yeah, I wish it could have been different, too," he said. Then, "Thanks, Ellen. I really appreciate you letting me stay like you did tonight. It...meant a lot to me."

"It's okay." She smiled, hiding her sadness. "Just don't disappear again. Laura and Patrick really do need you."

"I'll try to believe that," he said, and surprised her by bending his head and giving her a quick kiss on her cheek. "See ya."

Ellen blew her nose firmly after he was gone. Why on earth did she feel like crying? Because she had remembered how much she liked Tom, and how disappointed she had been in him? Or because he had made her realize that if her own mother had made the same choice he had, to walk away, life wouldn't necessarily have been the bed of roses she'd always imagined it would be?

Eenie, meenie, minie, mo, she thought tiredly, absurdly. What was right, what was wrong?

ELLEN FIGURED SHE ought at least to tell Linda about Tom's showing up and the time Laura and Patrick were spending with him. The cowardly side of her wanted to pick up the phone and do it as impersonally as possible, although she wasn't altogether sure whether it was the confrontation with her sister she was afraid of, or taking the chance of running into Nick.

The trouble was, reaching Linda by telephone was never easy. The line was usually tied up, and if Ellen did get through, invariably Linda was in a meeting of some kind or another. That was all the patients seemed to do: eat, sleep and go to meetings.

So for about the tenth time in a month she used her lunch hour to drive to the hospital. Linda was through with lunch, sprawled on the couch in the lounge watching a soap opera. Damn. Maybe she *could* have called.

When Linda saw Ellen, she stood up. "Hey, Joan, tell me what happens, okay?" she asked another patient. To her sister she said, "Hi, you planning to spring me?"

"Dream on," Ellen said lightly. "Anyway, what is it, two more days?"

"Yep." Leading the way, Linda gave a Cheshire cat grin over her shoulder. "Where are the kids, at the baby-sitter?" The question was casual, no big deal, but her eyes narrowed when she saw Ellen's expression. "What is it? Is something wrong?" she asked sharply.

"No, of course not. The thing is, that's what I came to talk to you about."

Linda stopped short in the hall. "What do you mean?"

"Can't we go to your room?"

"I'm going to scream if you don't tell me."

"They're with Tom."

Linda looked incredulous. "Tom? The jerk? The S.O.B.? The..."

At the nearby nurse's station, a nurse glanced up. Ellen said hurriedly, "Yeah, him."

Her sister swore pungently, but she did start moving again. Inside her room she whirled, back to the window. "Why did you let him take them? What if he doesn't bring them back? He could just disappear in that truck and we'd never find him! He could..."

"Linda." Ellen dropped into one of the room's chairs. "*You* let him take the kids for visits."

"As seldom as I can help it. I don't trust him."

"You don't really think..."

"Oh, I don't know." Linda hunched her shoulders and turned to stare moodily out the window. "No, I guess he wouldn't do that. I'm just afraid..."

"Of what?" Ellen prompted.

Ellen's view of the back of her sister's head was unrevealing, but Linda's voice sounded odd. "Maybe that they'll be too happy with him."

Ellen blinked. She'd told Tom that Linda was more honest with herself these days, but this self-analysis still startled her. "Laura and Patrick love you," she said softly.

"I know they do." Linda turned back to face her and tried to give one of her blithe shrugs. The twist of her mouth and the pain in her eyes were a dead giveaway. "But I'm not a very good mother, am I?"

Ellen felt a burst of anger instead of the expected sympathy. "That's what Tom said, too, that he wasn't a very good father. It's not fair to Laura and Patrick! Can't *one* of you do better?"

Answering anger wiped the self-pity off Linda's small-boned face. "At least I didn't walk out on them! Don't compare me to him!"

Ellen shot to her feet. "What was he supposed to do? Hold your head when you threw up in the toilet?"

"Be there for the kids!"

"It was *you* he walked out on, not them."

"What's the difference?" Linda asked with contempt.

"There's a big one. You and I ought to know."

"Oh, come on. Let's not harp back..."

"Why not?" Ellen said stubbornly. "We've never really talked about it. Does that mean you think that Mom stayed with Dad for *us?*"

Linda's mouth curled. "She just didn't have the guts to leave."

"Yeah, well Tom did."

"Give me a break." Linda began a restless prowl, her face set in hard lines. She reached the door and swung around with her back to it. "He just didn't want to deal with a problem."

Turning her head to follow her sister's progress, Ellen caught a flash of movement through the doorway. Somehow she wasn't surprised to see Nick in the hall. It was obvious from his arrested expression, from his stillness as their gazes locked, that he had heard at least some of what had been said.

In her blur of anger, Linda obviously hadn't seen him. Ellen realized that she wanted to finish what she had to say as much for Nick's benefit as for her sister's. Or maybe it really was just for herself.

"I don't think you were just a problem to Tom," she said clearly. "He really loved you. In fact, I think he still loves you, but he can't stand your self-destruction."

Linda froze, the anger wiped away. For just an instant, she was defenseless, the longing on her face heartbreaking.

Behind her, Nick smiled at Ellen. Dear God, she thought. His smile was the one of her dreams, warm with approval as it deepened the lines carved in his cheeks. She met his eyes, so blue they hurt to look at, and felt herself drowning in longing as powerful as Linda's. And didn't they want the same thing? To be loved no matter what?

The expression on her face yanked a slipknot around Nick's chest. That full, luscious mouth of hers was just tremulous enough to stir memories of its taste; the awakening he saw in her eyes made them soft with sorrow and need. She just stood there and looked at him, her tangled emotions so close to the surface that he wanted to take her in his arms and make dreams become reality. He wanted to kiss her and feel the response she couldn't deny. He wanted *her.*

As he stepped into the doorway, his voice was scratchy, rough with hunger. "Am I interrupting?"

Linda turned quickly, but her expression was guarded. Ellen blinked, pushed her hair back from her face and busied herself reaching for her purse. "No, I was just leaving. I need to get back to work."

"I'll walk you out," he said firmly, and felt gratitude that was damn near humiliating just because she didn't argue.

She stopped beside her sister and said quietly, "You know, Laura and Patrick can hardly wait until you can take them home. If you weren't a good mother, they wouldn't be so eager."

"I..." Linda's smile failed. "Thank you."

Ellen had passed her and was on her way to the doorway when Linda said, "Ellen?"

Nick could have touched her when she stopped. "Yes?"

"Is Tom... Well, is he still going to be around Saturday?"

"I don't know. I wouldn't be surprised."

"Oh." Linda gave a jerky shrug. "Well, it doesn't matter either way. I just thought... Oh, never mind. I'll see you later, okay?"

"Bye."

Outside the room, Ellen fell into step beside Nick. He snatched a glance at her face, expecting to see distress, or at least wariness. Instead she met his eyes with unaccountable serenity. "Do I get the doctor's seal of approval?" she asked.

He lifted the stethoscope hanging from around his neck. "Shall I stamp you with it?"

"Make it a gold star."

They were passing the nurse's station. He said gravely, "I'd be happy to make it more intimate than that."

For the first time, she didn't seem to want to look at him. "I know," she said, her voice just a little husky.

That was it. They walked in silence down the last stretch of hall, until the teenager who'd been watching their approach from a doorway sauntered into step on the other side of Ellen.

"Hey, wanna have a good time Friday night?" he asked cheekily.

The nurses were going to be glad to see the last of Billy. As one of them had put it, he was cute but obnoxious. A typically horny seventeen-year-old. Actually, Nick thought he'd done some growing up in here. He liked Billy's prognosis.

"Sorry," Ellen said. The delicious smile that spread across her face wouldn't do anything to cool Billy, Nick thought in amusement. "But thanks for all the whistles," she added. "They made me feel young."

"Young?"

"I'm thirty, you know."

"Uh, yeah, well . . ." Billy lagged back. Just as Nick straight-armed the door to the gray day outside, a wolf whistle rocked the hall. Ellen laughed.

"He's out of here tomorrow," Nick muttered. "Thank God."

"Actually, he's kind of cheered me up a couple of times," Ellen said. The smile still lingered around her eyes, but the strain was back between them.

"Me, too," Nick admitted. "He's not a bad kid."

Ellen stopped beside her car, parked in one of the first slots. "Do you ever think they're bad kids?"

"There was the one who picked my pocket during a counseling session."

"I guess that would do it."

"Hey." He touched her cheek lightly, remembering the first time he had done that, wondering if—this time—he could push a little harder. "I've missed you. As usual."

"Me, too, Nick." He was heartened because she didn't turn away, only resolutely faced him. Only then he discovered it wasn't them she was thinking about at all. "I want you to tell me the truth," she said. "Do you think Linda has any chance?"

Caught off guard, he said, "I'm no fortune teller. People often surprise me."

She just looked stubborn. "You must have some kind of gut feeling. I won't hold you accountable, you know."

He had a gut feeling, all right. It told him that his future rode on her sister's success or failure. Unfortunately, Nick could think of people whose hands he'd rather put his life into, starting with Billy.

Nick knew that what he said wouldn't make any difference one way or the other to the outcome. But he couldn't lie to Ellen.

"This time out . . ." He shrugged. "I don't think she's learned enough humility. She isn't taking responsibility for her own problem. I don't know what's going to make her do that."

Ellen didn't even flinch, just absorbed it. "Thank you," she said, and exhaled with a soft rush. "Nick, there's something I'd like to say."

That sounded ominous, but she didn't give him a chance to stop her.

"I just want you to know that I do appreciate your honesty, even if it means you don't always tell me what I want to hear."

"Thanks. I think."

When this time she turned away, Nick was too frustrated to let her run again. He'd been patient; too patient. He was sick of the subject of alcoholism, sick of her sister.

"Ellen." He put a restraining hand on her car door. She turned her head to look inquiringly at him, with maybe a little apprehension mixed in. "I've given you a chance to think," he said. "Now it's your turn to give me a chance. I want a day to remind you what we have together."

She opened her mouth, closed it, opened it again. "I . . ." Ellen drew a deep breath. "What exactly do you want to do?"

"I'll make it lady's choice," he said roughly. "Whatever you'd enjoy."

"Anything?"

"Anything," he promised recklessly.

There was that smile, trembling, soft, mischievous. "Okay," she said. "You asked for it."

CHAPTER THIRTEEN

THANK GOD SHE HAD the date with Nick to look forward to. "Otherwise, it's back to real life," Ellen muttered.

She was startled to realize she had spoken aloud. She'd been standing in the middle of her living room admiring its pristine state. Well, not quite pristine. The off-white couch had a couple of juice stains—at least she told herself they were juice, and there was definitely a scratch across the fine grain of her cherry coffee table. A month's worth of practice made her instantly recognize the dirty sock just poking a small toe out from under the entertainment center. Ellen sighed. The living room was in better shape than it had been any other time in the last month, anyway.

After tossing the sock in the bedroom hamper, she wandered without much enthusiasm into the kitchen to make dinner. Tonight was to be an indulgence: crab fettucini and asparagus, both of which Laura and Patrick would have called "gross." They probably would have clutched their throats and pretended to gag if she'd presented tonight's menu to them. Sometimes cooking just for herself hardly seemed worth the effort, but after a month of hot dogs and pizza, being on her own tonight was a luxury. At least, it should have been.

Why did she feel so aimless? Did she miss the children already? But when she closed her eyes, it wasn't Laura and Patrick she saw. She saw Nick, his rugged face almost homely but strong, mobile, *alive*. His eyes, intense, penetrating, caring. His wide, powerful shoulders, big hands, long stride. His voice, just rough enough to remind her of the rasp of his shaven jaw against her softer skin.

Ellen groaned. Who was she kidding? She would miss Patrick and the way he nestled against her when he was tired, Laura and her constant, wearing chatter that nonetheless showed a bright mind. But it wouldn't be the same, bone-deep kind of missing; she wouldn't feel as though a part of her had been lost. That was saved for Nick, a man she hadn't even known a month ago. It was scary how fast it had happened.

Next Saturday was too far away. She both longed for it and dreaded it. She had needed pushing; drifting as she'd been doing wasn't fair to Nick or her. If she couldn't live with the threat Nick's past cast on the future, then she should make a clean break. She owed it to both of them. But she suspected that he was right. She *did* need reminding why she had fallen in love with him in the first place.

Ellen made herself go back to her dinner preparations, though she couldn't quit thinking about Nick. Yes or no, right or wrong. Could she live without the joyful anticipation the promise of seeing him gave her? But how could she bear it if he started to drink again?

She had finished grating the Parmesan cheese and was chopping green onions when she realized that her agonizing was overlaid by uneasiness, nothing she could put her finger on, just . . . *there*. Hesitating, knife above the cutting board, she listened to the silence. It was too quiet. That's what was wrong. Damn it, what were the kids up to now?

Talking a mile a minute to their mother in her own kitchen, that's what, Ellen reminded herself, feeling an odd pang. Silence wasn't cause for alarm anymore. At least, it wouldn't be for a few weeks. Or would it be only days? Her worries easily found a new outlet. How long would Linda stay sober this time?

The whole day had been strangely anticlimactic. Mrs. Whalley had picked Linda up at the hospital. By the time Linda arrived at Ellen's in her own car to get Patrick and Laura, she had already stopped at the grocery store to restock on food.

Excited to see their mother, the children bounded out the front door, hardly bothering to say goodbye. Linda gathered up a motley armload of bags, day packs and loose toys, as untroubled as if she'd only left them there for the day. Collecting the rest, Ellen trailed her sister out to the car, unsure how she felt. Sad, relieved, resentful? Or maybe all of the above.

Tossing the last duffel bag of clothes in behind the grocery bags, Linda slammed the trunk. "Thanks for having Laura and Patrick," she said breezily. "I don't know what I'd have done if you weren't here."

Leaned on someone else, Ellen thought. But for the sake of the kids, she smiled. "You know I love them."

Patrick was already buckled into the front seat when at the last minute Laura surprised her. The six-year-old started to fasten her seat belt, then suddenly scrambled out of the car and ran to Ellen. She gave her a quick, convulsive hug and whispered, "I love you, Aunt Ellen," before running back to the car.

Ellen held back the tears until they were out of sight.

Now she wondered. And worried. Had there been wine bottles hidden under the lettuce and eggs in that neat row of brown paper bags in the car trunk?

Only if Linda had no intention at all of trying to stay sober. Chances are, Ellen thought, she was worrying unnecessarily. The trouble was, she didn't have a clue as to what was really going on in her sister's mind.

She was pretty sure all those people at the Al-Anon meeting would tell her it was none of her business. Linda was an adult who had to take responsibility for her own problems. Easy to say, Ellen thought for the millionth time, with all too familiar frustration. Unfortunately, Linda's problems involved too many other people, and especially her children.

Would Laura and Patrick have to find their mother unconscious on the floor again?

Sighing, Ellen pushed the chopped green onion into a bowl and plugged in the electric wok. She'd have been tempted to abandon her dinner if she hadn't already spent so much effort on it. Somehow, sitting in solitary splendor to eat an elaborate meal no longer sounded very appealing.

"YOU KNOW I'VE NEVER been on one before," Nick said plaintively.

Ellen's hand stroked lovingly down the long sleek chestnut neck of the horse that she proposed he ride. "I believe you've already said so," she agreed, trying to hide a smile.

"Me and my big mouth," Nick muttered.

She shook her head, unable to keep her smile from widening. "Gets a person into trouble every time."

"All right, all right." He shoved his foot into the stirrup. For that smile, he'd do anything, even risk life and limb on an animal strong enough to ignore his wishes with impunity. Once up, he settled onto the saddle, grabbed the horn with one hand and stiffened when his underpinnings danced sideways. "What am I doing wrong?"

"Relax." Ellen laid a hand on his booted ankle. "You're squeezing with your heels. That means 'go' to Jamil. You're confusing him."

Relax. Right. He did loosen the grip his legs had automatically taken on the chestnut's broad barrel, though, and the horse promptly stood still, rock solid. Nick's heartbeat slowed slightly and he watched as Ellen swung easily up on a dappled gray mare, who shook her head until her silver mane rippled like a sea swell.

"All set?" she asked.

"As set as I'm ever going to be."

"Cheer up, it's fun." Ellen tossed him a smile brimming with humor, then glanced around at the pickup and horse trailer she'd carefully backed into a narrow space beside the gate and half a dozen other trailers.

The management of the Pilchuck Tree Farm was kind enough to let horseowners ride on the miles of narrow roads and trails that intersected their land. The borrowed pickup said, "Sweet Home Arabians," and belonged to the same friend of Ellen's who had loaned the horses. From the way Ellen handled the trailer, it was obvious she'd used it before.

"Okay, here we go," Ellen said, and urged her mare toward a narrow trail that went around the wide, locked gate.

Nick loosened his death grip on the reins and let his horse follow. The swaying gait felt insecure to him, and when the gelding stumbled on an exposed tree root, Nick's muscles all locked tight again. What the hell was wrong with him? He was usually able to enjoy almost any new experience.

Yeah, and he was usually the one in control. He was pretty sure this time the horse was.

Ellen, looking back, felt a surge of remorse. She'd told herself she wanted to share doing something she loved; but she wondered a little if she hadn't suggested horse-back riding because she knew that, for once, *she* would be the confident one.

"Hey." She pulled her mare up once they were on the hard-packed dirt road on the other side of the gate. "I promise we won't do anything but walk. Jamil is as gen-tle as they come. He's not going to take off on you."

Nick gave her a lopsided grin. "I'm okay. I thrive on challenges, right?"

She wrinkled her nose at him. "Sure. Want to race?"

"Uh...maybe later."

They shared a smile that twisted in Ellen's chest with sweetness edged with pain. She couldn't help remember-ing that day in the tulip fields, when she had realized how startlingly happy she was. It came so easily in Nick's company, the quiet joy that seemed to crystalize every small sensation. The sun was warm on her arms, and she was peripherally aware of the buzzing of a bee and the tiny quicksilver flutter of white butterflies. She loved the solid power of the animal under her, the smell of hay and horse and the wiry silk of the mare's mane.

She loved Nick. The knowledge spilled out of her heart, flooding her chest. Undeniable. Scary. It was ironic, she thought miserably, that this very happiness made her *more* afraid of the great clawed specter of al-coholism. Falling from such heights would hurt worse than a lesser tumble.

Damn. He'd asked for today to remind her of that happiness. She owed it to him, and to herself, not to let the day be shadowed by her fears. She had to try.

Ellen was startled from her thoughts by Nick's voice. "Why do you like horseback riding so much?"

A small laugh escaped her. "I take it you don't?"

He smiled crookedly. "Hey, give me a few minutes. Maybe when I can quit holding on for dear life..."

Ellen laughed again. "Why do I like it? Um..." It was hard to analyze such an instinctive pleasure. "For starters I've always loved horses," she admitted. "I dreamed about being a cowgirl instead of a ballerina. Whenever there was a horse around, I begged for the chance to ride. Dad..." She paused, corrected herself. "My stepfather used to take me to a stable near Granite Falls. He pretended it was just for me, but I always had a suspicion he enjoyed riding, too."

"Yeah, but what's wrong with petting them over the fence?"

"Which is as close as you want to get?" she teased. With a sidelong glance she saw that he had released the saddle horn and begun to relax, his big body moving naturally with the gelding's gait. "I love to ride," she said simply. "For me it's like parachuting must be for some people, or flying. The speed and the power and the grace..." Ellen shrugged, a little embarrassed. "I can be something I'm not on my own two feet."

He looked at her with amusement and a glint of something warmer. "If I were going to psychoanalyze you..."

"Which you're not," she interjected firmly.

"Uh, since I'm not, I'll only say that you're right. That's exactly why people do the damnedest sports."

"It's an escape from my own limitations," Ellen said. "Doesn't everybody have some kind of escape?"

"Are we getting personal here?"

"Sure." She slanted a saucy glance at him. "Why not?"

He met her gaze with pure, sexual intent. "No reason I can think of," he said huskily.

Ellen turned her head to hide the heat rising in her cheeks. Almost at random, she said, "Let's take this trail. Hold on tight."

Out of the corner of her eye she saw Nick convulsively grabbing for the saddle horn, and then she urged her mare up the muddy bank that ended in a narrow trail tracked with countless horse hooves. The sound of meandering water could be heard faintly through the woods that rose on both sides of the road and now the trail.

Nick grunted as his gelding bunched hindquarters for the precipitous scramble. "Fun," he mumbled.

Once up, brush scraped at his jean-clad legs and boots. Deeper under the tall Douglas firs, ferns grew in lush profusion with wisps of salal and blackberry. As close as they were to Highway 9 and civilization, the silence was profound. Moving water, the creak of the saddles, the soft whuffle as one of the horses blew out a puff of air; soothing. He *was* relaxing, Nick realized, despite himself.

"Have you ever fallen off?" he asked to Ellen's back.

She turned in her saddle, her expression unsuccessfully stern. "I have *never* fallen off. I *have* been thrown."

"There's a distinction here?"

An enchanting smile peeked out. "Sure. The one's incompetence. The other implies malicious intent on the horse's part."

Nick's gaze dropped to the top of the gelding's chestnut head. The finely pointed ears were swiveling to listen to the conversation. For the first time, Nick wondered what was going on inside that head. "Nice horse," he mumbled, and awkwardly patted its neck. He could have sworn he heard choked laughter from up ahead.

"What did you do to get thrown?" he asked.

The trail widened, and Ellen pulled her horse up and waited until he came abreast before allowing her mare to fall comfortably into step with his gelding. "Um, I got scraped off on a tree once," she said. "A bolt of lightning struck and my horse took off. I didn't duck quick enough."

The sky was reassuringly blue. "Is that the only time?"

"Heavens no!" she said cheerfully. "I got rolled on once. Barely jumped off before he went over. I didn't know I could move so fast. And then there was the time I pulled my horse up so fast he flung his head back and hit my nose. The next day I looked like Rudolph with two shiners." She gave him a sidelong look. "Am I making you nervous?"

"Yep."

Ellen reached over and laid a hand on his arm. "I meant it when I said Jamil was well-behaved. He wouldn't dream of bucking or running off with you."

Nick was trying to deal with the shock her touch gave him. Insane. She meant it to be casual, reassuring. He felt like he'd just bumped into an electric fence.

"I'll take your word for it," he said, even to his own ears sounding strained.

To his regret—relief?—Ellen took her hand back. Color had risen in her cheeks, and her voice showed some constraint, too, the cheeriness not quite coming off.

"I had a friend whose horse *walked* off with him," she said. "In college a group of us used to rent horses. The kind that plod along following each other. You'd have to use a cattle prod to get them out of a walk, unless the barn—and hay—are in sight. Anyway, the rest of us stopped to admire a view and got off. His horse just kept going. Plod, plod, plod, but nothing he did was going to stop it. We had to run after him and grab the reins." She laughed again. "And then there was the friend who tried to stop her horse by grabbing a tree."

"Did it work?" Nick asked with interest.

"Well, she stopped herself."

"But not the horse."

"Nope."

Nick pictured himself dangling from the branch of a tree while his chestnut gelding trotted on its merry way. His laugh was heartfelt. "Got any more of these stories?"

"Oh, I could go on all day. You'd probably never get on a horse again."

"I didn't have any immediate plans to, anyway."

Nick cursed himself even before a cloud crossed Ellen's face. She knew, as he did, that he'd never have reason to ride again if she wasn't part of his life.

He'd sworn he wouldn't refer to the future. Even tomorrow was a blank he wouldn't try to fill. Today would be as good as he could make it. Beyond that was out of his control.

That was when she surprised him by saying with what sounded like genuine curiosity, "What about you? Do you have something you love doing? That takes you out of yourself?"

Drinking. Booze had done it for him. Yeah, and he'd had ten years to find something else. Maybe that's why he'd torn a car apart and put it back together, why he was building a house. "I guess I don't," he said regretfully. "Maybe it's another one of those occupational hazards I keep talking about. I used to ski, and I played football in college. But somehow in medical school..." He shrugged. "You know, I never found time again. I guess nailing up two-by-fours doesn't qualify, does it?"

"Oh, I don't know. It's scary in a different way. And it must be satisfying."

"Yeah, but it doesn't exactly take my breath away. The closest I get to breathless is playing handball once a week. I'm afraid that isn't excitement, though. More like a few too many hours with my butt fastened to a chair." He clutched at the saddle horn as he ducked to miss a low-hanging branch. "Hell, maybe I'll take up horseback riding after all."

"Do you want to try trotting?" Ellen asked.

"Don't I remember a promise . . . ?"

Her smile flashed, dazzling, heartwarming. "We don't make promises, remember?"

His mouth almost dropped open. Was he hearing things? Had she actually just *teased* him about something that ought to be an open wound? Good Lord.

The least he could do was meet her halfway. "Sure, what the hell," he said rashly, and booted his heels against the chestnut's sides.

Nick almost lost his seat when the horse sprang forward. By the time Jamil settled into a bone-rattling trot, Nick was beginning to wish he *had* fallen off. He'd take bruises any day over compressed vertebrae.

"Relax," Ellen called. "Move your body *with* the trot, not against it."

Relax. Right.

FORTY-FIVE MINUTES LATER, they had circled back to the gate.

"Your legs might be a little shaky," Ellen warned, when she pulled her mare up. "Riding is harder work than it looks."

Nick's knees didn't buckle when he slid off, probably only because he was too macho to let them, Ellen bet. "I feel like I've been at sea for six months," he muttered. "Now I know why old cowboys always have bowed legs."

"I don't think you're in any danger of that from an hour and a half in the saddle."

As she dismounted herself, Ellen was conscious of Nick watching her over his mount's withers. Naturally she landed with something less than grace. The glint in his intensely blue eyes were approving, however.

"There's nothing wrong with *your* legs," he said, his tone less than analytical.

Ellen flushed at the look on his face. "Is that the doctor speaking?"

A wicked smile curled his mouth. "You might recall that I *have* examined them closely."

An image flashed into Ellen's mind. Herself stretched out on Nick's bed, naked and languorous. Nick starting at her toes and stringing kisses up her leg. That rumpled dark hair she'd wound her fingers in. Herself moaning. The hot feel of his mouth.

The memory was so vivid, she felt a surge of heat that shocked her into embarrassment. It wasn't fair. What did he expect of her today?

When he saw the tide of color in her face, something flickered in Nick's eyes and then he lowered his gaze to the saddle, not giving her a chance to think of a rejoinder. "So now what do I do? Is this horse going to kick me if I unfasten this buckle?"

Knowing she didn't sound quite normal, Ellen said, "He's going to be thrilled to have you unfasten it. We'll take the saddles off and walk them for a few minutes."

The saddles slung in the back of the pickup truck, bridles replaced by halters and lead ropes, Ellen and Nick cooled the horses. For the most part they walked in silence.

When the sweat-streaked coats had begun to dry to Ellen's satisfaction, Nick held the gelding while she loaded her mare, then watched as she led his horse into the trailer and loosely tied him.

A moment later Nick collapsed onto the passenger seat of the pickup with a groan. "What makes me think I won't be able to walk tomorrow?"

"You will be a little stiff," Ellen said guiltily. "The ride was probably too long for a beginner. I didn't think..."

"Hey." His grin carved grooves in his cheeks, and Ellen caught a brief glimpse of his younger self. "You know me. I don't dip my toe into anything. If I'm going to try something, by God I'm going to try it. Who needs to walk anyway?"

"Your patients might lose some confidence in you if you wobble in."

"Never," he said grandly.

She wouldn't lose confidence in him if he were in a wheelchair, or confined to a hospital bed. The thought shocked Ellen. If she trusted him, if it came that instinctively, why was she holding back?

The answer wasn't hard to find. She could trust him with her money, her heart, her life. But not with a bottle. It was a lesson she'd learned too well from her stepfather, who had loved and guarded his family from everything but himself.

"Do you have time for dinner?" Ellen asked, looking over her shoulder to back the horse trailer from its niche.

Nick's eyes, deadly serious, caught hers. "You know I do," he said quietly. Then his tone changed, though she could hear the effort in it. "You going to take me out on the town? I don't suppose there's a hot tub on the agenda?"

"I'm afraid not. Actually..." She straightened the wheel, stole a look at him. "I was planning to make dinner. But if you'd rather..."

"You know the answer to that, too."

She knew, all right. He wanted whatever she was willing to give him.

Ellen just wished she knew what that was.

DINNER WENT OFF surprisingly well. They talked about gardening, politics, cooking. Ellen teased Nick about his ineptitude in the kitchen. Watching him hack up the salad makings, she said, "If you were a surgeon, I think I'd give the hospital board a quick call."

"Are you maligning my coordination?"

"Well..." She peered dubiously at the peculiar bits and pieces of carrot he'd dumped into the salad bowl. "Maybe it's aesthetics."

"Just watch. Practice makes perfect."

"Honestly, Nick," she said later, dishing up the salad. "What *do* you eat? Don't you ever cook?"

"I can pour myself a bowl of cereal. I'm a whiz with the toaster. At lunch I usually eat the hospital food. If I remember dinner, hey, there are plenty of good restaurants. I eat a well-balanced diet even my mother would approve of."

Ellen just shook her head. "Men *can* learn to cook, you know."

His grin stole her breath. "But why bother, when women are willing to do it?"

She waved her knife at him. "If I thought you meant that..."

"You'd carve my heart out?" The amusement on his face was suddenly gone, and his voice was as stark. "It's all yours."

Ellen was swamped by pleasure weighted with pain. Why was he doing this to her? Why was she letting him? In a desperate effort to salvage the earlier mood, she said lightly, "That sounds gory."

His gaze bored into hers; a muscle on one cheek jerked. "Maybe you weren't cut out to be a surgeon, either," he said, then grinned faintly. "Hey, a pun. What the hell, if I haven't lost my sense of humor..."

Relaxing, Ellen said, "I can't imagine you without one."

"Oh, I've lost it a few times." His mouth twitched. "On purpose, sometimes. My patients don't always appreciate humor."

"I guess there've been times I would have found it hard to laugh about my life, too," Ellen admitted.

"You've surprised me a few times," Nick said, his rough voice softening. "Like today."

"You mean..." She flushed, remembering her impulsive rejoinder. *We don't make promises, remember?* She might be grateful for that one moment of insouciance, but that didn't mean it had been honest. She wanted a promise from him. Dear God, she wanted one.

"Dessert?" she said quickly, starting to rise. "I made blueberry pie."

He pushed back from the table, too, reaching for her empty plate as well as his. "Next best thing to heaven," he said blandly.

Damn. Ellen knew what he considered heaven. Her.

Nick followed close behind her into the kitchen, and every nerve in her body flinched at the sound of his footsteps, the clatter of dishes. Her spine tingled and she'd have sworn that even the ends of her hair prickled.

This was ridiculous. All day she had felt as if she was on a first date, except they knew too much about each other. The surface awkwardness was underlaid by dark currents of emotion. Desire and tenderness, fear and longing. All swirling beneath the chitchat.

Most of all she was conscious of the end of the evening drawing near. Would Nick politely say goodnight and go home? Something in his eyes, some tension in his body not quite disguised, gave her an answer. On a stab of panic she wondered. What would *her* answer be?

She wouldn't think about it. Wouldn't worry until the moment came. As she poured the coffee, Ellen said the first safe thing that came into her head. "Have you ever had a pet?"

Nick looked at her strangely. "Is that apropos of something? Are you missing the kids? Place too quiet?"

No, I was just trying to make conversation. "Well, I do miss Laura and Patrick," she said hurriedly, grateful that she didn't actually have to lie. "I don't really suppose I want a pet, though. Not when I'm gone all day and don't have much of a yard."

"A cat." He leaned comfortably back in the chair and took a swallow of the hot coffee, his big hand wrapped completely around the mug and his legs outstretched under the table. He looked contemplative. "I think you're a cat person."

Interested despite herself, Ellen said, "Some people would take that as an insult."

"Why?" he asked, his blue eyes direct.

"Cats are famous for being totally uninterested in anybody else's wishes or opinions."

"I'd call that independence," he said, shrugging. "If you're going to identify with your pet, it beats being a dog person. Snarling and barking some of the time, fawning the rest of the time."

"How about you?" Ellen said. "What do you identify with?"

"Would you believe a guinea pig? Quiet and cute."

To laugh with him felt good. When his smile died he lifted the fork in a salute. "You make a great blueberry pie."

"Thanks. I actually enjoy cooking. I'll probably turn into a plump middle-aged lady sampling everything on the stove."

A shadow of emotion crossed Nick's face, disappearing before Ellen could analyze it. But then he said softly, "I wouldn't mind."

She suddenly saw the same thing he was seeing; the two of them, together. Mowing the lawn, going to PTA meetings. Coaching seven-year-olds playing soccer, baking cookies, wishing each other hello and goodbye, morning and night, day in and day out. Waists thickening, gray hairs showing, the years passing comfortably. But always, always, holding each other nights, never letting go.

Was that what it would be like?

She realized that their dessert plates were empty along with their coffee cups. The small silence that had fallen between them began to feel cavernous. He was watching her, and she knew damn well that he could read her mind.

Fine, she thought, maybe *he* could tell her what she wanted. Only, of course, she knew. She wanted him. Now and always. She just wasn't sure she was brave enough to try and hold him.

Her voice showed the strain when she said, "Can I get you some more pie? Coffee?"

He shook his head. "Maybe I should say good-night."

"Do you have to go so soon?" How conventional she sounded.

"I don't have to go anywhere," Nick said. The mask was suddenly gone, letting her see the hunger in his eyes. When he spoke again, his voice had roughened. "If I stay... Hell, I was going to say I wouldn't make any promises. I never make them anyway, do I? But I want you, Ellen. This call is up to you."

She sat there paralyzed, excitement curling in her stomach while apprehension tightened her chest. Why couldn't he have swept her into his arms, seduced her?

Because he wanted honesty. He wanted her to be mature enough to know her own mind. To come to him wholeheartedly. And tonight...tonight she could do that, if only for a few dark hours.

She sounded as shaken as she felt when she said, "I'd like you to stay."

Desire—or was it triumph?—flared in his eyes, and he reached across the table and took her hand in his. "You won't be sorry," he said huskily.

Ellen realized that, whether he knew it or not, Nick had just made her a promise.

CHAPTER FOURTEEN

"THANKS FOR LETTING ME have the kids today." Tom shifted uneasily from foot to foot in the doorway. The carpet there was worn so badly, in spots the fabric backing showed. "I'm uh, glad you're doing okay."

It was weird, Linda thought, seeing him right now. He was Tom, the boy/man she had loved, but he was different, too. Even when he'd picked up and dropped off the kids these last couple of years, she hadn't really looked at him. She'd had too much resentment.

But now... Now she could see the little changes. Lines at the corners of his eyes, deeper ones in his cheeks. Maybe a few gray hairs at his temples even though he was only thirty, like Ellen. He looked older, wiser, sadder. Linda felt older and sadder, but she wasn't so sure about wiser. But maybe... maybe it wasn't too late.

"Would you like to stay for dinner?" she asked.

She saw the shock, the wariness. "Are you sure?"

Linda bit her lip and nodded, trying to smile. "I'm sure."

"I, uh, yeah, I'd like that." Tom closed the open door. "Is there something I can do to help?"

"Daddy!" Laura bounced into the living room. "I thought you were gone."

"Your mom invited me to stay for dinner."

"Hey, cool! Patrick, Dad's staying!" Her piquant face lit with hope. "You going to stay the night, too?"

Startled, embarrassed, Linda let her gaze shy away from Tom's. "No, of course not!" she snapped, knowing she sounded like a grump. "He's...he's just visiting."

When she looked back at him, he didn't show anything, but his voice had gone flat when he said to his daughter. "Sorry, kiddo."

Trying to ignore the way Laura's face had fallen, Linda went into the kitchen. Its shabbiness embarrassed her, too, but she told herself it was Tom's fault as much as hers. If they had stayed together, they would've had something nicer by now.

Linda didn't have any choice but to serve what she'd planned for dinner. Tacos were Laura's favorite, and cheap, too, which meant they had them often. She wished she'd known Tom would be staying, that she were making something fancier. Something special, that he would remember when he was on the road.

But he ate with apparent relish, teasing the kids, teasing her.

"Knock, knock," Laura told him.

"Who's there?"

"Boo."

"Boo who?" Then he threw back his head and laughed as Laura proclaimed triumphantly, "You don't have to cry, it's just a joke!"

Watching Tom, Linda felt like she'd been hollow and was suddenly being filled with hurt and hunger and a horrible loneliness that slammed against the walls of her chest. It felt so damned right, having him here. Wasn't being with him some of the time better than never? It had been so long, she had trouble remembering how she'd felt when he was on the road, when he called to casually tell her that he wouldn't be home today after all. He was here *now*, that was what counted.

After dinner Laura said hopefully, "Can Daddy stay to watch our movie? I bet he's never seen it."

"Did Mom rent you a movie? What is it?"

"*Honey, I Shrunk the Kids*. It's my favorite. I've seen it zillions of times. Patrick thinks it's cool, too. You like that giant ant, don't you, Patrick?" She flung out her arms and lunged at her brother, snapping her teeth.

Patrick hunched away from her. "Stop it! You're scaring me!"

"Laura!" Linda shook her head. "You know better. And it's up to your dad whether he wants to stay."

"Sure," he said easily. "You're right. I've never seen that one."

Linda let herself get talked into making popcorn and hot cocoa, though of course Patrick spilled some on himself and cried. They had fun, though. It was like a party. Linda should have been cleaning the kitchen and doing some ironing, but she didn't care if she had to wear a wrinkled blouse to work tomorrow. Tom was here, big as life, sitting on the other end of the worn couch. He bounced Patrick on his knee and casually ruffled Laura's hair once in a while. Best of all were the smiles he gave Linda, conspiratorial, amused.

"I like the giant Cheerios best," he announced, when the movie was over.

"Bedtime," Linda said, lightly whacking Laura on the bottom when she scrunched up her nose in protest. "Go brush your teeth."

"I can tuck 'em in, if you've got something else to do," Tom said, not as if it were any big deal. Linda wondered if he thought she'd say no and didn't want to show his hurt.

"That would be great," she said. "I can get the kitchen cleaned up."

"Cool!" their daughter proclaimed.

Tom rolled his eyes. "What's this 'cool' stuff?" Linda heard him ask, as the three vanished into the small hallway. Smiling, she went into the kitchen.

A few minutes later she ducked in to say goodnight herself, leaving Tom to finish a story. By the time he appeared in the kitchen, she had the dishes washed and was drying her hands. Seeing him standing in the doorway, she said, "Would you like a cup of coffee?"

"Sure." He smiled, that crooked, warm, magical smile that had always lifted her heart. "Thanks for letting me stay tonight. I've . . . missed you guys."

Linda made herself say it. "I've missed you, too."

"Yeah?" His smile was gone. "You could have fooled me."

"It hurt, you leaving."

"So much, you never wanted to see me again?"

Linda ducked her head and tried to breathe slowly, deeply. If there had ever been a time to try and make it right, this was it. So she said the truth. "I wanted to pay you back. I wanted you to hurt, too."

He actually groaned then, and turned to rest his forehead against the door frame. "Linda . . ."

"I'm sorry." She bit her lip and didn't move. "It wasn't very grown-up of me."

"Well, it worked," he said, his voice choked. "I hurt, all right."

She realized suddenly that she was crying. "I'm sorry," she said again, uselessly.

"Oh, God." Just like that, he'd crossed the kitchen and taken her in his arms. She wiped her wet cheeks on his chest and wrapped her arms around his waist. His embrace felt like it always had: strong, safe, forever. "I've missed you so badly," he said, the words muffled against her hair.

She wanted to lift her head, find his lips. But first there was something she had to ask, something that had torn at her every time she thought of Tom.

Pulling back a little, trying not to sound as though she really cared, Linda said, "Did you . . . I mean, was there anybody . . . anybody else?"

Tom's gray eyes met hers with scalding honesty. "I tried. There've been a couple of women. But they just didn't work out. Neither of them was you."

Linda didn't know whether she felt relief or pain. Both, maybe. She said shakily, once again, "I'm sorry."

"How about you? Did you find someone?"

She could only shake her head.

His fingers tightened on her shoulders. "Can I kiss you?" he asked, his voice low and raw.

Linda touched her tongue nervously to her lips and gave a tentative nod. Tom's kiss was as unsure. His mouth touched hers softly, as though for the first time, but it sent sweetness trickling through her. With a shudder she slipped her arms up around his neck, and instantly the kiss deepened. He pulled her against him, and the feel of his long, strong body was as familiar as yesterday, as necessary as air.

They didn't talk. He left his shirt in the living room, hers in the hall by the bathroom. For a single, wondering moment they paused in the doorway to look at their sleeping children before Tom swept Linda up in his arms and shouldered his way into her bedroom.

He stripped her clothes off with endearing clumsiness, the tremor in his hands giving away his hunger. The only sound was their harsh breathing, the scrape of his zipper as she tugged it down to free him. She stroked him, her fingers remembering how best to please him. It was enough to snap his control, and suddenly he was devouring her mouth as he pushed her down onto the bed and kneeled between her legs.

"Now," she said. "Now!"

He hadn't even gotten his jeans off. She didn't care. It had been too long. Forever. Yesterday. Her memories blurred with the present as he took her in one long thrust, fusing their bodies. She wrapped her legs around him, accepting his urgency, letting it shatter her. She came around him, then again when he gave a ragged cry and let himself go. She was there to catch him. That was the way it had always been.

But would he be there to catch her, when she needed him?

WHEN ELLEN GOT to her mother's, the garage door was open, and she saw that Linda was already there, running her hand across the scratched top of the table that sat, graceful and solid, in the middle of the garage.

As Ellen walked in, she heard Linda ask Mrs. Whalley, "Why don't you take it to one of those places that refinishes furniture?"

Ellen's mother looked stubborn. "Because your father made it. You know how poor a job he always thought they did."

"Come on," Ellen said. "It'll be fun. I'm dressed for action." She pirouetted so they could see her paint splattered T-shirt, worn jeans and canvas tennis shoes.

Linda gave a quick, disarming grin. "Yeah, okay, let's attack it."

Shades of a quilting bee, Ellen thought a few minutes later, if a little less romantic. Sitting on the concrete floor, she worked on the legs with paint remover and steel wool while her sister and mother scraped the varnish off the top. She'd almost forgotten what the table looked like, how fine the cherry grain was. When she and Linda had been children, their mother had run a home day care for a few years and the furniture had all gotten battered. Ever since, her mother had swaddled the table in a lacy cloth. Why she'd suddenly become determined to tackle refinishing it, Ellen didn't have the faintest idea.

But what the heck. It was kind of fun, the conversation desultory, the tension that was so often between the three of them lacking.

"Where are the kids today?" her mother asked.

"You remember Lori Gardner?" Linda said absently. "The receptionist in our office? She invited them over to play with her two. They're about the right ages. She lives out in the boonies, no kids around."

"Oh, good, Laura and Patrick need friends."

Linda's face popped down into Ellen's line of vision. "How you doing down there?"

"At least I get to sit."

"Um. Those legs are going to take forever, aren't they?"

"The curve makes it hard," Ellen admitted. "How on earth did Dad get them so smooth?"

In unison they all said, "The right tools!" and laughed. How many million times had they heard George Whalley say that? He'd look at a poor job—not just on furniture, on anything—and shake his head in sorrow. "If they'd just use the right tools," he'd say.

"This is going to be gorgeous." Ellen wrapped the steel wool around the gently curved leg of the table. "Don't you dare use a tablecloth after we put all this work in!"

"But I wouldn't want it to get scratched," Mrs. Whalley protested.

"We'll put a cast-iron finish on," Linda said. "I'll threaten my kids on pain of death. And it's not like you're going to be flinging sharp things around."

"No, I suppose not," Mrs. Whalley said, sounding uncertain, her voice having that faint quaver that gave away her age.

Linda plunked down on the opposite side of the table from Ellen and began to tackle another of the legs. "I've been seeing Tom," she announced abruptly.

There was something in her voice that said, "What do you want to make of it?" Defiance. Well, Ellen could understand that. After convincing your family that the guy was a louse, rehabilitating his image would be a little awkward.

"Yeah?" she said neutrally. "I'd forgotten how nice he was."

"I guess I had, too," Linda said. Her hands stilled, although she didn't look up. "Do you think I'm nuts, Mom?"

Ellen held her breath. Don't be critical, she prayed. Not now, please. Save it.

"He's the father of your children," Mrs. Whalley said with dignity. "Of course I don't think you're crazy."

Linda's face softened, became beautiful. "Thank you, Mom," she said quietly. "I guess maybe it was my drinking . . . He's not a bad person."

"I'd think more of him," Mrs. Whalley said, "if he'd paid the child support promptly."

"That was partly my fault," Linda said. Color rose in her cheeks. "I . . . I made it hard for him."

Hallelujah! Ellen thought. She grinned at her sister under the table. "What's all this humility?"

Linda's smile blossomed, ever so slightly mischievous. "It's Nick's fault. He's big on humility."

"Yeah." Ellen looked away. "Yeah, I know."

"Ellen . . ."

"It's okay." She managed a smile for her sister. "I'm seeing him again, I guess. He went horseback riding with me yesterday."

Linda made a face. "Horseback riding?"

"That was kind of his reaction. But we agreed on equal time."

Leering, her sister said, "Let me guess what you did on his time."

Ellen stuck out her tongue. "Are you trying to tell me that Tom kissed you a chaste good night?"

"What do you think?"

"Girls!" Mrs. Whalley said sternly. "Don't squabble! Besides, this is hardly an appropriate subject for conversation."

"Oh, why not?" Linda said, then flashed a grin at her mother. "Okay, okay. I'll leave the bedroom door closed."

Hers had stayed open, Ellen suddenly remembered. Her hands slowed as she again heard Nick say, *You won't be sorry.*

Was she sorry? Did she regret a single moment? The first kiss, when they'd risen from the table and he had cupped her face in hands so gentle she felt them tremble, when their mouths had touched and tasted so softly? The feel of his big hands moving down her arms, kneading, sliding over to engulf her breasts and mold them?

She didn't remember how they had gotten to the bedroom. Nothing as dramatic as the first time. He hadn't swept her up in his arms; he'd been too busy kissing her. She had felt so small and vulnerable. Emotionally fragile. As though he sensed it, Nick had been incredibly gentle.

In the bedroom he had undressed her with such care that the very act of doing so was a caress. Her cotton shirt felt like silk when he slipped it from her shoulders and the texture of her jeans gave her sensual pleasure as they traveled down her long legs with a little help from Nick's deft fingers. At last she stood naked before him. Nick's eyes blazed with such hunger, such love, that she moaned.

At the throaty sound his teeth gritted and he began ripping his shirt off. Something brave and wanton had made Ellen step forward and cover his hands with hers. He had stopped, stood motionless, only the gasping rise and fall of his chest giving away his urgency.

She had begun to touch him, then, to tease and caress as though he, too, were naked. Through the thin fabric of his shirt she found the small hard nubs of his nipples. Down over the powerful muscles of his chest and stomach; she closed her eyes and *felt*, her fingertips acutely sensitized. He was warm, the finely woven cloth deliciously sensual. His jeans, she discovered, were rougher, rasping against her palms. Inside them he was rock hard, and with her touch she made him harder. She sank to her knees and rubbed her cheek against him, teased and tormented until he was groaning and the hands that tangled in her hair tightened, pulling painfully.

Ellen stood, then, letting her body slide up his. By the time she worked the zipper down, her hands were shaking. Nick's face was taut and flushed, his eyes molten with sexual excitement. She was weak suddenly with desire; she *needed* him. When his big hands splayed across her buttocks, pulling her against him, she melted.

"Nick," she breathed. "Please, oh please..."

His voice was a husky growl. "With pleasure."

He laid her back across the bed and went with her. His shirt was open, baring his chest. She slid her hands inside, dug her fingernails into his back as he pushed his jeans down and entered her, quick and hard. It was joy and pleasure and pain all wrapped up, all splintering into shards of exquisite sensation as he moved in her. At her involuntary cry, at the small convulsions that shook her, Nick let himself go.

She had never felt anything like it. Without Nick, she never would again.

Was she sorry? Ellen wondered now, recalled to the bare garage. Did she regret the day with Nick, the night? Even the smallest, most vulnerable moment?

No. Never. The answer was breathtakingly simple, although only a tiny part of all she felt. She would never, ever regret anything that had happened with Nick.

Ellen let out her breath with a long sigh, and looked at her sister, sitting cross-legged on the concrete floor just on the other side of the table. On Linda's face she saw memories as precious and as painful as her own. Their eyes met with complete understanding, and Ellen felt as close to her sister as she ever had. They were women who each loved a man, who had decisions to make. For each, love should have been enough but wasn't. Their childhoods had taught them that. *I love you* didn't guarantee happiness.

But it could! Ellen's heart cried. It could!

SHE TRIED TO BELIEVE that in the days that followed. She saw Nick twice more that week; Sunday afternoon, after he had admitted a couple of new patients, and lunch on Wednesday. The other days he called, and Ellen clung desperately to hope. It was so easy just to forget Nick's past, to pretend he was an idealistic man who treated alcoholics because he believed it could be done, not to assuage his own ghosts.

They had fun, they talked, they laughed. They made love again on Sunday, long and slow. Tenderly, lingering over the funny moments as well as the passionate ones. It was so easy to shut her mind to her fears. For all that Nick wouldn't make promises, he was a miracle worker. All she had to do was look at Linda, who glowed with happiness these days.

Once she said something like that to Nick, and he frowned. "I'm glad she's doing well, Ellen, but you'd better not count on anything."

"But why would Linda start drinking now? It's been a couple of weeks. If she had a real craving or...or something, wouldn't she have already gone off the wagon?"

"She didn't come to the AA meeting this week."

Ellen's throat constricted. "But I've *seen* her! She's doing fine."

"But she's too busy to come to AA?"

"Well...She and her ex-husband..."

"What if something goes wrong between them?" Nick said urgently. "What if she loses her job? What if...hell, what if she has a crummy day at work, gets a flat tire on the way home and then the kids drive her nuts? So far she's handled the good times. Can she handle the bad times?"

"You're scaring me," Ellen said.

He lifted her chin and looked ruefully down at her. "I don't want to do that. I just don't want you to be let down if your sister slips. Because then you might give up on her."

They both heard the unspoken words. *Then you might give up on me.*

Would she? Did Linda matter that much? Ellen didn't like to think that her happiness rested on her sister's thin shoulders.

When Nick kissed her, Ellen quit thinking about it. Trust didn't come easily; love did.

CHAPTER FIFTEEN

THAT NEXT SATURDAY, Nick had to work. Ellen had called her mother and suggested they take Laura and Patrick to Seattle's Woodland Park Zoo. After they had picked up the kids, they left Linda and Tom standing on the front doorstep of Linda's small, shabby house in north Everett. Although both were dressed, Ellen had a feeling Tom had spent the night. Linda looked ever so slightly smug.

"Thanks for giving us time alone," she whispered to Ellen, as she handed over a bag of toys to entertain the kids in the car.

"No problem. I've missed Laura and Patrick."

"Today's our last day. Tom's leaving tomorrow. Back on the road." She made a face. "I'm kind of dreading it, actually. So having today..."

"Hey, I'm looking forward to this, too. Just have fun, okay?"

"Thanks," Linda said again, her smile both sweet and sad.

Ellen *had* missed the kids. That was the truth. Just getting used to being alone again was harder than she had expected. In one month her niece and nephew, with more than a little help from Nick, had dumped all her priorities on end. Now that she was sorting through them, trying to put everything back where it had been, she was discovering that some weren't worth keeping.

The dumbest things had seemed important to her. Who cared whether her books were in alphabetical order, for heaven's sake? The first couple of times Patrick had pulled them all off the shelves to build a fort, she'd spent half an hour restoring order; the last time, she'd just shoved them back on the shelf willy-nilly. Studying the bookcase last night from the couch, she'd decided she didn't really care whether Fogel came before Foner.

So it was with a wistful kind of pleasure that Ellen watched as Laura eagerly asked questions of a remarkably patient zoo docent who had a display of gorilla bones and fur laid out on a table, while Patrick stood with his nose pressed to the glass of the animal enclosure. Inside the natural display a juvenile gorilla drummed his chest in a comical imitation of the hulking giant lounging in the straw nearby. Even closer to the glass a large hairy mother cuddled a tiny baby with huge, dark eyes that were uncannily human. They had been lucky today to find the gorillas where they could see them so well, Ellen thought; much of the enclosure, which looked vaguely jungle-like, including a waterfall, was out of sight of the human intruders.

"Patrick's fascinated," Mrs. Whalley murmured.

"Um hm. Whenever we went to the library, he always wanted books about animals. He'd love a pet."

"Right now he looks like he'd love a gorilla."

Ellen laughed. She and her mother sat on a strategically placed bench, enjoying the chance to rest. Actually, Ellen wouldn't have minded pressing her nose to the glass next to Patrick's, but she was worried about her mother, whose steps had been getting slower in the last half hour.

"Kids are fun," she said, surprising herself. "I don't know why I've never much thought about having my own."

"Maybe because you need a husband first?"

As if somebody had flicked on a slide projector, Ellen saw Nick. Who else? Despite his intimidating size, gravelly voice and restless energy, he still personified gentleness. He was the father her children were meant to have, she thought, with the kind of certainty that was wrenchingly painful to deny.

"You can't marry just to have children," she argued, as much with herself as with her mother.

"No, but if you're ever going to have them, you can't be afraid of getting married."

The conversation was well-worn. This was *not* the first time they had had it. "I'm not afraid," she insisted. "Just cautious."

"Now, now," her mother said with mock severity. "Didn't I raise you not to tell lies?"

"I wouldn't say that. I think you encouraged me to tell all kinds of lies." Shocked by the sudden harshness in her own voice, Ellen couldn't look at her mother. Instead she stared blindly at the gorillas in their cozy family groups.

Where had the bitterness come from? It had risen in her throat like bile. She was *happy* these days. Why was she still nursing such anger?

"I'm sorry," she said, turning impulsively to her mother. "I don't know what's gotten into me."

Mrs. Whalley's brown eyes were terribly sad. "No?"

"Can we go look at something else now?" Laura asked from right beside them.

The pause was too long, but Ellen summoned a smile. "Sure. Better yet, how about a pony ride?"

Patrick hung just behind Laura as usual, and now his face lit with joy. "Can we?"

"Of course you can."

At the pony ring Laura and Patrick joined the line of other waiting children eagerly watching the fat, patient ponies being led by teenagers around the circle, a child clinging to each saddle horn. Laura clutched the two dollars for herself and her little brother. Ellen and her mother found an empty bench in easy sight.

They sat in silence for a moment. Ellen looked at her mother and saw the face she had known all her life, but changed now by the years until it was brittle and lined like the faded leaves that fell in the fall. One part of her wanted to go back to pretending, but another part of her knew it was no use. "Will you tell me something?" Ellen asked.

Her mother's back was very straight. "I've always been willing to answer your questions."

Ellen had just been afraid to ask them. Perhaps because of seeing Nick again, she felt strong now, at least in this small way. "Did you ever try to force Dad to quit drinking?"

"What do you mean? You know how hard I tried! Constantly. I poured out bottles and hid the car keys. I begged. Oh, how I begged. You heard me. How can you ask . . ."

"But did you ever threaten to leave him? Did you ever mean it?"

"Mean it?" Her mother looked away. She seemed to be gazing at her grandchildren, although Ellen doubted that she saw them. Her expression was curiously remote, so it was doubly a shock to see the tear roll down her cheek.

On a surge of guilt Ellen laid a hand on her arm. "Mom, you don't have to..."

"No." Her voice was strained but strong. "You have a right to ask. I threatened to leave your stepfather twice. I suppose you were too young to remember. The first time George tried to quit, I think he really did, but he just couldn't do it. And," her sigh was small and shuddering, "I didn't have the courage to go through with it. The next time I threatened, he cried. He told me to go if I had to." She groped in her purse, produced a tissue to blow her nose with. "I think... I think he knew I couldn't do it. For you and Linda, I should have. But losing your father was so hard. Being on my own... I couldn't go through that again. You're right to be angry. I know I was a coward. I just hope that someday you'll at least understand."

How could she not? It came like a revelation, the peace that Ellen had spent the years seeking. Understanding wasn't hard. Why had she thought it was? All it meant was truly growing up, looking across the years with an adult's eyes and not a child's. It meant facing her own cowardice, seeing that choices were not simple. There had been no yellow brick road that took only courage for her mother to follow, any more than the way was clearly labeled for her now.

"I do understand," she said, and reached out to grip her mother's hand. "I do. I just didn't want to. It was easier to blame somebody."

The tears ran more freely down her mother's cheeks as she looked at Ellen, and the fingers that grasped Ellen's in turn tightened. "It seems inadequate, but... You know I've always loved you."

Were her own cheeks wet? "Oh, Mom, I love you, too. I always have. Maybe that's why I was so angry."

"Do you know that he loved you, too?" Mrs. Whalley searched her face with sudden urgency. "Will you believe that?"

Beyond words, Ellen nodded. Strangely, through the tears she was smiling.

"Do you know why he...why he..."

There was only one answer. "He thought he was doing it for us."

"Everything he did was for us. Except..."

The one thing he couldn't give them. That was what Nick had said, wasn't it? He had lost his soul and couldn't give what he didn't have. George Whalley had believed that in dying he gave them a gift of love, the only one he had left, and how could Ellen argue? It was wrong, insane, even warped; but she should never have doubted his love.

"I'm sorry, Mom," she said shakily. "For all these years."

"Oh, Ellen you have nothing to apologize for. If anybody is to blame..."

"No more blame. Please, Mom. No more."

They had managed entirely to forget the children. It was a shock to hear Patrick's small voice.

"Are you crying, Grandma?" He looked more interested than upset.

"Why... I believe I am," she said in surprise, and firmly blew her nose.

Ellen gave a watery chuckle. "Do you have another tissue in your purse?"

"Of course. Don't you carry them?"

Ellen suppressed a smile at the familiar motherly tone. "I guess I'm out," she said meekly.

"Why are you crying?" Patrick asked.

"Because... Oh, I suppose because your aunt and I were talking about sad things. Maybe because I'm a little bit happy, too."

"I don't cry when I'm happy."

"Never?"

He shook his head.

"Then maybe you haven't been happy enough yet."

Patrick frowned and thought it over. "Would I cry if you bought me a puppy?"

They all heard Laura's indignant cry at the same time. *"Patrick!"*

Ellen looked up. "Uh oh, it's your turn. Come on." She swept Patrick up on her hip and carried him to the head of the line. A mother shepherding her own herd stepped back to give Patrick room.

His sister heaved a dramatic sigh. "He was *supposed* to go get you, so you could watch us. What took you so long?"

"Grandma was crying," Patrick said.

Laura rolled her eyes. "That's dumb. I don't believe you. Go on." She pushed her brother ahead of her. "You go first."

"But..." The words were cut off as a smiling teenager lifted him into the saddle of a white pony. Eyes wide, he grabbed the saddle horn in a death grip.

"This is Ginger," Ellen heard the girl say, as she led the pony away.

Laura went next, trying to look nonchalant as she threw her leg over the back of a portly black pony.

Laughing, Ellen turned to her mother. The laugh seemed to catch in her throat when their eyes met. It was the first time since she was a small child that they had been able to look at each other without the barriers resentiment had built. So easy, and it had taken so many years. Absurdly, she felt the sting of tears again.

"Mom, do you suppose I could have another . . . ?"

Mrs. Whalley handed her a tissue. "If I buy you a package the next time I'm at the store, will you put them in your purse?"

Another damp chuckle. Some compromises were easier than others. "Thank you, Mom," Ellen said docilely, and her mother gave a satisfied nod.

THREE DAYS LATER, Ellen's fragile peace dissolved. When the telephone rang she was ironing a blouse she wanted to wear to work the next day. She plunked the iron in its stand, tripped on the cord that had somehow wrapped around her ankle, and took three rings to free herself.

The minute she heard her sister's voice, a frisson of unease ran down her spine.

"Where's Mom?" Linda demanded.

"Uh . . ." She had to stop to think. Tuesday evening. "Bingo," Ellen said. "You know she plays once a week out at Tulalip." The Indian tribe was making a killing running a bingo hall.

"Oh."

"Is there something wrong?"

Her sister's voice was elaborately casual. "No, I just wanted to talk to her. She'll be home tomorrow, won't she?"

"I don't know. I guess so. Except she is taking that quilting class. I think that's on Wednesdays. Listen, are you sure . . . ?"

"It's no big deal." There was a pause. "Well, maybe you could help me. Is there any chance you could loan me a little money?"

Ellen felt a familiar sinking sensation. "Is it something special, or...?"

"I don't get paid 'til Friday. You know I had a month without pay. I'm just short, that's all."

"Okay," Ellen said quietly.

"Can I come by this evening?"

"Sure. But aren't you getting the kids ready for bed?"

"Hey, it won't kill them to stay up late this once. I need the money."

"Fine," Ellen said. She sounded as artificially casual as her sister had. "How are things going otherwise? Have you whipped your office back in shape?"

"Why bother?" Linda snapped. "Jerome's giving me a hard time. I was a little late this morning and he was all over me. I don't have to take that. I can get another job."

"Linda..."

"Don't get preachy with me," her sister warned. "I'm not in the mood, okay? Listen, I'll be by in half an hour or so."

Ellen slowly hung up the telephone. That sinking feeling had magnified into dread. She tried to tell herself Linda had just had a bad day—and maybe she hated to be in the position of having to ask for a loan.

But Ellen failed to convince herself. There had been something about Linda's voice. She hadn't slurred words, nothing that obvious. Maybe it was the hostile edge, the *I'm misunderstood* plaint that Ellen had heard too often before. Linda had been deflecting criticism that hadn't been made—which meant she knew she deserved it. And what was it Nick had said? *What if she has a crummy day at work? Can she handle the bad times?*

With mounting apprehension Ellen waited for her sister's knock. It was typical of Linda—the old Linda—that she didn't show for nearly an hour. When the knock fi-

nally came, Ellen glanced at the clock. Ten-fifteen. Linda
would have to be getting Laura and Patrick up in less
than eight hours.

When Ellen opened the door, Linda made no move to
come in. Behind her Ellen could just make out the car in
the driveway and the huddled dark shapes that must be
the children.

"Sorry I'm so late," Linda said quickly. "There were
some other things I had to do."

Ellen bit her lip. "Here's the check," she said, handing it over. "Is that enough?"

Linda barely glanced at it. "Yeah, sure. Thanks. I'll
pay you back. Maybe not this Friday, but two weeks after that. Okay?"

"There's no hurry." Ellen searched her sister's face and
surreptitiously sniffed. If Linda was drinking, Ellen
couldn't smell it on her breath, but neither did her sister
want to meet Ellen's eyes. "Are you sure everything's all
right?" she asked.

"Why wouldn't it be?"

"Is Tom back yet?"

"Are you kidding?" Linda's laugh was unpleasant.
"He got a chance to pick up another load. What's a few
more days to him?"

Ellen felt her way. "You are . . . you are still seeing
him?"

"Oh, I don't know. What's the use? I mean, he hasn't
changed."

"But driving the truck is his job."

"Well, maybe I don't want a man who always puts his
job ahead of me." Linda shrugged. "Listen, I'd better
get home. I'll see you later, okay?"

Was it her imagination, or did Linda sway ever so
slightly when she started down the two steps? Ellen stood

there, paralyzed by the certainty she didn't want to acknowledge. Oh my God, she thought suddenly. The children were in that car with her sister.

She hurried to the edge of the porch. "Linda!"

But she was too late. The car was backing out, heading with deceptive care down the quiet night street. Ellen clapped a hand over her mouth and watched the red taillights flicker at the corner.

She didn't pray for divine intervention very often, but now she did. *Dear Lord, keep them safe. Please, please, keep them safe.* Or else I'll never forgive myself.

SHE LAY IN BED knowing that the only thing in the world she wanted was to talk to Nick. She wanted him to tell her she was wrong, Linda wasn't drinking. She wanted him to tell her what to do. She just plain wanted Nick.

But what right did she have? They were living on borrowed time, skimming the surface of their feelings, because she refused to trust him. Tonight her worries cut too close to the heart. How could they talk about Linda without talking about themselves? No. She *couldn't* call him, not tonight, no matter how desperately she ached to.

Nor could she talk to her mother, who would only worry more than she doubtless already was. Ellen had friends, but all they could offer was sympathy.

Looking into the darkness with only the small bright numbers on her clock to keep her company, Ellen faced her aloneness.

Scarier yet, though, was the thought that came unbidden. What if this was Nick she feared for, worried about, doubted? What if she *knew* that Nick was drinking? What if she did trust him, and he betrayed both of them?

Even if she married him and he never had a drink again, would she still lie in bed on nights he had to be out, wondering just as she was now, hurting, destroying his love and hers by her doubts?

Would even the promises she craved be enough?

"I'M AFRAID WE LOST this round." George Grun sat on the edge of Ellen's desk, idly swinging his leg. Casual, condescending, friendly in a way she never quite trusted. He shook his head. "Pete Bronowski really analyzed the data on this one. He ended up convinced there's room in the market for a new cost-analysis program, especially when it's clearly better than anything available. He was influenced when the engineer whose project this is suggested ways of keeping development expenses down."

In other words, they hadn't believed her figures.

Trying to keep her face expressionless, Ellen realized her stomach was burning. She'd have an ulcer if she stuck around here much longer. In the past she would have been able to shrug the whole episode off; she did her job, they paid her for it. Kashiwa was a successful corporation. What difference did it make if what she accomplished had no cosmic significance?

But today she'd had enough. She asked it flat out. "Why do we bother, George? Nobody ever pays any attention to our figures. Why doesn't the company just skip this stage?"

"Now, you know better than that," he said heartily. He laid a beefy, ostensibly comforting hand on her shoulder. "Development costs are something that have to be factored in. Bronowski isn't ignoring us; we're just not seeing the big picture."

How many times had she heard that, always reverently, as though it were beyond her capacity for understanding? Maybe the trouble was that she wanted to see a big picture once in a while. It didn't even have to be big,

Ellen thought. Just *whole*. Otherwise, one of these days she'd be sitting here in her teeny tiny cubby, peering at her teeny tiny sliver of the apocryphal "big picture," and she'd suddenly flip. Go stark raving bonkers. Run naked through the warren of offices. Stick out her tongue at the magisterial Pete Bronowski. Slap George Grun's groping hand the next time he laid it on her. The possibilities were endless. She was still enjoying them when George finally, reluctantly, withdrew his hand from her shoulder and went off to console some other sucker who'd just found out two months of hard work had been worthless.

Lunchtime and the chance to get away from work lured Ellen like an exotic oasis in the desert. After an almost sleepless night she was exhausted. It had been all she could do to drag herself out of bed this morning. What she needed, Ellen decided, was books. Elliott Bay and the University of Washington bookstore were too far, but one of the chain stores at the mall would do. They were perfectly adequate for a quick fix.

Naturally, her phone rang just as she was standing up. "Damn," she muttered, tempted to ignore it. A glance at the clock told her it was still five minutes to twelve, though, which meant she was being paid to answer the miserable thing.

Sighing, she snatched it up. "Hello?"

Some sixth sense told her even before he spoke. "Ellen, this is Nick."

She sagged back into her chair and dropped her purse with a plop. "Nick," she said inanely.

"How are you?"

"Fine," she lied. "How about you?"

"I miss you." His voice was rough. "I'm really calling about Linda. She didn't show at the outpatient AA meeting again last night. I've tried to call a couple of times and she hasn't answered. Have you talked to her? Is she still doing okay?"

She had been trying not to think about Linda. The reminder brought her worries crashing around her. Definitely an ulcer, Ellen thought, swallowing against the acid that burned in her chest.

"I saw her last night. She borrowed some money."

The silence in her ear told Ellen that Nick interpreted that about the way she had.

"Has she been drinking?" he said at last, baldly.

"I don't know, Nick!" It was a cry from her heart. "I don't want to be unfair to Linda . . ."

"But you think she has been."

Ellen closed her eyes. "Yes."

"Oh, hell."

She opened her eyes but didn't see her surroundings. "What should I do?" she pleaded.

He was unexpectedly sharp. "Damn it, Ellen, you know the answer to that."

"But . . . What about the kids?"

"Does she drive with them when she's been drinking?"

Ellen remembered the taillights receding into the darkness last night, the careful flicker at the corner. "Not usually," she said slowly. "It's one thing she's always been careful about. But it seems like every time she starts again, she goes downhill faster. And sometimes she'd have to pick them up at the baby-sitter's or something, wouldn't she?"

"Maybe you have to confront her."

"I guess so." Ellen closed her eyes and rubbed at her forehead. "But I'm pretty sure she'll deny she's drinking. And I can't kidnap Laura and Patrick."

"No, you can't." The rough voice was suddenly gentle. "But you can appeal to the mother in her. She loves those kids."

"But what if she doesn't love them enough?" Ellen said in distress. "Or what if she's lying even to herself?"

There was another silence, then Nick said, "Not being able to do anything is hard, isn't it?"

"I think," she said dully, "that it's even harder than trying to do something and failing."

"Well, this time you haven't failed. Don't give up on her, Ellen."

"No? When *should* I give up on her?"

Nick let that pass. "It's a rare alcoholic who makes it the first time, or the second time, or even the third time. Sometimes they have to slip before they pick up the phone and call AA. I quit once for a couple of months before I started drinking again. Sobriety didn't take for me until I'd been through treatment three times."

"Didn't *take* for you?" Ellen echoed. "That sounds almost like you *know* . . . "

"What?" She hadn't heard him sound like that in a long time. Harsh. "That it's permanent? Is that what you want me to say?"

"Yes!" She almost shouted it. "You know what I want!"

"And I can't give it to you," Nick said wearily. "I have a good friend who's been sober for twelve years. He was my buddy from AA, the one I leaned on in the early days. His wife just left him and he hit the bottle. After twelve years."

Ellen was silent. What was there to say? Hopelessness weighed her down. She just sat, clutching the phone, listening to the faint sound of breathing that told her Nick was still on the other end of the line. She had been right last night, not calling Nick. She had known what it would come to.

"Ellen, can we have dinner tonight? I want to see you."

She wanted to see him, too, so badly it hurt. But that wasn't why she *had* to see him.

"I already have plans for dinner," she said, proud of how level her voice was. "But if you want to stop by afterward..."

There was a momentary silence. His voice gave away no more than hers had. "About seven," he said. "I'll look forward to it," and hung up.

Ellen slowly followed suit, looking at the wall clock. She had just created the worst deadline she had ever faced. In six hours and thirty-five minutes she had to give Nick an answer. Though in her mind she knew what it ought to be, her heart wasn't so sure.

Panic grabbed at her. How could she let him go? How could she not?

CHAPTER SIXTEEN

LINDA'S HAND SHOOK as she poured the beer from a tall can into a glass. Drinking it that way was classier, slower. It made her feel in control. Not that a beer really counted anyway. What was it, three-percent alcohol or something? You couldn't get a flea drunk on that.

But oh it tasted good going down, foamy and cold, with a bite that she craved. She closed her eyes and let the relief wash over her.

She shouldn't be having even a beer; she knew that. But today had been lousy. Jerome had given her a hard time. She'd been ten minutes late again this morning, no big deal. But he'd stared hard at her and asked if she was hitting the bottle again. As if it was any of his damn business. She did her work, didn't she?

She had stared hard back at him and asked if he wanted to give her a breathalyzer test. Or was he going to start random drug testing?

"No, I'll tell you what," she had said in a flip way she knew he hated. "I'll walk a straight line for you. Now, come on, watch." She dropped her purse on the desk, held out her arms, and with exaggerated care followed a line in the linoleum. When the receptionist laughed, Linda gave Jerome a saucy smile. "Is that good enough for you?"

"I pay you from nine o'clock."

"Patrick didn't sleep well last night. We were all tired this morning." Not quite true, except the last part. She *was* tired. By the time she'd picked up the check at Ellen's and found a bank machine, then gotten home and put the kids to bed, she'd needed a beer just to unwind. It must have been midnight by the time she fell asleep.

But Jerome's face softened at the mention of her son, just as she'd known it would. He was a sucker for the devoted mother image. And that wasn't a lie. She *was* a good mother. It wasn't like she'd been out partying or anything. Anyway, Jerome was probably just jealous. He didn't like the idea of her out with anyone else. She hadn't told him that her ex was back in the picture. Jerome never had liked Tom. Or vice versa.

It was just as well she hadn't announced their reunion to the world anyway. Because it wasn't going to work. Like she'd told Ellen, Tom hadn't changed at all. After he'd picked up that extra load, he had promised, cross his heart and hope to die, that he'd be back in town today. She had hurried straight home, figuring she could leave the kids at the baby-sitter's until six, giving her some time with him alone. But guess what? No Tom. He still cared more about that damn truck than he did about her and the kids.

Anger and hurt gave her the momentum to pour another beer. She leaned against the counter in the kitchen and looked around. The breakfast dishes still sat dirty in the sink and there were crumbs of dried clay under the kitchen table. The place was a mess. She ought to be doing something about it.

Why? she thought, with profound depression. This house was a dump, the linoleum cracking and the sink chipped and stained. The carpet was a badly worn shag, harvest gold even, for God's sake. No matter what she did, the house was still a dump. She didn't want to live like this. She especially didn't want to have to borrow money from Ellen. She always felt like she should account for every penny. $1.10 for bread, $2.06 for a gallon of milk.

$3.50 for a six-pack. That'd go over real well.

The first gulp of her third beer was sliding down her throat when the phone rang.

She felt a leap of hope and grabbed the receiver. "Tom?"

A faint crackle of static made him sound far away. "Hey! You must miss me."

"Where are you?" she demanded.

"St. Louis. I got a chance to pick up a load in Philadelphia. Really a good deal. I just delivered it." Someone spoke in the background and Tom said, "Hold on a sec, will you?" She heard his voice, muffled by the hand he must have put over the receiver. Then he came back on. "Toys, can you believe it? Too bad I couldn't hijack some. Anyway, Seattle's my next stop. The thing is, I can't load here until morning. So I won't be in until Sunday morning."

Disappointment, surprisingly sharp, lent an edge to her voice. "What am I supposed to do, keep your dinner warm?"

"How about I take you out for breakfast Sunday morning instead? The kids, too. We could go really big time, make it stacks of pancakes at Denny's."

"You promised you'd be home today."

"Don't start that."

"It's the same old thing. I can't count on you."

He swore. "You know it's important for me to pick up extra loads. I can't roll empty. You know what it's like."

She knew all right. The memories hit her like a fist. The bed in the back of the cab, a warm cocoon that kept out the night. Just the two of them, as though they were all that existed in the world. That's what it had felt like, that first year they were married. She'd make him a sandwich and climb forward into the cab, and he would give her that slow sweet smile she had always loved. With one hand he would shove a cassette into the tape deck, maybe Bonnie Raitt, and they would sing along. They had sounded good together. Sometimes they'd really rocked. The strange countryside would slip by the windows, never quite real, just scenery passing. The road signs were what mattered, and the two of them. They were always hurrying, but it wasn't important. No matter how tired Tom was when they stopped, he always held her, kissed her, made love to her. Even his incessant care of the truck hadn't bothered her. Back then, she'd gotten the kind of pleasant glow you get when you watch your husband doing chores around the house. After all, the truck was their home, right?

She had been happy. At eighteen, being a trucker had seemed romantic. "Loner" had been his CB tag. It sounded stupid now, but in those days... In those days he hadn't even minded her having a few drinks. It made her talkative, and then she was good company, kept him awake, made him laugh.

And then she got pregnant. First she was sick to her stomach, and it was hard to eat right in diners. Her back began to hurt and climbing into the cab was a bitch. She had claimed not to mind when they agreed that he should leave her behind. After all, this was how she'd imagined it, right? Vine-covered cottage and blond, blue-eyed babies. Good smells floating from her kitchen, floors shining. Running out to meet him with a smile. But she was so lonely.

God, so lonely.

She was still lonely.

"I know what it's like," she said, very softly. Her eyes stung. "But I'm not eighteen any more. I want something different. Something more."

"The only thing you've wanted for years is booze. Has that changed?"

"Did you ever think that if my life was better, maybe I wouldn't have had to drink?" Linda cried.

"Oh, that's good. Go ahead and blame it on me. Then if you slip this time, it won't be your fault."

She *wanted* to blame it on him. If only she could! But there was a voice in the back of her head. She could hear just fragments: "change yourself . . . take responsibility . . . *your* problem . . ."

Dr. Braden. Of course.

"Do you know how hard it is?" Linda begged. She didn't know whether she was asking Tom, or Dr. Braden. Except, of course, that Nick did know.

"If I'd thought you ever really tried . . ." Tom said.

"I just couldn't do it! I was so lonely."

"So it comes back to blaming me."

Linda closed her eyes and slid down to the floor, back against the cupboard. "No," she whispered. "No, I'm not blaming you."

"Then who?"

For a moment she couldn't answer. Then she screamed it into the telephone. *"Me! Damn it, me!"*

"Linda . . ." For the first time, he sounded uncertain.

"You don't want to understand, do you? Goodbye, Tom." With sudden fury she erupted to her feet and slammed the phone into its cradle. Then she stood there, tense muscles quivering.

What had she done?

The anger drained away, washed out by hopelessness. The dirty kitchen, Jerome, Tom, her children's anxious eyes, they were all her fault. And she was helpless to change herself. She was too weak against the wanting inside her.

"It's not fair!" she cried, and her voice echoed in the empty house.

There was only one way to muffle her desperation, her self-pity. But as she gulped the beer, tears ran down her cheeks into her mouth. She could taste the salt of them mixed with the alcohol she needed.

Oh, damn, Linda thought suddenly. She had to pick the kids up.

TWENTY MINUTES LATER Linda was ready to go home again, Laura and Patrick strapped into their seats in back. She was doing okay. Maybe a little fuzzy around the edges, but no big deal.

At the head of the driveway she stopped with her turn-signal on and looked carefully left, then right. The baby-sitter lived on a winding country road with a stripe down the middle. People drove too fast on it, Linda thought. She was always careful here.

Another long look left and she started forward. Too late, out of the corner of her eye, she saw the car coming from the right.

The next few seconds were a blur made up of screeching brakes and the squeal of tires. There was nothing she could do; no time to do it in.

How the other car missed her, she never knew. With a bellow of horn, it kept going, leaving black tire skids painted across the road.

Some glimmer of composure allowed Linda to put her car into reverse and back it into the driveway. She heard the kids, their voices high and anxious, but couldn't answer.

"Why are we going back, Mommy?"

"Why did that car honk at us?"

Linda set it in park, her hand shaking. All of her was shaking. She wanted to throw up, but couldn't summon the will to get out.

She had almost killed her children. One small moment of inattention because she'd had a couple of beers—no, she made herself be honest—because she was drunk. Another driver's skill had saved them.

This time, she couldn't blame anybody else. Not Tom, not her mother or even her dead father whose genes she had inherited. Nobody. *She* had chosen to pour a beer because she'd had a lousy day. Because it was easier than resisting the unbearable temptation.

She leaned her forehead against the steering wheel and closed her eyes.

NICK TURNED OFF his car's ignition. In the sudden silence he didn't move, just sat looking at the charming, perfectly cared for exterior of Ellen's townhouse. Gray shingles, white trim, purple columbines and meadow rue in a tub. For the life of him, he couldn't make himself move.

From the minute he had hung up the phone from that last conversation, Nick had had a feeling of dread. It had been there in her voice, the finality. Had he pushed her into making a decision before she was ready? he wondered. Or was there any chance at all that he was wrong? That she really did just want to see him?

For what? To cuddle and talk about her sister's failure? A failure that Ellen would surely see as symbolic?

Reluctantly he climbed out of the Saab. Walking up the driveway to her porch, he felt like a condemned man. No, worse. He remembered the last time he had gone into treatment. He could still close his eyes and feel every last sensation, every footstep.

He had to do it. He had told himself that, over and over, willing his feet to move forward. He'd been trying frantically not to think about alcohol, about the glass cold in his hand, tipping it up, heat and pleasure pouring down his throat. He was sweating, his hands shaking. *He had to do it.* Life or death. He almost wanted to choose death. The other times he had entered treatment, he had gone through the motions, telling himself it would be easy. Sure, dry out and the craving would go away.

That last time he knew better. He knew he was saying goodbye forever to the one thing that made him feel right. *Never again.* He would never again taste smooth whiskey, never again feel that warmth blossoming in his chest. Never.

He'd also been sure nothing in his life would ever again be so hard.

He had been wrong.

This was.

He rang the doorbell and stood waiting, knowing the sight of her would feel like a kick in the chest.

The sun was setting behind him, and when Ellen opened the door the golden light touched her, turning copper hair to fire and adding the peaches to a creamy complexion dusted with freckles. She was achingly beautiful, slender curves and soft mouth. *His.*

Why? Why her, out of all the women in the world? Why the one woman who would be afraid to love him?

"Hello, Nick." Her tongue moved nervously over her lips. She started a smile that she couldn't quite finish. In lieu of it, she stood back. "Come in."

"Thank you," he said quietly, making no effort to reach for her or kiss her. If she had wanted his kisses, she would have stepped forward with a saucy flick of her hair. She would have smiled, and there wouldn't have been dark circles under her eyes. His heart constricted further and Nick walked past her into the narrow foyer and then the living room.

"Sit down, please."

Ellen waited until he sat at one end of the blue-and-white striped couch, then perched at the other end.

"Can I get you some coffee or something?"

He couldn't stand it any more. He wanted to shout, "Let's can the pretense!" but managed to swallow it along with his fear. The burden was hers; he was damned if he was going to help her out. And that's what making her angry would do.

"No, thanks," he said. And waited.

Talk to me, he pleaded silently. Tell me how you feel. Tell me how angry you are at Linda. Tell me how angry you are at me. Tell me anything, but talk.

Instead she fidgeted, reminding him of one of his patients. Except, he'd never had one who affected him the way she did. She had on black jeans that hugged her narrow hips and long legs, and a loose-fitting, deep green polo shirt that succeeded in being both chic and comfortable. She looked slender, delicate. Vulnerable.

And desirable. Too damned desirable.

In the waiting silence Ellen bowed her head. With one hand she lifted the heavy mass of red hair off her neck, revealing its creamy length. Still Nick didn't say anything, although he wondered if she could hear his heartbeats.

He heard her sigh, saw her straighten her back. When she nerved herself to look at him, he could see her determination.

"Nick, I had a wonderful time with you last weekend. And...and on Wednesday. But..." She fidgeted some more. "It was a lie. I wanted everything to be okay, but it's not. Pretending isn't fair to you."

He wouldn't let her off the hook. "I'm a patient man," he said.

Her lashes fell and she looked away. Her voice was strained. "Nick, I just can't deal with it. I sat here last night agonizing about Linda, and I knew how much worse it would be if it were you. I wouldn't trust you, and that would eat away at both of us. This is...is very hard, but I didn't want to say it on the phone."

Every muscle in his body went rigid. Hard? She'd just ripped out his heart and she said it was *hard?* Was he supposed to sympathize?

"Love is supposed to mean taking risks," he said, from between clenched teeth.

Her chin came up. "If you want to quote greeting cards, how about 'Love means never having to say you're sorry'?"

"Then quit saying it!" Hardly conscious of doing it, Nick shot to his feet and stood towering over her. He was dimly aware that his own anger was a defense.

Ellen stood up, too. "Nick, please try to understand."

"I don't want to understand!"

He expected her to shout back, but her anger melted, leaving her eyes haunted and her voice shaking. "You and I have lived on opposite sides of alcoholism. I've spent too much of my life with constant uncertainty, constant anxiety. I remember when I was about twelve, walking up the hill from the school-bus stop, dreading getting home. I never knew what it would be like. Whether Dad would show up for dinner or whether he'd call at eight o'clock from some bar. Whether he'd be in one of his jovial drunk moods or an angry one. Whether Linda would be screaming at Mom or have stayed at a friend's for dinner. It was hell," she said simply. "I swore then that when I was all grown up, I wouldn't live like that."

"And you think that's what I would subject you to?"

"Isn't that what it was like for your ex-wife?"

She'd hit below the belt. He knew he flinched. Uselessly, like a mantra, he said, "It's been ten years..."

Ellen interrupted relentlessly, "You keep saying that. What's it supposed to mean?"

Nick opened his mouth, then closed it. What *did* it mean? Did time translate into the miles he had traveled from a disaster? Did the years give him confidence? Or were they only a reprieve? Was that what he lived in fear of?

"It's something I'm proud of," he said at last. "A fight that I won."

"But you're still not sure you'll win tomorrow or the next day."

"Overconfidence..."

Her voice rose. "What about simple confidence? 'I can do it.' What about that?"

"I *have* confidence!" He was angry again. "I don't get up in the morning and wonder if I'll get drunk today!"

"But you never forget you're an alcoholic, do you?"

He swung jerkily away and strode across the room, then turned to face her. "I *am* an alcoholic," he said flatly.

"Why?" She was begging. "Why can't you forget it?"

The answer was inescapable, painful. "Because I don't dare."

Ellen's face was bleached pale except for bright spots of color on her cheeks. "I can't live like that," she said, shaking her head. "I can't spend my life wondering. It would kill me."

His pain and his fear and his need combined ruthlessly to squeeze Nick's chest. Under that crushing pressure his heart skipped a beat; breathing seemed beyond him. But a sense of self-preservation created a tide of anger that allowed him to move and speak.

"Just tell me one thing," he said harshly. "What the hell use is life if you don't take risks? Do you think some man is going to come packaged with guarantees?"

"I . . ." She stopped helplessly. "Nick, I . . ."

He was across the room in two long strides. Ellen came unresisting into his arms. "You know what we feel like together," he said, desperation bared. "Isn't it worth taking a chance on?"

Nick didn't give her time to answer. He bent his head and kissed her, forgetting tenderness in his hunger. If she had stiffened, pushed him away, not responded . . . But she didn't. Instead she melted against him, parted her lips for him, kissed him back. He groaned and let himself forget, just for a second, that he would never kiss her again. He wrapped his hands around her hips and pulled her hard up against him, drowned in her taste and feel, burned in her fire.

When he was able to lift his head, he was breathing in gasps and his voice was thick. "Isn't this worth anything?"

He read the answer in her eyes, the terrible conflict that was tearing her apart. He let her go and stepped back.

"I didn't know you were a coward," he said.

His accusation sparked something in her, because her face came blazingly alive. "I may be a coward," she said strongly, "but I'm not the only one!"

"What the hell does that mean?"

"I think you use being an alcoholic to protect yourself!" Ellen said, her eyes glittering with tears and temper. "I think if you would just look straight at it, face it once and for all, you'd be free to move on. But you won't even talk about it! Well, fine. If it's too ugly to live with, let it go! But you're not willing to, are you? No, you're going to spend your life behind some wall you've put up. 'I am an alcoholic.' Well, don't expect me to think of you any other way, then!"

"What are you suggesting?" he said. "That I quit going to AA? Maybe have some social drinks? What, damn it?"

Even the color in her cheeks was gone now. Her eyes were huge and dark against her white face; only her hair crackled with life.

"I'm not suggesting any of those things," she said quietly. "All I ever wanted was for you to be sure enough of yourself not to live in fear of the past. If that was too much to expect, I'm sorry."

He abruptly turned his back on her, raked unsteady fingers through his hair. "Oh, hell," he said.

The telephone began to ring, startling them both. Ellen took a deep breath to regain some semblance of control, closed her eyes for a second, then picked it up. "Hello?"

"Ellen?"

She scarcely recognized her sister's voice in the slurred syllables. "Linda, is that you?" she said in alarm. She'd been conscious enough of Nick's presence, but now, his attention arrested, he turned his head to watch her.

"Yeah." There was a long pause. "Listen, I...I screwed up. I need a favor."

The pain that already encased Ellen's heart seemed to crack and she knew she was crying. "Oh, Linda," she whispered.

"It's Patrick and Laura. I'm...well, I guess I'm drunk again."

"I can tell," Ellen managed to say.

"I almost killed them. I thought I could drive, and I was wrong. I need you to take them tonight. Maybe for a couple of days. Like this, I'm not any kind of mother."

What good would a few days do? Ellen wanted to cry. But what use would it be to argue? "Yes," she said huskily. "Yes, of course I'll take them."

"Can you pick them up? We made it home, but..."

"No! No, you shouldn't drive. I don't mind. Really."

Linda sounded like she was trying hard to articulate. "Okay, I'll wait 'til you get here."

"I'll be right there. Don't go anywhere. Please, don't go anywhere."

Whether Linda heard her, she didn't now. Her sister had hung up.

Ellen dropped the phone into the cradle. "Oh, Lord," she said, turning to face Nick.

"Drunk?" he asked.

"Yes. She..." Ellen swallowed. "She wants me to take the kids tonight. She said she isn't any kind of mother."

"Drunk, she's not," he said bluntly.

Ellen was shaking. "Nick, I . . . I'd better go."

"So this is goodbye."

She didn't want it to be. She wanted him to open his arms so that she could walk into them. He was so big and solid and steady, his embrace so comforting and his passion so life-affirming. How would she survive without him?

She had stood there wordless too long. His face closed and became expressionless except for his eyes, dark with pain and shielding anger. He nodded at the telephone. "If you can't live with uncertainty, what the hell is that?"

"She's my sister."

He looked at her for a long moment, then said roughly, "Why couldn't you have loved me no matter what, too?"

Tears burned in Ellen's eyes. She opened her mouth to say—what? I do love you no matter what? But Nick shook his head hard, stopping her. "No, don't say anything. That's not a question that can be answered."

Watching him leave, walk out of her life, was a nightmare. When he stopped in the doorway, back to her, Ellen's heart jolted with hope and agony.

But he didn't even turn his head. "Linda knows the AA number. But tell her we have a spot for her if she needs it. And . . ." He hunched his shoulders. "If you need me, call."

And then he was gone.

She didn't even have time for tears, although she couldn't stop them. As they rolled down her cheeks, blurring her vision, she gathered her keys and purse, a box of tissues. She managed to empty her mind enough to drive, though she pulled up in front of Linda's small house with absolutely no memory of the trip.

A glance in the rearview mirror had her fumbling for a tissue. She couldn't go in like this.

But as it turned out, Linda was just drunk enough not to be observant and the children were too frightened and despairing.

Some clothes and toys were ready for them in a pathetic row of brown paper bags. They had obviously been shoved in willy-nilly and Ellen had no doubt half the essentials would be missing. This was hardly the time to worry about that, however.

Laura stood stiffly waiting by the door, a small blond statue. Patrick clung to his mother's leg. "Mommy," he begged, "please can I stay? Please?"

Linda's eyes were bloodshot, unfocused, but her words were almost steady. "It's just for a couple of days. I love you. I love both of you. But I'm no good for you. Not like this. I'm going to get some help. You have to behave for Aunt Ellen while I do that."

"Nick said to tell you that he has an opening for you if you need it."

Linda tried to smile. "I called somebody from AA. She's coming to get me. I've really only been drinking for a couple of days. I just need a little help. The rest I have to do myself. But thank Nick for me."

Ellen couldn't tell her sister that she'd have to thank him herself. She just nodded and began to collect her niece and nephew's possessions. "It's going to be fun to have you guys visit again," she said with transparent brightness.

Patrick's lower lip trembled. Laura gave mother and aunt a stony look. When Ellen glanced back at her sister, she saw the bottomless grief in her brown eyes. One more wound dealt to her children.

Ellen ushered Laura and Patrick out. On the doorstep she smiled shakily at Linda. "This is the first time you've ever asked for help yourself."

Linda hugged her like a child, wiping her tears on Ellen's collar. But when she spoke, she sounded all grown up. "It's the first time I've ever known that I needed help."

CHAPTER SEVENTEEN

ELLEN TOOK ONE DAY off work, trying to help Laura and Patrick accept the latest upset in their lives. As she played with them, pretending that this was just another cheery day with Auntie Ellen, she started to think again, as she had a million times, how unfair it was that their own mother should cause their sorrow. But this time she stopped herself. Linda had changed; perhaps she would slip again, but this time she had reached for a foothold herself. Surely that was all a child could reasonably ask of her parents: that they do their best.

On Friday she had no choice but to go back to work. The children were quiet and withdrawn when she left them at the baby-sitter's. Memories of their bewilderment made the day interminable. A couple of days, Linda had said. What did that mean to Patrick, who had no real concept of time? Or even to Laura, who had learned not to trust her mother?

Ellen would stare at a column of figures on her screen and suddenly see instead the tears running down Patrick's plump cheeks, the betrayal in Laura's blue eyes. Biting her lip, Ellen tried to make herself concentrate, but for the first time in her life, numbers, tidy and predictable, no longer gave her comfort. The certainty they represented was so far from reality, messy and uncertain.

She absolutely refused to let herself think about Nick. When his name or a fleeting image crept into her thoughts, she shoved it ruthlessly back into the recesses of her mind. She felt empty, hollow; as though nothing existed below the surface that other people saw.

When Ellen picked the kids up at their baby-sitter's, she managed a smiling face. It was short-lived, though, because the first thing Patrick said was, "I want to wait for Mommy."

His sister beat Ellen to the punch. "Don't be dumb," Laura said scornfully. "She isn't coming for us. She sent us to Aunt Ellen's because she didn't want us around."

For a split second Ellen's appalled gaze met the baby-sitter's over the children's heads. Then she crouched down to their level and said emphatically, "That is *not* what your mother said, Laura. She loves you. She sent you to stay with me *because* she loves you. Your mom is sick right now, just like she told you. Until she gets better, she knows you'll be safer with me."

"Will she ever come back?" Patrick asked in a small voice.

Ellen hugged him. "Yep," she said, giving him another squeeze. "I bet she even calls tonight." She'd damn well better, Ellen thought grimly.

Laura said suddenly, "We had a police officer come to our school last week. He talked about drugs. He said you just say no. That's what's wrong with Mommy, isn't it?"

"Well . . . Sort of. Alcohol *is* a drug, but it's one most people can handle when they drink only a little. But your mom can't handle it. Neither could her father. I guess she inherited her problem from him."

"Why can't she just say no, like the policeman said?"

"Because nobody told her to say no, back when she had her first taste of it. Nobody told her it wasn't okay for her. By the time she realized she shouldn't have ever tried alcohol, it was too late. Her body *needs* it. That's why she's sick.'' Ellen realized that for the first time, she believed the explanation. It *wasn't* Linda's fault.

Laura pursed her lips. "What's in . . . in . . . ?"

"Inherit?"

"Yeah. What's that mean?"

"It means that her father passed that part of himself along to her, just like he gave her blond hair and long fingers and a special smile. Just like *your* mom gave *you* blond hair."

"Oh." Her expression closed. "Can we go home?"

"You bet." The baby-sitter had tactfully disappeared, and now Ellen called, "Thanks, Lisa."

In the car, Laura asked, "What's for dinner?"

"Uh . . ." Ellen drew a blank. "Frog's legs?"

"Gross! People don't really . . ."

"They really do," Ellen assured her. "It's considered a great delicacy."

"You don't expect *us* to eat them."

"No, I don't expect you to. I was kind of hoping you *would* eat beef stroganoff."

"Gross."

Ellen sighed. She glanced in her rearview mirror at Patrick, buckled in his car seat behind her, to see him staring out the window, apparently oblivious to the conversation. He looked so sad—no, that wasn't right. Empty, she thought, just like she felt. Hiding way inside himself.

Not fair.

"I have a better idea," she announced. "How about McDonald's?"

WHEN HER MOTHER called later, Ellen admitted that dinner had been bribery. "Patrick's so *quiet*," she said. "He sits there in the living room, crashing his trucks into things, never saying a word. The only thing he's talked about is when Mom is coming to get him. It's going to be hard on Linda. He isn't going to want her to leave him at all. She probably won't be able to go to the bathroom alone."

"Can she now?" Mrs. Whalley asked in mock surprise.

"Well . . ." Ellen had to laugh. "You've got a point."

Then her mother's voice became more serious. "I'm going to tell Linda that if she wants to put him into counseling, I'll pay for it. I can manage. For Laura, too, if Linda thinks she needs it."

"That's . . . generous of you." Ellen sank onto a kitchen stool and curled one foot around the leg. Along with McDonald's she had succumbed to begging and rented a movie. Berenstain Bears, which seemed innocuous enough and was popular with both kids. From the living room she could hear Sister Bear's whiny voice. "I think therapy is a good idea," Ellen said. "I'll talk to Linda about it. I wish she'd call," she added, glancing at the clock.

They agreed that they should all have dinner together soon—but, what with her mother's quilting, her volunteer work at the hospital, a senior center dance and a tour of a museum exhibit, she seemed to be booked for the next week. Hanging up, Ellen reflected on how depressing it was to have a mother with a busier social life than her own. Yeah, and whose fault was that? she reminded herself, which naturally left her even more depressed.

The phone rang only a few minutes later. Ellen started to reach for it, until she heard the thunder of feet. Wisdom being the better part of valor, she pressed herself against the wall. Patrick won the race, but Laura's longer arm reached over her brother's head to snatch victory from him. "Hello?"

"*I* wanted to answer it!" Patrick screamed, but when his sister said, "Mommy?" he fell silent, his expression of hope pathetic.

Grateful for small and large favors, Ellen left the room so that they could talk to their mother in privacy. When her turn came, she shooed them back to the Berenstain Bears and picked up the receiver. "How are you, Linda?"

"Ugh," her sister said. "Does that answer your question?"

"Did you go to detox or something?"

"No, Karen—she's this nice woman in AA—anyway, she came and got me and I'm at her house. She held my hand and washed my face and cheered me on. I hadn't been drinking long enough to really withdraw or anything. I was just hung over yesterday and depressed. You know Nick's slogan."

A week ago Ellen would have smiled. *Life's a bitch and then you die.* Right now it struck her as all too appropriate. "Yeah, I remember," she said wryly.

"Are Laura and Patrick mad at me?"

"Laura is," Ellen said honestly. "And Patrick..." She hesitated.

"I can imagine," Linda said. "I'll come and get the kids tomorrow."

"Are you ready?"

"As ready as I'll ever be," Linda said honestly.

"When's Tom coming home?" Ellen asked.

"I don't know if he is."

Ellen sank onto a kitchen stool. "What happened? Was it your drinking or..."

"Yes and yes," Linda said wearily. "I kept expecting him and he kept calling from Philadelphia or St. Louis or someplace like that to tell me he wouldn't be home for three more days. I couldn't handle it." She was silent for a moment. "Am I unreasonable to want a husband who doesn't disappear for weeks at a time? Who's there when he says he'll be there?"

"No," Ellen said. "No, I don't think you're unreasonable. It's not fair to you and the kids."

"Hey, you're the one who always said, 'But it's his *job!*'"

"I just didn't like you using him as an excuse."

Another long silence. "I guess I did. Even to myself."

"Are you going to try to work things out?"

"I don't know," Linda said. "I don't know if I'll have the chance."

OVER THE NEXT WEEK, Ellen's numbness gradually wore off. An ache took the place of her hollowness, becoming a constant companion. She would wake in the morning and feel the desolation before she remembered its cause: Nick was gone, out of her life. She cried sometimes, burying her wet face in her pillow.

Then, because she had to, she would get up. The shower might wash the tears away, but the hurt stayed inside her constantly.

This was the freedom she'd wanted, Ellen reminded herself without success. She had been afraid to depend on anyone else, afraid to live with uncertainty. Well, fine. Now she didn't have to. She only had to live with herself.

And that meant finding the peace she had sought. Or, maybe, the courage to risk it.

THE DAY WAS HOT enough that the Olympic Mountains looked hazy in the distance. Nick stripped off his shirt once they'd heaved enough bundles of cedar shakes to the tar-papered roof.

Beside him worked Vince Jarman, the friend he had told Ellen about. When Vince had come to Nick a couple of days before, drunk, dirty and desperate, Nick hadn't hesitated to take him in. He owed him more than that. Talking hadn't come easily, though. Sober, Vince had clammed up. And what the hell was there for Nick to say? Was he supposed to tell his old AA buddy how peachy life was, when he'd taken to dreaming every night about getting drunk and wondering when he woke up in the morning why he didn't?

Last night they'd looked at each other across the living room and realized they had nothing to say. Nick had tried. "Do you want to talk about it?" he asked.

Vince slumped lower on the couch. "Not yet."

If they couldn't talk, what *were* they supposed to do? Nick wondered, looking at his friend's bleary eyes and haggard face. He knew Vince must feel like hell. But the things he might have suggested to someone else didn't fit here. Friendship got in the way.

He'd been startled when Vince said suddenly, "How about we roof your place tomorrow? I might as well be useful."

Since Vince was a successful contractor and Nick's entire experience consisted of reading a book about roofing, he was grateful for the offer, in more ways than one.

Somehow it was proving easier to talk while they worked than it had been the night before, sitting in the living room looking at each other. Their hammers tapped rhythmically, driving nails through the shakes. Nick braced his foot against a tacked-on two-by-four and inhaled the tangy scent of the split cedar. The sun was hot on his back, the view sublime. He'd have felt contented if...

Nick slammed the door on the inevitable, futile tail to that thought. *If he were building the house for Ellen as well as himself. If Ellen were bringing a picnic later. If he could call Ellen tonight, see her, kiss her, hold her.* If, if, if.

One day at a time, he reminded himself, wiping the sweat from his face.

A comfortable silence had fallen between the men, which Nick interrupted. "You in a mood to tell me about Patty?"

Vince slammed his hammer down on the next nail and the cedar split. "Damn," he muttered, tossing the broken shake off the roof. They both heard it hit the ground. He took another one from the bundle, tacked it in, then said, "Yeah, what the hell. Seems almost funny. She stuck with me through the drinking, doesn't mind my putting hours into AA, and now... Now, damn it, she walks out on me! I just don't get it."

"You must have been having problems," Nick said neutrally.

Vince sighed. "Oh, yeah. She says I'm a workaholic, don't have time for her. But I was working for her, too. I didn't get where I am by taking weekends off! She knows that. Why would she want me to change?"

"Has she always wanted you to take it easier?"

"She's been after me these last few years. Especially since she quit working. She liked her job with the phone company, you know, but they're trying to cut back, and when they offered some great incentives for people with twenty years in to take early retirement, Patty grabbed it. Now she doesn't know what to do with herself.''

"Maybe it *is* time for you to cut back.''

"Don't you start, too,'' Vince growled.

They worked in silence for a few minutes. The sun was hot on Nick's back and he took a swipe at a horsefly that buzzed eagerly around his face. Groaning, he shifted his weight on the steep pitch of the roof, in the process dropping a couple of nails that rolled off the edge. Maybe this was one of those jobs he should have subcontracted out, he thought. He didn't feel patient enough for it. Although he and Vince were moving surprisingly fast. Maybe what he *should* do was keep his mouth shut so he didn't lose his volunteer labor.

"Taking a drink again,'' Vince said suddenly, "I didn't think I'd ever do that. All those years for nothing.''

"Why did you do it?'' Nick asked. "What were you thinking?'' He wished his interest were academic.

Vince laughed without humor. "You want to know the truth? After all those years, I took a drink because I was mad at Patty. I guess I wanted to make her feel guilty. Really noble, huh?''

"Does she know?''

"Not from me.'' His hammer kept its rhythmic beat. "Haven't talked to her.''

"You don't want to check into the hospital.'' It wasn't really a question; he knew the answer.

"Nah. I think the detox was enough. Hey, it was only a three-week binge. I'm handling it.'' Silence but for the hammers. "Thanks to you,'' he admitted.

"I owed you more than one,'' Nick said. "I can understand why having Patty leave threw you.''

"You've never gotten over Marie walking, have you?'' Vince asked unexpectedly.

Nick didn't answer right away. When he finally did, he surprised himself. "Two months ago, a year ago, five years ago, I'd have told you I had gotten over her. I never even think about her anymore. Can't picture her face. But, you know, I've gotten to wondering lately if I haven't avoided relationships because I didn't trust myself enough. I hurt Marie, what's to say I won't hurt another woman? Let's face it, it's easier to keep your grip when things don't change. I think maybe I've been afraid I couldn't handle getting hurt—or knowing I hurt somebody else."

Vince kept working. It was a minute before he said, "Something happen to bring this on?"

"Yeah." Nick swiped at his sweaty face with one forearm, pushing damp hair back. "I fell for a woman. Trouble is, she's a relative of a patient. Grew up with an alcoholic parent. She doesn't want to take a chance on me."

"She doesn't sound worth the heartburn."

Nick grimaced. "Oh, it's more complicated than that. Ellen—that's her name—she's the one who got me thinking. She accused me of using my alcoholism as a barrier, something to keep safe behind. She said maybe if I trusted myself, she could trust me."

This time Vince quit hammering. "I trusted myself," he said bleakly.

Nick felt a smile coming on. Maybe a little wry, but a smile nonetheless. "Hey," he said, "you had good reason. The worst happened, you fell off the wagon, and look at you. Sober as a judge. You got help, you're coping. It's tough, but I'll bet in a week you'll be back at work. What's more, I'll bet you're going to start taking those weekends off, aren't you?"

"What? So I can sunbathe, take up golf? Stupidest damn sport..."

"Take up mountain climbing." Nick gestured toward the precipitous edge. "You like heights, right?"

Vince gave a crack of laughter. "Patty doesn't."

The silence this time was considerably more peaceful, the air cleared between them. It left Nick free to think.

Had he been shortchanging himself? Was there something to Ellen's accusations? Sure, he'd destroyed his marriage and hurt Marie. But that *was* ten years ago. Ten long years in which he'd stayed sober, built a respected treatment program, written a book. He'd made friends, learned to tear a car apart and put it back together again, designed a house. He'd fallen in love again, with a woman who was nothing like Marie. Just as he was nothing like the young man who'd been so cocky he wouldn't face his own problem.

How long had it been since he was really tempted to take a drink? He dreamed sometimes, but those were nightmares, memories of helplessness. Once in a while he would watch someone lift a glass, swallow, and he could feel it going down his own throat. But tempted? *Really* tempted? Walking into a liquor store tempted? Ordering a drink tempted?

Nick couldn't remember the last time. Years. He knew he couldn't drink. Period. That last time he'd entered treatment, walked into the hospital under his own power, he had chosen life. If he could do it then, shaking, sick, what made him think he would choose differently now?

Nothing.

I won't ever take a drink again. He tried it out. There was an echo, a younger self glibly promising. It hadn't been a conscious lie; but neither was it a conscious truth. It was just something to say, something that sounded easy, that would get Marie off his back. But now? He tried it again, silently, but shaping his lips to the words. *I promise...*

"Cross my heart and hope to die," he muttered.

Vince, who was straddling the peak of the roof, glanced up. "Did you say something?"

"Just talking to myself."

"Bad sign."

"Tell Ellen that. Maybe she'll feel sorry for me."

His friend grunted. "I'll try it out on Patty first."

"You do that," Nick said, suddenly serious. He hooked the hammer on a bundle of shakes and looked straight at Vince. "Don't let her go. Patty's been through a lot for you. I think she's just trying to tell you something loud and clear."

Vince pulled a bandanna from a back pocket and very deliberately tied it around his head. "She should have shouted," he said at last. "But I'll tell you what. I'll make you a deal. I'll go after Patty if you promise not to give up on your Ellen. Women are supposed to like persistence, right? Give her a call. See what happens. What do you say?"

I'm a patient man. Wasn't that what he had told Ellen? Had he not been patient enough? "I don't know," Nick mumbled.

Vince tossed him a small brown paper bag of nails. "Speak up."

"Am I supposed to use one of these to write it in blood?"

His friend became very still, then smiled. "A promise is good enough."

Nick swore. "Damn it, Vince, you know how I feel about that."

"Hey, it's not so tough. You made yourself a promise a long time ago. And you kept it, didn't you?"

Nick glared at his friend. "The only thing I've ever promised myself is that I'd get through the day. You're the one who taught me that."

"Yeah, well, add up ten years of promises."

"Vince, I don't need this."

Despite his bloodshot eyes, the grin that spread across Vince's saturnine face was still wicked. "Sure you do. You give me a hard time, I give you one. But, hell, we're friends, you don't have to promise me anything. Save your promises for someone a little softer and sweeter."

"Right." Nick found himself laughing. There always had been something about Vince that dragged him out of despondency. He hadn't changed at all, even if he had spent three weeks trying to blast all his brain cells.

And maybe Vince had something. What the hell, Nick thought suddenly. He didn't think he could bring himself to promise Ellen that he'd never drink again. But maybe he could come close enough. *I'll do my damnedest. I don't think I'll ever drink again. I'm really pretty sure.*

How could Ellen resist? he thought ruefully. She wanted "'til death do I," and he was offering "pretty sure".

It was almost funny, because he didn't want "pretty sure" from her, either. He wanted promises. He wanted forever.

Maybe those kind of promises weren't any easier for her than they were for him. Maybe she was just as afraid to believe in forever. Maybe love demanded promises you weren't sure you could make come true.

Maybe trusting that you could keep those promises was a leap of faith for everyone.

Nick tilted his head back and let the sun temporarily blind him before he closed his eyes. When you got right down to it, he thought, promises were kept one day at a time. And he was an expert on that.

ELLEN CAREFULY PULLED the letter from the printer and laid it on her desk beside the other one. Neither was on company letterhead, which seemed to her symbolic.

"Dear Sirs:" began the first. "Enclosed is my application to the Graduate School of Business Administration..."

She read it over, took a deep breath, and signed at the bottom. Her fingernails were digging into her palms when she read the other letter.

"Dear George: Please accept my resignation, effective August 15..."

Her heart was drumming, her palms sweating. Ridiculous. Scary. This time her signature was barely a scrawl. But hers. Permanent.

She could still take it back. If she crumpled both letters and wadded them into her wastebasket, nobody would ever know.

You can't change another person. Only yourself. That's what they had told her at the Al-Anon meeting. She'd spent a lifetime trying to change other people. Now it was time to work on herself.

Nick had been right. Admitting that was downright humiliating. Somehow she had let herself become a coward, hiding in a job that didn't excite or challenge her, refusing love because it didn't come with a warranty.

Well, she was still a coward, not brave enough to call Nick and say, "I'm willing to try." But she could learn to be! She could take this first risk, trusting that her savings would tide her over the two years to a graduate degree, that she could find a way to make a living doing something she cared about.

On a rush of determination, Ellen slipped the first letter with the completed application into a manila envelope and sealed it. Already stamped, it went into her out basket for the mail department who sent somebody around twice a day.

As for the other... Ellen let herself hesitate only for a second. She would put it on George Grun's desk herself. If he was there in his office, she would offer her resignation personally as well as by letter. From that, there would be no going back.

TOM'S CALL CAUGHT Linda so off balance that she didn't know what to say. He asked to speak to the kids, and while they talked to their father she kept on with dinner preparations. The motions were purely mechanical, though. She kept hearing his voice over and over.

Hello, Linda. She seemed to hear it lowering, saying soft and intimate things. *Touch me.* Nibbling at her neck. *Shall I brand you for life?* Yes, yes, please.

Why didn't you come home? she raged. Why did you run away again?

But she couldn't say it. She didn't know if she *wanted* him to come home. She loved him, she ached for him; but she didn't know if she could live with his frequent absences. Saying goodbye again and again, always waiting, it hurt too much.

"Daddy wants to talk to you," Laura said, holding out the receiver.

Surprised again, Linda blinked and stared at the phone, her heart lurching. "Me?" she said stupidly. "What does he want?"

Her daughter shrugged her indifference. "I don't know."

Setting the spoon down, Linda took the receiver. She tried to sound like she did when answering the phone at work. "Yes, Tom?"

"I need to ask you something," he said abruptly.

"Like what?"

"Do you love me?"

Linda opened her mouth to ask what difference it made. That wasn't what came out, though.

"Yes," she said, and felt her eyes burning. "You know I do."

"I love you, too, you know."

That was what made it so hard. He loved her, all right. Just not enough.

But before she could say anything, Tom said hurriedly, "I just had to know. Listen, I'll see you soon, okay?"

He didn't wait for an answer.

IT WAS A WEEK before Tom showed up. He caught Linda by surprise again, because she didn't recognize the white Subaru station wagon that pulled into the driveway. It was brand new. She could see the dealer's sticker in the side window.

She had no trouble recognizing Tom the minute he climbed out and reached up above his head to stretch. She stood well back from the window and watched as he opened the rear of the wagon and collected a couple of grocery bags, then nudged the hatch door shut with his shoulder.

Linda's heart was drumming. She got to the front door just as he inserted his key. When she pulled it open, he was the one who was surprised.

He stood stock-still on the doorstep. "You're home. I thought . . ."

"Just for lunch. Sometimes I don't feel like going out or anything."

"Oh." He awkwardly shifted grocery bags. "I thought . . . when you got home . . . Well, I was going to make dinner and have the table set and everything."

Linda looked over his shoulder at the station wagon, then back at him. "I guess you'd better come in."

"Can I put these in the kitchen?"

"Sure, I'll take one."

In the kitchen they both set their sacks on the counter. He reached in his. "I'd better put the ice cream in the freezer."

Peach sherbet. Her favorite. Neapolitan for the kids.

"I guess I should put the steaks in the fridge, too."

"What are we supposed to be celebrating?" Linda was proud of how casually it came out. She leaned against the edge of the counter and tried to look as casual.

Tom stopped halfway to the refrigerator, his back to her. "I sold the truck."

"You . . . *what?*"

He turned slowly, the packaged steaks dangling from one hand. "I thought the station wagon would be good with the kids. Maybe we could get a dog or something."

"A dog?"

"Sure, we can buy a house with a fenced yard. I mean, unless you'd rather get a cat . . . I just thought for Laura and Patrick . . . But they'd probably like a cat, too."

"A cat," she echoed. Was she dreaming?

"The thing is . . ." He looked down at the steaks as though the label on the package was important. "Well, I decided you were right."

She felt really dumb, just standing here staring at him with her mouth hanging open. "I was right about... what?"

"Both of us need something different. The truck...well, that was all I knew how to do, and I was really proud of it. But I want to be here to tuck the kids in at night, and...and eat breakfast with you in the morning, and..." He was running out of steam. "I guess all I'm trying to say is that I love you."

"You sold the truck?" It was just sinking in. "But you loved it."

He looked so awkward and nervous, even boyish. Funny, when she'd just realized that he had become a man. "I love you more," he said simply.

She started to shake. "You did that for me."

"Well, of course I did." In one long stride he'd tossed the package of meat on the counter and taken her into his arms. "I never realized that you really needed me."

Linda tilted back her head so she could look into his gray eyes. "I tried to tell you, but I didn't know how."

"Maybe we were too young," he said, tenderly wiping away a tear she didn't know she'd shed. "But we're not now. I can get a job driving a truck locally. I can be here every night and we can have a house and...jeez, maybe a vegetable garden. I've always wanted to grow sunflowers. Who knows, maybe when the kids are all grown up and on their own we could buy a rig again, go out on the road, just the two of us. What do you think?"

"I think," she said slowly, "that would be wonderful. I loved driving with you. I missed you so much."

"It was never the same without you." He tried to smile. "Nothing was."

"Tom, I'm . . . I'm trying. But it's hard. I can't promise I won't drink again. Sometimes it just takes me over."

"I'll help," he said softly. "You can do it, if I help. This time I'll be here. I can promise that."

Fresh tears spurted. "God, I love you."

"Yeah." This time his smile twisted her heart. "I know."

CHAPTER EIGHTEEN

"NO ICE CREAM?"

Mrs. Whalley, Laura and Patrick all stared incredulously at Ellen, who gestured helplessly. "Sorry."

Mrs. Whalley shook her head as though in sorrow. "I'll tell you what," she said, turning to her grandchildren. "Why don't you guys come home and spend the night with me? We can stop for ice cream on the way."

"Oh, boy, just what they need," Linda murmured, but indulgently. "What do you think, sweeties? Do you want to stay overnight with Grandma?"

They all sat around Ellen's dining room table. The grown-ups had progressed to coffee and lemon meringue pie, which had looked suspiciously unfamiliar to Laura—and Patrick, of course, had followed his big sister's lead.

"Wow, sure," Laura agreed. Patrick looked more doubtful, but the two weeks since his dad had come home had worked wonders. Besides, visits with Grandma invariably included treats.

"This way the three of you can talk to your heart's content," Mrs. Whalley said, collecting sweaters and toys. "Any time tomorrow is fine, Linda. No hurry."

After they had departed amid kisses and hugs, Tom grinned lazily at his sister-in-law. "I wouldn't mind another piece of that pie."

"Tell us more about what you're going to do," Linda said. "I never dreamed you were thinking about quitting your job. Boy, was that a bombshell."

"I haven't been thinking about it very long," Ellen said ruefully. Actually, she was surprised at how well her mother in particular had taken tonight's announcement. "I've been bored for a long time, though," she admitted. "And... oh, I suppose it was Nick. I remember, months ago, him asking whether my job was satisfying. I tried to tell him how good the pay was and what a wonderful corporation Kashiwa is and on and on. And he just said, 'Yes, but you didn't answer my question.' It was the first time I had really honestly asked myself that."

"Yeah, I know how that is," Tom said. "Making big changes is pretty terrifying stuff."

"I guess we've all done that lately," Ellen said. "More coffee, anyone?"

Conversation drifted pleasantly. Tom talked about his new job driving a truck for a soda pop distributor. "It's different," he said. "I think I'm going to have to turn into a salesman, too."

A little later, Ellen said impulsively, "I'm so glad to see you two together again. It never seemed quite right..."

"Hey, if we can try again, maybe you and Nick should," her sister suggested.

"It's not exactly the same thing..." she evaded. Tom and Linda just looked at her. Ellen met her sister's steady gaze, then Tom's. When he lifted one brow, Ellen threw up her hands. "Okay, okay! I'll admit it. I'm scared."

"Scared of what?" Tom asked bluntly.

Ellen twined her fingers together and stared down at them. "That he'll start drinking again."

Linda shook her head. "That's crazy. The guy is famous for his alcohol treatment. He's got himself so together I always feel like I'm unraveling in front of him. I mean, why would he take a drink?"

"Why does he still go to AA meetings?" Ellen retorted. "Why doesn't he seem to trust himself?"

"What do you mean, trust himself?"

"Why won't he promise . . . ?"

"*Promise?* Is that what you want?" Linda looked disbelieving.

To hide her perturbation, Ellen pretended to take a sip of coffee. "What's wrong with that?"

"Come on." Linda rolled her eyes. "You of all people! Don't you remember how Dad used to promise Mom everything under the sun?" She mimicked her father's voice. " 'I'll be home at five.' 'Of course I'm not going to drink.' 'I'll call AA tomorrow.' If I had a penny for every promise . . ."

Hearing the echo of her own bitterness, Ellen looked away. "If Nick would just talk about those years. But, no, it's like some closed door. How can I help but compare him to Dad if he won't talk to me?"

"You want to know what it's like?" Linda's voice had altered and she looked unexpectedly angry. "You want to know what it feels like? To need something so badly you'd kill for it?"

Tom reached for her hand. "Linda . . ."

She shook her head hard but let him keep her hand. "No! Ellen wants to know. I'll tell her."

And she did. For nearly an hour she talked, as though Ellen had opened some Pandora's box of anguish and shame.

"I wanted somebody to make it right for me," Linda whispered at last. "I wanted it to be somebody else's fault. If Tom was different, if he didn't leave me alone so much . . ." She squeezed his hand, then finished starkly, "It's hard to know that the person you have to hate is yourself."

After Linda and Tom had left, that was what Ellen remembered. It ran through her head when she brushed her teeth and prepared for bed. She remembered it in her dreams, then over the morning coffee that slowly awakened her enough to function. Nick, too, must have hated himself.

No wonder he hadn't wanted to talk about it! Why had she been so determined that he reveal himself at his most vulnerable? Why had his humiliation been a condition of her love?

Ellen knew the answer, of course. She had been so afraid, although she still wasn't sure what she feared most. On the surface, she had been terrified that Nick would let her down, betray her as George Whalley had. But underneath lurked something scarier still. What if *she* let Nick down? Either way, she had turned her love into a spotlight, harshly searching for flaws. As though she were perfect, Ellen thought wearily.

The truth was, she had used Nick's alcoholism as an excuse not to risk failure. Dumb. The marriage vow said for better or worse. She'd been afraid to face the worse.

She still was. She also had a feeling that being brave didn't mean losing all fear. It meant living with fear— your worst fears. Just like Nick had been doing for ten years. *Her* worst fear just happened to be a replay of her childhood.

Would Nick still have her? He had said, "If you need me, call."

She dialed without letting herself have second thoughts.

IT SEEMED TO TAKE forever to reach him. First the switchboard operator, then a nurse. "I'm afraid he's not available at the moment," the woman said pleasantly. "May I take a message?"

How could she leave a message? What could she say? Oh, yes, tell Dr. Braden I love him?

"Uh, this is Ellen Patterson. I guess I'll call back..."

The woman's voice changed immediately. "Oh, Ms. Patterson. I'm sure Dr. Braden will want to talk to you. He's in conference, but let me put you through."

Startled, Ellen wondered how much the hospital staff knew about Nick's romance, but then the phone was ringing once again. This time Nick answered himself. Impatiently.

"Dr. Braden here."

Her mouth was suddenly, impossibly dry and her heart beating so hard she could hear it. "This is Ellen," she said. "I was hoping to talk to you for a minute when you have a chance."

"Ellen." His voice, too, had altered. "Is this about your sister?"

"No. It's...about us."

There was a long silence. Then, with apparent calmness, he said, "I'm afraid I'll have to call you back."

After she had hung up, as she sat waiting for his return call, Ellen wondered how he felt, if he had understood. She pictured him, distracted, trying to comfort a distraught family. Even though it was Saturday, maybe she shouldn't have called him at work. Maybe she should have waited until evening.

When the phone rang, she snatched it up. "Hello?"

"Can I come over?" he asked, without preamble.

Ellen nodded, then realized he couldn't see her. "I...was hoping you would."

"I have another appointment. It'll be about an hour."

"That's fine." The conversation sounded absurdly ordinary. She wanted to tell Nick she loved him; instead she agreed that she was home and she didn't mind waiting.

Then he said abruptly, "Oh, hell. Somebody's knocking on my door. Ellen . . . Can you sum it up in one sentence?"

Impossible, she thought, but it didn't turn out to be so hard. "I was wrong," she said simply.

"Don't go anywhere," he said, and hung up.

THAT HOUR WAS the longest of Ellen's life. Excitement and fear were inextricably mixed, fizzing in her veins like ginger ale. She picked up a book, laid it down, brushed her hair and rebraided it, then changed her mind and shook it out. She watered her ferns to the point of drowning, jumping every time a car passed. When the phone rang, she thought she might have a heart attack.

"Hello, this is Casey's Carpet Cleaning," a woman said cheerily. "We're having a special right now, two rooms for . . ."

"Call me next week," Ellen said, and slammed down the phone.

Desperate to do something, she dragged the vacuum cleaner out of the closet and started to vacuum. Such was the power of suggestion on the unconscious mind, she thought ruefully. But what the heck. It was useful, and she couldn't hear every car passing.

When the doorbell rang, she froze like a wild doe, then leaped into action, frantically bundling the vacuum cleaner back into the closet. At the door Ellen realized her pulse was racing and her hands were shaking.

She also realized that for the first time in weeks she felt gloriously, terrifyingly alive.

Swallowing, she opened the door. Nick stood waiting, bigger than she remembered, dark hair disheveled and his eyes so vivid a blue she couldn't look away.

They stood there in silence for a moment, just gazing at each other. And then Nick drew in a ragged breath that was near a groan and took one long step across the doorstep. He gathered her into his arms, holding her so tightly it hurt, but she hadn't the slightest desire to protest. His face was buried in her hair, his heart slamming against the wall of his chest under her ear.

Some need made Ellen tilt her head back to see him. "Nick..."

"Don't say anything," he muttered. "Not yet." The sheer, desperate hunger in his eyes shredded her veneer of poise, and she heard herself moan as he bent his head to claim her mouth.

The kiss was urgent, primitive, and pleasure shuddered through her. Ellen melted against him, her senses spinning until she scarcely knew up from down. He was everything, the raw power of his mouth all she felt. She hung on to Nick for dear life and wondered how she had ever thought she could live without this. Without him.

When he lifted his mouth from hers, it was only to kick the door shut and sweep her up into his arms as effortlessly as though she were a child. Ellen clung to his broad shoulders, her gaze locked to his as he strode down the hall and through her bedroom door.

Beside the bed, he let her down slowly, holding her hips to his. There was a hot light in his narrowed blue eyes and his jaw muscles knotted as he lifted one hand up very deliberately to cover her breast. She looked down at his hand, engulfing her softness, and the heavy warmth of desire stirred inside her like a living being. She had an odd moment of presentiment, of knowing what it would feel like to carry his child. Their child. When she met his eyes again, tension shimmered between them, stealing Ellen's breath and her heart.

"I love you," she whispered.

His voice was thick, uneven. "Do you have any idea how empty life without you looked?"

Her lashes fell and she nodded. "I was...scared. You could hurt me."

"If you need promises," he said roughly, "I..."

"No!" Ellen covered his mouth. "No promises. You were right. Just...just tell me you love me."

His eyes blazed into hers. "I love you. Dear God, I love you."

"That's all I need. Just you." She reached up and touched his face, the rough texture of his hard cheek and the worn lines that spoke of suffering and caring.

His own hands came up to cradle her face and his thumbs trailed over her lips. Ellen nipped his thumb, drew it into her mouth and tasted it with her tongue. Nick half laughed, half groaned. "We should talk," he said huskily.

"Not yet," Ellen whispered.

"No." His voice was a growl. "Not yet."

This time he claimed her lips with shattering possessiveness, sliding his tongue into her mouth with an insistence that demanded a response. Ellen shivered as a tremor rippled down her spine. She parted her lips, accepting an intrusion that presaged the one to come, reveling in the challenge he offered. Every nerve end crackled; instead of becoming weak and pliant, she had a heady feeling of her own feminine power.

Nick's eyes glittered with a hot blue light when he lifted his head only long enough to pull her shirt over her head and unhook the front of her bra. His breath rasped in his throat as he cupped her breasts in his hands and gently squeezed. Slowly, maddeningly, his thumbs circled her nipples, which hardened to his touch.

"Ah." The sound he made was both ragged and sensuous.

Ellen gave a soft cry when he bore her back onto the bed, one knee planted between her legs. Now his mouth could follow where his hands had led, and she arched into him when he suckled and tasted and taunted her nipples in turn.

"Beautiful," he said hoarsely, lifting his head, sliding his palm over her breasts and down the taut line of her stomach. "So beautiful."

Ellen murmured her own pleasure, pushing his shirt off over his head and taking fierce satisfaction in the smooth shift of muscles beneath her hands. He was so solid, so powerful, so gentle.

When his hand slipped lower, Ellen lost the ability to think. The ache that she had lived with these last weeks had become a need so stark that her last inhibitions fled. She writhed under his touch, wrapped her legs around his in an desperate effort to pull him closer. Her skirt and panties were gone, and she struggled to rid him of the last barriers. At her touch he drew a ragged breath, groaned, and with a husky laugh rolled onto his back, taking her with him.

"Now," he said, in a voice that didn't sound like his own. "Show me that you're ready."

She should have felt embarrassed, sitting astride him like some Valkyrie, tangled curls tumbling over her bare breasts. But despite the heat of passion in his eyes, there was something vulnerable about his expression. Perhaps he needed her this time to come to *him,* to erase his last doubts.

And so with agonizing slowness she settled onto him, the wrench of pleasure at their joining almost unbearable. Bracing herself against his sleek, muscular chest, she led and he followed, arching, driving, becoming indissoluble. The world was nothing; only Nick, holding her, beneath her, inside her, mattered. Suddenly she no longer led or followed. Their mating had become fierce, primitive, beyond control.

When she shattered around him, Ellen cried out, and Nick pulled her into his arms and rolled her onto her back, burying himself inside her one last time. He shuddered wildly, groaning his pleasure against her temple.

Afterward, Nick seemed as reluctant to move as she was. They lay in a tangled, sweat-slick embrace, wrapped in tenderness. Slowly Ellen became aware of the normal day sounds: cars passing out on the street, a clock ticking, a child's laugh, muffled by the walls of her condo. Sunlight streamed in between the curtains. Nick stroked damp tendrils of hair off Ellen's forehead and cheeks, his hand lingering in a caress.

"We do have to talk," he said quietly.

She wished they didn't, that they could start afresh from this moment. But if love was that uncomplicated, they wouldn't *have* to talk. "I know," she said. "And I have an idea. Why don't we go up to your house?"

"*Our* house," he corrected her, his gaze searching hers. "At least, that's what I want it to be."

"Ours." Ellen savored the idea. Then she raised herself on her elbow to smile saucily at him. "In that case, no brown. And you should be thinking about where the pasture will go."

Nick looked alarmed. "Uh… We'll discuss it. Later." He tugged her onto him, then reached up to feather one fingertip over her lips. The expression on his face changed and his voice roughened. "Much later."

"Mmm," Ellen agreed, wriggling just to see what effect it would have on him. The result was gratifying, and excitement quivered in her belly. "Later," she murmured.

WHERE THERE HAD BEEN a skeleton now stood a home. Cedar shingles capped the steep-pitched roof and sunlight glinted off the tall windows. A breeze stirred the long meadow grass and tossed a strand of Ellen's hair across her face. Scarcely noticing, she pushed it back and smiled glowingly at Nick.

"It's beautiful."

"I should make you tour the roof so I could show you every nail I hammered in."

She wrinkled her nose at him. "I'm not crazy about heights."

"Neither am I," he said ruefully. "You're not the only one who does things you're afraid of."

On an impulse she wrapped her arms around his neck and stood on tiptoe to press a kiss on his mouth. "I love you," she said against his lips.

He groaned and deepened the kiss, to which Ellen responded as helplessly as she had to him from the first day she met the force of his gaze.

When he lifted his head, she whispered, "Will it always be like this?"

Nick had a sudden image of Marie looking up at him and asking the same thing. "Always," he had told her, his younger self confident that he could manipulate the future. Now he knew better.

"I'll do my damnedest," he said gruffly, surprising himself with the resolution in his voice.

Ellen studied him with wide, inscrutable eyes, and he couldn't help wondering whether she had wanted always, too. But then her mouth curved into a smile that heated his blood. "It's in our hands, isn't it?" she said, and kissed him again.

They wandered slowly through the house and at last out onto the beams that would eventually be covered with decking. The valley floor sprawled out below their feet. Faintly hazy, the Olympic Mountains made up the horizon.

Nick sat on a board that lay across the beams and pulled Ellen down beside him. Though they still held hands, the silence that drew out seemed to put distance between them.

"What changed your mind?" Nick said abruptly.

She averted her gaze. "Maybe I just learned to be braver."

He looked at her profile, loving the curve of her cheek and flare of her nose, the velvet matte of her skin and the soft fullness of her mouth. "When you decide to be brave," he said roughly, "you don't go halfway. Do you do everything so wholeheartedly?"

Her chin came up and she met his eyes. "With you, I can't help it."

His mouth twisted. "But you tried."

"Failed, you mean." Ellen's fingers tightened on his. "Nick, you have to understand. I don't remember my own father. The two people who meant the most to me were Mom and my stepdad. They loved each other. I could see that, but I could also see that it wasn't enough. I thought..." she hesitated and softly, apologetically, touched his cheek, "I thought a promise of love wasn't enough."

He was surprised by his own wariness. "What makes you think it's enough now?"

"I've just realized that really living means taking a chance. When you were gone, I had to face how little joy there is in my life. You helped me come alive. With the hospital you help so many people." Her eyes shimmered with tears and she blinked to control them. "I know you. That's all. You wouldn't make the same choices my stepfather did."

A muscle twitched at the corner of his mouth and then he pulled her tightly into his arms. He just held her, his mouth against the top of her head.

"I realized something, too," he said finally, in a voice that felt like it was torn out of his heart. "I realized that if you need promises, I can give them to you. Promising forever to someone is never easy. It shouldn't be any harder for me than it is for any other man. I'm not the same as I was when I failed Marie. I didn't mean a lot of things I said then. Now..."

"No." Ellen lifted her head sharply, banging his nose. When she had kissed it better, she said more softly, "I meant it, Nick. Your job is giving life to people. You won't steal it from yourself." She exhaled in a rush. "You weren't the coward. I was."

"Damn it, no." He cupped the back of her head and tilted her face up so that she had to meet his eyes. "You were brave enough to chase me out of the hole I've been hiding in. You think your life had no joy? Look at mine! My apartment could be a hotel room. I was so busy fixing everyone else's lives that my own was a vacancy sign. I was trying to fill in the blanks with a house. Wood and concrete, what was it supposed to do? Without you, I don't think I'd have ever had the guts to love anyone again. You were right. I've been running scared."

Ellen was filled with shame that rushed in a wave of heat over her cheeks, and she would have liked to hide her face. Huskily, she told him the truth. "I only said that because I was trying to hurt you."

"It was true."

Nick bent his head to brush his lips across hers, a whisper of sensation that nonetheless made warmth tremble inside her. The shaven line of his jaw scraped against her more delicate skin, a reminder of all the places she was soft and he was hard. But the look in his eyes made her forget the feelings his kiss had aroused.

He said flatly, "I didn't want to tell you what being an alcoholic was like because remembering scares me. It made me wonder if I've come far enough. If it's the kind of thing you can ever leave behind."

"Oh, Nick." Her lips touched his cheek in feather-light reassurance. "I love you," she whispered. "I love you so much. Sometimes I'm scared of how much."

He made an incredulous sound, and closed her into an embrace that would have hurt if it had been any tighter. "Ellen . . ."

Her smile was shaking when she looked up at him. "Do you know how happy we're going to be?"

"You can live with being scared?" Uncertainty was an edge in his voice.

"I wouldn't want it any other way." Her smile steadied a little when she saw the blaze in his eyes. "Doing something easy would never make me so stupendously, incredibly happy. It's like . . ."

"Horseback riding? Skydiving?" His grin would have been wicked, except for the unguarded, heart-shattering love in his eyes. "Making love on a rooftop?"

"Nick..."

He stood, sweeping her up into his arms, and strode toward a ladder.

"Nick!"

He stopped, let her slide down until her feet touched ground. "Scared?"

"Terrified," she said huskily, her lips a hairbreadth from his.

"Me, too," he murmured. "We can be scared together. Forever and..."

She laid her fingers against his mouth. "No promises, remember?"

He kissed her fingertips, then said steadily, "That's one promise I can make. I'll love you for the rest of my life."

"You know what?" Ellen slid her hands inside his shirt and felt his strong heartbeat. She smiled lovingly up at him. "For us, I think that *will* be enough."

Harlequin Superromance®

Family ties...

SEVENTH HEAVEN

In the introduction to the Osborne family trilogy, Kate Osborne finds her destiny with Police Commissioner Donovan Cade.

Available in December

ON CLOUD NINE

Juliet Osborne's old-fashioned values are tested when she meets jazz musician Ross Stafford, the object of her younger sister's affections. Can Juliet only achieve her heart's desire at the cost of her integrity?

Available in January

SWINGING ON A STAR

Meridee is Kate's oldest daughter, but very much her own person. Determined to climb the corporate ladder, she has never had time for love. But her life is turned upside down when Zeb Farrell storms into town determined to eliminate jobs in her company—her sister's among them! Meridee is prepared to do battle, but for once she's met her match.

Coming in February

my VALENTINE 1992

Celebrate the most romantic day of the year with
MY VALENTINE 1992—a sexy new collection of four
romantic stories written by our famous Temptation
authors:

GINA WILKINS
KRISTINE ROLOFSON
JOANN ROSS
VICKI LEWIS THOMPSON

My Valentine 1992—an exquisite escape into a romantic
and sensuous world.

 Harlequin Books®

VAL-92-R

Janet Dailey
Americana

A romantic tour of America through fifty favorite Harlequin Presents novels, each one set in a different state and researched by Janet and her husband, Bill. A journey of a lifetime in one cherished collection.

Don't miss the romantic stories set in these states:

Available wherever Harlequin books are sold.

HARLEQUIN
PROUDLY PRESENTS
A DAZZLING NEW CONCEPT IN ROMANCE FICTION

One small town—twelve terrific love stories

Welcome to Tyler, Wisconsin—a town full of people
you'll enjoy getting to know, memorable friends and
unforgettable lovers, and a long-buried secret that
lurks beneath its serene surface....

JOIN US FOR A YEAR IN THE LIFE OF TYLER

Each book set in Tyler is a self-contained love story;
together, the twelve novels stitch the fabric of a
community.

LOSE YOUR HEART TO TYLER!

The excitement begins in March 1992, with
WHIRLWIND, by Nancy Martin. When lively, brash
Liza Baron arrives home unexpectedly, she moves
into the old family lodge, where the silent and
mysterious Cliff Forrester has been living in seclusion
for years....

WATCH FOR ALL TWELVE BOOKS
OF THE TYLER SERIES
Available wherever Harlequin books are sold